LACHLAN

Immortal Highlander Book 1

HAZEL HUNTER

ALLURE PRESS

HH ONLINE

Hazel loves hearing from readers!
You can contact her at the links below.

Website: hazelhunter.com

Facebook:
business.facebook.com/HazelHunterAuthor

Newsletter: HazelHunter.com/news

I send newsletters with details on new releases,
special offers, and other bits of news related to my
writing. You can sign up here!

Chapter One

KINLEY CHANDLER HAD expected a perfect day. So of course, she got one. Gray-green sagebrush and bright bush sunflowers carpeted the bluffs above the golden sands where she walked. As dawn peeked over the horizon, the Pacific spread its endless indigo skirts to tease the shore with lacy white flounces. Manic, black-tailed gnat catchers flitted about in pursuit of their insect breakfasts. They uttered scratchy, catlike calls whenever Kinley strayed too near. The rising sun felt good on her face as it heated the briny breeze of the San Diego coast.

This is where I should be.

As she skirted a tidal pool, Kinley wondered why she hadn't come here more often when she'd been stateside. She'd never hiked the entire half-mile trail through the reserve. Atop the cliff in the distance, above a private beach, was the million-aire's sprawling, fake Italian mansion. Once it had annoyed her, but now it didn't bother her at all.

She could stay right here, happily.

Forever.

"Captain," a soft voice said, accompanied by a tentative touch on Kinley's left forearm. "Time to wake up."

The beach from Kinley's memory winked out of existence as her nose filled with the bleak cologne of old wounds, bleached linen and hand sanitizer. She breathed through the frantic fear bubbling up inside her as she reminded herself that this was America, not Afghanistan, and she no longer occupied a combat zone, but a room in San Diego's finest VA hospital.

She didn't have to fight anymore. She'd lost her last battle, and she was going to be a good loser.

Opening her eyes meant seeing the pitted ceiling tiles that had been her only sky for the last two months. The machines connected to her body beeped like robotic wrens. Their smudged screens displayed dismal numbers. She focused on them, as evaluating her condition always drove off the pathetic panic caused by her PTSD. She could see that her pulse was too low, and her body temp too high. Her blood oxygen level hovered a digit above borderline. The fever meant she probably had a budding infection in her mangled right leg. If her shredded gut had gone septic she'd already be comatose or dead.

Kinley focused on the ward nurse's round face. Brisk smile, forced cheer, dark circles under her eyes—a burnout or a treasure in the making.

"Heya," Kinley said.

"Good morning," the tired woman said as she began detaching lines and rearranging bags of fluids. "Feeling up to your appointment with the new therapist?"

"Can't wait," Kinley said. An orderly pushed a wheelchair into her room, and only when he parked it next to her bedside did she comprehend that it was for her. "I thought she was coming to me this time."

"She wants you up and about, Captain." The nurse drew back the bed linens. "Here we go." She nodded to the orderly, who helped shift Kinley into a sitting position. "One, two, three."

Being moved woke up her broken body, which

protested with a dozen different spikes of pain. The wheelchair rocked as they settled her emaciated ass into it, and her IV line tangled with the stethoscope around the nurse's neck. Kinley felt her patchwork abdomen throb in protest, but kept silent. If she complained they'd pump her full of opiates, and no way did she want to be high with the new shrink. No one knew about her PTSD except a medic who had been with her during one of her worst episodes on her second tour. He'd knocked her out, and then later told her how to deal with it so she could remain on active duty.

"Hang on," the nurse muttered, and extricated herself from the tangle. "There." She shooed away the orderly and peered at Kinley's battered face. "You okay?"

Sweat beads popped along the edges of her lank hair as the pain swelled, and for a moment she thought she might puke or pass out. She shoved it back and bared some teeth.

"Never better."

"We'll take it slow," the nurse promised as she wheeled Kinley out into the corridor of Medical Palliative Care Ward Four, which most of the staff referred to privately as Morgue Prep. "Have you met Dr. Stevens yet?"

"Maybe. All these shrinks look alike to me."

Kinley couldn't get comfortable in any position, so she opted for the least painful, which meant on the only uninjured part of her body: her left forearm. Though she didn't feel much in her right arm, the cast was too heavy to lift.

"She seems pretty nice. Very experienced." The deliberate heartiness in the nurse's voice took on an edge. "You're going to give her a chance, aren't you?"

"I won't make this one cry, like that kid who wandered into my room," Kinley said. "Unless she's a wimp around the really disfigured terminals, like the last one."

"You're going to live, Captain," the nurse chided, making the lie sound almost believable. "You'll turn around any day now, and start healing, and get back on your feet."

"Sure," Kinley said and glanced at the dressings covering her mangled right leg. Her surgeon would be amputating it mid-thigh, assuming she ever got strong enough to go under his blade again. "Any day now."

Dr. Geraldine Stevens occupied a smallish office just outside the psych ward, and came out with a ready smile. "Good morning, Captain

Chandler." Thankfully she didn't try to shake Kinley's hand. Her gaze shifted to the nurse. "I'll call when she's ready to return to her room."

Kinley had already seen the inside of the office too many times, so she eyed the new shrink. Dr. Stevens sported a gray blazer with a turquoise-blue linen dress that looked new. But her charcoal pumps looked old enough to be comfortable. She was somewhere between forty and fifty, a head shorter than Kinley, and about twenty pounds overweight. Her careworn look suggested that she was actually concerned for her patients. Or she might be married to a jerk who made her life hell at home. The doc hadn't opted to wear perfume or makeup, but she had some product in her curly brown hair that smelled of cherries and almonds.

Behind her the Veteran Administration's ICARE program poster hung like subliminal propaganda.

I care, she cares, everybody cares. We're all such good liars.

"Do I pass inspection?" Dr. Stevens asked as she sat down behind the desk.

Let the mind games begin, Kinley thought. "Do you want to?"

"Everyone wants approval, Captain. If we didn't, we'd live like tigers or polar bears, and eat each other." The shrink fussed with some drawers until she found a pen. "Before Dr. Patterson left for Chicago, he briefed me on your case."

"Did he say nice things about me?"

Probably not. Patterson had been a humorless ass who hadn't been able to look at Kinley for more than three seconds at a time.

"Did you want him to?" Dr. Stevens said, smiling at her witty turn around as she opened a thick patient file. "You were injured during the rescue of a downed air crew. According to your commendation, you ran into crossfire to pull them out of the wreckage, which insurgents subsequently blew up with an improvised incendiary device." She frowned. "You didn't suffer any burns at all?"

Kinley had never been burned in her life. Not once. In the explosion it was as if the fire went *around* her. But she couldn't explain that without sounding like she needed to be transferred to the psych ward.

"I was thrown clear," Kinley said and shrugged. "Luckily, right into the Hawk."

The explosion had blasted her head-first into

the side of her team's Pave Hawk rescue helicopter. She hadn't even dented the reinforced steel
hull, but the impact had smashed her nose,
cracked her cheekbones, and dislocated her jaw. A
secondary blast had dropped the wing of the
downed plane on her leg, crushing it. At some
point during that party she'd also taken six bullets
in the back and gut. They'd patched her together
as best they could at Bagram. Eight weeks later
her body and face resembled something a very
drunk Picasso might have drawn.

But hey, at least she hadn't been burned.

"You're very fortunate, given the circum-
stances," Dr. Stevens said and flipped through
more pages. "During your sessions with my prede-
cessor you've insisted that, aside from your physical condition, you feel fine."

Shifting in the wheelchair made Kinley's
lower spine burn like a lit fuse. "I do. I got out
alive, my brains aren't scrambled, and everything can be fixed or cut off or whatever. Life
is good."

"Dr. Patterson mentioned you feel so fine, in
fact, that you've been refusing pain medication."
Dr. Stevens arched brows that had been plucked
too thin. "According to your chart you're also not

eating much, and several nurses have noted that you sleep most of the day."

"That's from the TV." She put a little more weight on her forearm to keep the pain bomb in her back from detonating. "Game shows and soap operas are better than tranqs."

"Are you pretending to be asleep so you don't have to eat or speak to anyone? Is that why you haven't had any visitors since you were admitted? Have you even told your family that you're here?" When Kinley didn't answer Stevens closed the chart and gave her a direct look. "Captain Chandler, you should know that I've been working with disabled veterans for twenty years now."

Why did they always offer that as reassurance? Maybe it was in the VA shrink handbook: *Assure patient of your proficiency in dealing with ruined soldiers. Gain their trust. Then screw with their minds a little more.*

"Good for you, Doc."

It was a shame Stevens hadn't read her entire file, or she'd know exactly why Kinley had never had any visitors.

"I know military culture," the shrink insisted, "and the highly unrealistic expectations soldiers have of themselves and others. You're constantly pressured to 'accept the suck', as they say."

"It's actually 'embrace the suck'," Kinley said, her mouth hitching into a smirk. "Although my personal favorite has always been 'If you can still twitch, don't bitch.'"

Dr. Stevens didn't return the smile. "I think you're hiding your condition from your friends and family. You also seem to have no interest in recovery. Unless you start fighting for your life, Captain, you won't be twitching much longer." She paused to look into Kinley's eyes. "You'll be dead."

"Well, then, I guess I'll have to work on my attitude," Kinley said. She knew doctors always liked to hear that kind of suck-up bullshit. It might also stop the nurse from putting her on a gastric feeding tube. "I am pretty tired now, though. Could I go back to my room, please?"

"I have a better idea." The shrink stood and took a giant purse from the bottom drawer. "Your primary has cleared you for a short day trip. Let's go for a drive."

❧❧❧

THE CHANCE TO leave the VA hospital silenced Kinley, who had never expected to see the outside world again. Even the discomfort caused by being loaded by the electric lift into the handicapped van didn't seem so bad, not while sunlight poured over her like warm, liquid gold. But as the shrink drove north from downtown and took the I-15 out of the city, Kinley began to feel uneasy.

"Are you sure this is a *short* day trip?" she asked. "Because it looks like we're heading for Seattle. Not that I'd mind, but I think the charge nurse might freak out."

Dr. Stevens shook her head. "We'll arrive at our destination in twenty minutes, and spend an hour there before we return to the hospital. You'll be back in time for lunch."

Kinley guessed the vagueness was calculated, an attempt to coax her into asking questions about where they were going, or chatting about how wonderful it was to be out in the real world again. She also knew the surest way to confound a shrink was to use their tactics against them.

"That's good. I have things to do."

Like asking about a transfer to hospice, where she could die in fucking peace.

Once they left the city behind, hills and valleys rose and fell on either side of the interstate, and Kinley could see mountains ahead. They passed

Lake Elsinore, and then left the freeway to head west toward the rugged chaparral-covered mountains. The road bisected acres of sparsely-strewn sage and scrub oak, punctuated by huge boulders that gleamed gray and orange in the morning light. Once they had passed a small fire station, Kinley saw a sign indicating where Dr. Stevens was headed, and almost laughed out loud.

"You're taking me to Horsethief Canyon?" Kinley said. She hadn't been there in years but, as the signs on the freeway said, it was part of the Pine Creek Wilderness. "Are you serious?"

"It's a lovely spot for a hike," the other woman said as they slowed and turned. She parked the van in an empty lot with bike stands and a water trough. "There's a paved riding trail here we can use for you."

Kinley could have made a fuss about not being well enough to hike anywhere, even in her wheelchair, but going along with the crazy shrink's idea was easier. This might be her last trip outside, too.

"Okay."

Dr. Stevens unloaded Kinley and her chair, grabbed her purse, and almost set it in Kinley's scrawny lap. But she must have seen Kinley tense or maybe she'd just thought better of it. She left it behind the driver's seat, locked the van, and pushed Kinley across the lot to the promised trail. The weeds that crisscrossed it jostled her wheels, but Kinley ignored the discomforts as she looked ahead toward the slopes. California's long drought had left much of the area barren, and she could see an old watering hole that had dried up, but the raw, rough rock formations were stunning. More water-polished stones marched up to the edge of a cliff, and made her imagine the waterfall that had once cascaded down them. Before the drought it must have been a magical spot to go swimming.

"I don't think we'll go that way," Dr. Stevens said when they came to the fork in the trail, and turned to push her up toward a large oak grove. "We should have a better view past the trees."

When they reached the oak grove Kinley looked up at the canopy of the gnarled tree limbs. Here the trees looked much more mature, with thick, curving trunks and densely-leafed branches. Dandelion seeds floated like so many unused wishes through the dappled shade between the oaks. Beyond them Kinley could see a gap in the brush, and part of a dried-up riverbed. What lay

on the other side of the grove must be the old
waterfall overlook.

As Kinley caught the scent of the oaks—a
slightly smoky and heavy fragrance—she thought
of someone she hadn't in years, and smiled. Her
grandmother Bridget would have loved the spot.
She'd always taken her tea out in the afternoon to
sit under the giant black oak. As a little girl Kinley
would sit there and listen to stories about brown-
ies, kelpies and selkies that her grandmother had
told her.

Even as a child Kinley had been a skeptic.
"Do you really believe in such things, Gran?"

"I do, for we've magic in our family," Bridget
said firmly. "That's why I'm able to find your toys
when you forget them. Lost things call to me. My
own mam could charm wild birds with her
singing. They'd come and eat seeds, right from
her hand. She always said it comes from our Scottish blood."

"Then what's my magic?" Kinley asked.

Her grandmother tapped her cheek. "I can't
tell you yet, sweetheart, but whatever it is, it's
strong. I've felt it in you since the day you
were born."

Bridget had been babysitting her when

Kinley's parents had left for a weekend getaway, and had helped her through the horror and grief after their plane crashed in the sea. She had even gone before a judge to argue that although she was seventy and a widow, she could raise her granddaughter better than the foster care system.

Bridget Chandler might have looked like a sweet old lady, but she had a will of iron. The judge had granted her full custody of eight-year-old Kinley.

"Still awake?" Dr. Stevens asked.

Kinley nodded as the old guilt dragged at her. Bridget had taken care of her for the first few years, but as the old lady aged and grew frailer the situation reversed. A month before graduating high school Kinley had come home to find her grandmother under her oak tree, looking as if she had fallen asleep. The stroke she'd suffered had been so massive that it had killed her instantly.

At the funeral at Bridget's church, Kinley had sat alone in the family pew. Both of her parents had been only children born to older parents. They hadn't had her until they were in their mid-forties. Her grandmother had been her last living relative.

There hadn't been much money left after the

funeral expenses, so enlisting in the Air Force had allowed Kinley to go to college and get her degree, and make a new life for herself.

The military had become her family after that, and now they were gone too. Kinley had no friends outside the service, and no hope for the future. Reconstructive surgery could restore some of her face, but the nerve damage would always make her resemble a post-party piñata. Once they took her leg she'd be crippled for life. No man would fall in love with a disfigured amputee. She'd be alone, again, and this time it would be forever.

There really is no coming back from this.

Kinley had always thought as much, but when she saw the oak grove, and what lay beyond it, she understood.

"I think this is a good place to take a break," Dr. Stevens said, breathing a little hard. She set the hand brake and looked around before she eyed Kinley. "How are you feeling?"

"Okay." Her back screamed, her leg throbbed, and her eyes stung with unshed tears, but she also felt oddly, utterly calm. Letting her expression go soft and wistful, she asked, "Can I borrow your phone? I'd like to call home."

"Of course," Dr. Stevens said and reached to

her jacket pocket, but then she glanced back to the lot. "I left it in the van." For a moment, she studied Kinley's face. "I'll go and get it, if you promise to stay right here."

One last lie, and she would never have to tell another. "I'm not going anywhere, Doc."

The shrink hurried off, no doubt elated by what she thought was a break-through. Kinley felt a little guilty as she watched her go, but that melted away as soon as she looked through the oak grove. Once the other woman was out of sight, she released the hand brake, gripped the left wheel and rolled herself forward into the trees.

The incline of the trail sloped down, helping her propel the chair toward the edge of the cliff. The overlook was a drop of at least seventy feet onto the rocks. Death would be instantaneous, and the whole thing would look like a tragic accident.

Kinley didn't feel afraid.

Gran, I'm coming. Please, please be waiting for me with Mom and Dad.

Bits of dandelion fluff caught on her eyelashes, somehow spangling her vision. The roar of her heart in her ears turned to the sound of wind through the trees, whispering all around her. This was good. She was going to have a good death. Since her life had sucked, that was a nice surprise.

Suddenly, halfway to the edge, her wheelchair stopped, hurling her to the ground—but Kinley never landed. Inexplicably she kept falling, her broken body plummeting through endless shadows, with the old oak trees stretching and curving until they formed a tunnel around her.

I must be dead.

But if she was, how could she still think?

Memories began pouring through her, from the blurry images of her parents waving goodbye to the years with her grandmother to the morning she had set out from base on her last search and rescue mission. Her sucky life had been too short, but Kinley had only one true regret: she'd never shared it with someone.

She'd been too busy taking care of her grandmother to get involved with anyone in her teens. At college she'd had a brief fling with a jock, who had turned out to be a selfish ass. The service had supplied an endless amount of men, and as much sex as she wanted. But the stress of being in a war zone had made real relationships impossible.

If only I'd met someone to love!

The tunnel of trees closed over her as she headed into darkness. But as she plunged downward a strange warmth spread through her body. As her pain vanished, relief flooded through her. Tears sprang to her eyes at the sudden and sweet release. But in moments, a new, powerful energy replaced it. It surged down her body and into her limbs until sparks flew from her fingertips. Kinley screamed as she emerged from the tunnel and landed in darkness on her hands and knees.

As she struggled to catch her breath, Kinley stared at the ground. It wasn't rocks at all, but... mud? Stinging, icy rain poured over Kinley as she scrambled up from the slush. But as she looked down at herself, she froze. All the surgical pins holding together her shattered leg had disappeared. She was putting her full weight on it and all she felt was strong, sturdy support. Her back felt brand-new. She pressed her now-unbroken right hand against her abdomen, which felt flat, firm and unmarked. The last time she had touched her belly it had been spongy and latticed with long, stapled incisions.

Kinley's hands shook as she brought them to her face. She felt her straight nose and high,

curved cheekbones. Smooth skin covered everything, and she could feel her fingers against it.

"Oh, my god. How…?"

Drenched and shivering, she wrapped her
arms around her miraculously healed waist and
turned around, squinting against the downpour.
She stood in a clearing of wild grass surrounded
by oak trees, but nothing looked like Horsethief
Canyon. Thick stone posts poked up from the
grass in a rough circle around her. They resembled oversize gray bullets and on each were primitive carvings of swirls, animals and huge, sideways
letter Z's. The symbols glowed a fiery orange-red
that quickly faded.

From beyond the dark oaks came the sound of
metal clashing and deep, male voices shouting,
and then dozens of men fighting with swords
burst into the clearing.

Chapter Two

KINLEY'S TRAINING KICKED in as she took cover behind one of the stones. She hunkered low to make herself as small a target as possible. When she heard no gunfire being exchanged she took a chance and peeked around the edge at the fighters. As she took in their strange clothing she blinked, sure she was having some kind of psychotic break. She ducked down, rubbed the rain out of her eyes, and took a long, deep breath. As the rain slowed to a drizzle, she forced herself to look again.

This time they were only fifty yards away. Even in the darkening twilight she got a very good look.

"What the hell?"

One side appeared to be ancient Romans wearing red tunics under iron and bronze armor. The men had GI-cropped hair, and short, broad swords. But that's where the resemblance to Romans ended. Their eyes were strange, almost reptilian, and their skin was so unnaturally pale they appeared to be painted white. They fought viciously against huge warriors in white, gold and black Scottish tartans belted over brown leather vests and trousers. Judging by their ruddy, tanned flesh they were human, but Kinley had never seen an entire army of towering, brutally muscled men. They looked just like the medieval high-landers she'd seen in the documentaries her grandmother had loved watching.

Why were there Romans and Highlanders fighting in a San Diego canyon, of all places? Maybe it was some kind of ghastly alternate history matchup reenactment. The next wave might be Nazis and Spartans.

"I'm dreaming," Kinley muttered, sinking down behind the stone. "That's why I'm healed. I must be in a coma or something."

But then a decapitated head rolled past Kinley to stop and stare at her feet. Beneath its death-blinded eyes thin lips grimaced to reveal long, thick, white fangs. Then, incredibly, it dissolved into smoldering ash that gave off a rotted stink before it melted into the mud.

"*Jesus*," she gasped, backing away from it. She clung to the stone as she stared at the puddle that a second ago had been a severed head. "Oh, man," she muttered, covering her nose with her hand. "If I'm dreaming, why do I smell that?"

"Clan McDonnel," a deep voice shouted, and then bellowed, "Heid doon, arse up."

Thanks to years of listening to her grandmother's brogue Kinley had no trouble translating: *Head down, ass up*. She looked out to see that the men were almost on top of her. The savage words seemed to electrify the Scotsmen, who surged forward in a deadly wave of slashing iron. Their fury cut down every Roman in their path as they fought toward the center of the grove. In another minute they'd swarm around the stone behind which she crouched.

Kinley blinked as buried memories burst inside her head. Stark and vivid, images and sounds bore down on her one after another: landing the bird by the smoldering wreck of the transport plane; grabbing the carry-alls and the portable Jaws of Life; bullets suddenly pinging off the Hawk; heart hammering, hands cold, voice tearing out of her throat as she shouted to her crew to take cover; the crackle of the radio as her lieutenant called to base; the body pile inside the wreck; the stink of fuel and plastic and death; slipping in the blood pool; the smash of glass, the huge waft of heated air, and then the world on fire.

"No," Kinley gasped.

She wasn't there. That was then. She pushed down the pulses of churning panic. Though fear and confusion threatened to sweep her away, she focused on the battle. She was here, she was present, and she was not going to lose it.

One of the largest Scottish warriors plowed through the Roman line, hacking through with long swords in both hands. Despite her shivering terror Kinley couldn't stop watching him. She'd never seen any man move the way he did. He had a sinuous suppleness, as if his bones were made of water. How could such a huge man move like liquid?

The big Scotsman flung back his sodden mane of dark hair as he kicked a wounded Roman aside and skewered two more. Lightning blazed across the dark sky, illuminating his handsome face for a moment. His lack of hesitation told her that he felt no pity for his enemy, but the bitter disgust in his expression assured her that he took no pleasure in killing, either.

He's not a machine, Kinley thought, her heart clenching as she recalled the same expression on the faces of her fellow soldiers. *He hates it, but he's doing what has to be done.*

One of the Romans danced around him, thrusting his heavier broadsword at the Scotsman's legs. "Why do you persist, Lachlan McDonnel? Your clan shall never kill us all. We are too many."

"Aye, you're a plague," Lachlan agreed. His dark eyes glittered as he chopped off the Roman's sword hand, and impaled him with his second blade. "And now they've one less leech."

As if they'd overheard him dozens of Romans surged out of the trees, swarming around and cutting off McDonnel from his men. Kinley saw how most of them drove back the Scotsman's comrades, while six of the largest Romans encircled him.

"Well, well, we've caught the Laird of the McDonnel," one taunted, and licked his lips. "We'll feed well on your carcass, Pritani swine."

Romans holding the line suddenly started flying through the air like toy soldiers, and Kinley saw one huge Scotsman knocking them out of his way with a giant hammer as he plowed a path toward Lachlan.

"They call us Scots now," Lachlan yelled, then beckoned to him. "But I'll let you have a try at the first nibble."

They all bared their fangs, and crouched as if to spring on him en masse—except for one who stood behind him, his sword pointed at the Scots-man's neck.

Even with all his courage, strength and skill, the laird of the McDonnel would never survive the attack. He would be stabbed in the back and dragged down by the cowards, helpless to stop them from tearing him to pieces. Fury boiled up inside Kinley as she shot up from behind the stone, and ran toward the ambushed Scotsman. She couldn't think, not with the roaring in her head and the pounding in her chest, but it didn't matter. Nothing did but this brave fellow soldier.

Lachlan McDonnel couldn't die like this.

Her body heated as she reached out, and something raced through her arms and exploded from her palms. Kinley froze as two streams of fire shot from her hands, blasting all six of the Romans back from the laird. The stench of burning flesh and melting armor wafted over her as she gaped, completely stunned. The flaming streams stopped as instantly as they had started, but one by one the fanged men dropped to their knees and keeled over to melt into the ground.

When Kinley turned her hands palm-up she couldn't see a mark on them.

Her bones shook inside her limbs as she felt the shock sinking in. She'd just murdered six men. Burned them alive. Burned them to death. *With her hands.*

"No, I can't...*no.*" Kinley frantically shook her head. "This isn't real. I can't do this. I want to wake up." Forget the perfect body, the new face, all of it. She was going back to the real world, the world where she wasn't a murderer. "I want to wake up *right now.*"

All of the men stared at her for a frozen moment before the Romans collectively turned and ran for the trees. Kinley curled her fingers over into fists, and looked up to see the Scotsman whose life she'd saved, now striding over to her.

"Come here to me," he said.

He snatched her up in his arms, and before

she could speak kissed her, his mouth hard and hungry.

Kinley hung suspended as Lachlan ravished her mouth, his tongue bold and hot against hers. A cool scent flooded her head, something like the rain but more, so deep and dark that she felt as if she were being held under water. When she realized it was coming from him she snapped out of her trance. Then terror spiked inside her, crashing through the delicious sensations like a rampaging animal. He was kissing her like a lover but smearing her with the blood of the men—the things—that he'd killed.

Horrified, Kinley shoved with all her strength against his chest, wrenching her face aside to scream.

"Gently, now, gently," he said. His huge biceps bulged as he set her down, but he wouldn't release her. "I'll no' harm you. None shall for as long as I draw breath, *faodail*."

Twisting out of his grip, Kinley staggered backward and turned to run, but his men had surrounded them, and they looked at her the same way the Romans had...the same way the insurgents had...the same way the medics had...

The laird caught her arm and spun her around. "Lass, you cannae—"

Kinley punched him in the face, hard and fast. It hurt like hell, crunching her knuckles and jamming a pool cue of pain up to her shoulder. A heartbeat later something came down like a cinderblock on the back of her neck, and she collapsed at the Scotsman's feet.

Men shouted over her, and strong hands lifted her from the mud to cradle her against a broad, hard chest. Dizzy and confused, Kinley listened to the heavy thud under her cheek until it lulled her into oblivion.

Chapter Three

BENEATH THE BLACKEST skies in Scotland a large, rocky island awaited the dawn. Shaped like an immense claw swatting the icy strait that embraced it, Skye had been known by many names over the millennia. Norse invaders called it the isle of cloud, while the Celts had dubbed it the winged island for the sweeping shape of its coast. Since the Scottish had taken it back and settled it they had the final word in naming it: Skye, the misty isle.

To the south, in the heart of the island's Black Cuillin mountain range, lay two ancient secrets: Loch Sìorraidh, the largest body of fresh water on Skye, and Dun Aran, the stronghold built by Clan McDonnel. No outsider had ever beheld the mirror-still waters of the magical loch, or the immense, broad stone towers and soaring ramparts of the castle. Its foundation, hewn from the veins of basalt and gabbro that made up the Cuillin, lay deep within an extinct volcanic crater. From far below the earth a subterranean spring, heated to boiling by the molten stone beneath it, surged up to feed a huge cistern that warmed the rest of the stronghold.

Lights shimmered in the depths of the loch, growing brighter until they took on the shape of warriors. Waves churned as the McDonnel men began to rise from the waters to walk to shore, their wounds rapidly shrinking and disappearing as they were healed by the life-giving waters. Each man took up one of the torches they had left burning on the rocky shore. From there they mounted the hidden stone stairs and climbed up to the entrance of Dun Aran, where the clan's mortal servants waited to welcome them home.

Evander Talorc's tall, lanky form moved with silent purpose as he caught up with Lachlan McDonnel. He handed off his spear to a clansman as he regarded the soaked, unconscious woman in his laird's arms.

"You need not attend to the wench, my lord. Give her to me."

Lachlan eyed his stern-faced seneschal. While Evander was one of his most lethal fighters, he had a hard head and a cold heart. "You've done enough, man."

"Have you forgot I am seneschal, my lord?" Evander said. His tone suggested the answer was a resounding yes. "This wench attacked you. She is a threat. 'Tis my duty to deal with her now."

"Do you no' ken when to piss off, Evander?" said Tharaen Aber, Lachlan's bodyguard, as he moved between them. His dripping, silver-streaked black hair framed a face made jagged on one side with thin, gray lighting tattoos. "Shall I explain with my boot and your arse?"

The seneschal took a step closer. "Since you're an arse watcher, I reckon it'll be a change."

"Leave him be, Raen," Lachlan warned before he jerked his chin toward the loch. "Stand first watch, Talorc."

The seneschal gave them both a narrow look before he turned and walked back toward the shore.

"There's stew and bread set out in the main hall for ye," Margret Tally, the clan's chatelaine, called out to the men before she smothered a yawn. "More in the kitchens as well if you've a mind to waste the night drinking again. *Saints defend us*." Her drowsy eyes widened as she stared at the limp form in Lachlan's arms. "Who is this, milord? One of the legion's blood thralls?"

"We dinnae ken, Mistress Tally," Lachlan said as he passed the old woman. "Heat some wash water, and brew a calming blend with some honey. She's had a shock."

"Ye're *keeping* her, milord? *Here*?" the cook called after him.

"See to your work, Meg," Raen told her before he followed the laird into the main hall.

Lachlan had no intention of handing off the drenched, half-naked lass who had saved his life to anyone else. As he crossed the hall his clansmen parted to make way, but as he reached the steps to his tower chamber he could feel their eyes and hear their mutters.

The short, stocky form of Neacal Uthar stepped into his path, his usual cheerful grin not quite reaching his eyes. "Stay and drink with us, Laird. Meg and the maids can tend to the wee lass before she's sent back to her kin."

The clan's armorer and sword master, Neacal also served as the chieftain of the Uthar tribe, who numbered one in every five among the clansmen.

As such Neacal answered to no one but Lachlan, and held great sway over the clan. Keeping on his good side was one of Lachlan's perpetual aims, so he made no reproof for the unsubtle warning.

"Aye, but I owe her my life, and I'll thank her for it when she awakes."

"As you'll have it, then," Neacal said and nodded. He rubbed a hand across his bald head, and turned to toss a gauntlet onto the huge table where the men sat eating. Both arms sported huge tattoos of hammers that flexed with his muscles. "Break out the whiskey, lads. We've a victory to toast."

At the top of the tower stairs Raen reached the door to Lachlan's chamber before him, and opened it. "Neac's right, my lord. 'Tis no' your work."

"And 'twas it hers to save my hide?"

He carefully lowered her on his bed. His savior's long, slender form and gilded golden hair looked exotic against the plain weave of the linens, as if she deserved instead to be wrapped in silks. Her pretty lips looked a little swollen, which had been his doing. He'd meant to give her a kiss of gratitude, but tasting the lush sweetness of her mouth had made him go daft with woman hunger.

Raen came to stand beside him, his shadow stretching long and wide across the still, sodden form on the bed. "She's no' awakened, then?"

Lachlan shook his head and bent over her. She hadn't stirred once since they'd left the battle-field, but when he touched her neck the steady thrum of her heart danced under his fingertips. He breathed in her scent, which even after being doused in rain and mud smelled of strange flowers.

"Talorc shouldnae have coshed her so," he muttered. The feel of the soft, thin skin over her delicate bones made his jaw set. "She's all but a wisp."

"Doubtless his spleen prodded him. Evander has but two names for females: hoor, or hoor." Raen gave the woman a perplexed look. "What is this she wears now?"

Lachlan straightened and inspected what there was of her only garment. From her collar-bones to her thighs it clung to her, pale and thin as noble linen, but it had not been dyed or worked with colored thread. The tiny, flowerish marks on it seemed to be stained into the very stuff of the cloth.

"I cannae say," he said and plucked at the strings knotted at the back of her neck. "I've naught seen the like. Appears to be tied on her."

"Seems finely made," his bodyguard said as he touched the blade-straight hem. He turned it up to reveal dense needlework of perfectly uniform stitches that appeared to have no beginning or end. "A bodice, donned in haste, mayhap? Or some new manner of mantle?"

"Aye," Lachlan said, "but would she scamper about without kirtle or drawers?" He gently rolled her to her side to expose the three ties on the back. As he did he saw the odd white and blue strip encircling her left wrist. "Look at this cuff."

They discovered they could not unlatch the strange, tight bracelet, which had tiny English letters and numbers stained on it like the flower pattern of the woman's garment. It felt like painted parchment, so Lachlan cut it off with his dagger. Once he flattened it he was able to read the words.

"'Chandler, Kinley, CPT.' Kinley would be her given name, I think, and Chandler her surname. Or she might be a slave, owned by a candle-maker." He turned the flimsy strap and tried to sound out the last four letters. "You-saff?"

"Sounds Moorish," Raen said. He frowned and nudged up one of the gown's tiny sleeves. "My lord, she's marked. Could she be one of ours?"

The inked design on Kinley Chandler's arm had been fashioned with colors more vivid than any Lachlan had ever seen, and were far more intricate than any known to his kind. The red, blue and black art showed a stylized bird clutching a banner. Beneath the starred and striped design had been written two more odd words.

"Aff-sock. You-saff again," Lachlan said. "And such skinwork, there never was." He met Raen's troubled gaze. "Ken you any mortal clans by such names?" When his bodyguard shook his head, he tried to think of why the lass might have been inked. "Have the mortals given up branding yet?"

Raen shrugged. "She's no' a slave. Her hands are too soft."

When his servants delivered a steaming ewer of tea and a mug of Meg's brew, Lachlan told Raen to bring one of his semats as he stripped off Kinley's wet gown to reveal her fetching, willowy

body. As he gently washed the mud and gore from
her flawless skin he felt desire pour hot and heavy
through his veins. She had the loveliest breasts he
had ever seen, high and ripe with dark pink
nipples. All of her had been fashioned with long
lines and sweet curves, from her delicate shoulders
to the lyre of her hips. A neatly-trimmed thatch
of gilded curls over her womanhood made his
fingers itch to touch her there. His gaze reluctantly shifted from her sex to her right hip and
thigh, which bore more tattoos.

Written along Kinley's thigh the words "These
things we do, that others may live" stretched in
bonny, flowing script beneath a scattering of stars.
Reading it on her skin made something twist in
his heart. Above it on her flank a shield with a
red-hilted sword sprouting golden wings had been
inked, along with the words "Air Combat
Command." The final mark beneath the emblem
seemed to be only more numbers.

"Fack me." He felt completely bewildered
now. Air combat? Surely the lass had appeared
out of thin air, but how could she lead or fight
in it?

Raen returned from his dressing room with
the semat, and helped Lachlan ease Kinley into

the old, soft shirt before they swaddled her with a warm woolen. The raucous sounds of the men celebrating in the hall below drifted into the room until the bodyguard went and shut the door.

"Mayhap I need this more than the lass," Lachlan said and drank some tea.

Though he wanted to hover by the bed, he forced himself away. Instead he sat down in his great chair by the hearth to stare into the flames as he recalled everything that had happened from the moment he'd first seen Kinley Chandler. Raen offered to bring him food, which he refused, and then the bodyguard tended to the fire.

"She's fashed me but good," Lachlan said finally. "I cannae even tell if she's Scots, Britanni or, Gods save us, a Norsewoman." A thought occurred to him. "I spied her first by the stones. Do you ken the direction from whence she came?"

"I didnae see her until she ran at the undead, my lord." His bodyguard hesitated before he added, "The fire she used to burn them, to me it looked as if...but I'm addled, surely. She must have thrown torches."

"No, lad. The flames came from her hands. I saw it myself." During his long life he had witnessed many outlandish things, but never the like of this woman. "She has skin like a newborn. Did you see? No' a mark on her, anywhere."

"'Tisn't natural," Raen said, sounding as grim as Lachlan felt. "We should watch her teeth."

"If the legion turned her, she would never have attacked them, or saved me." He rubbed his brow. "Tomorrow we'll send word to the druids. Mayhap they can make some sense of her."

His bodyguard glanced past him and tensed. "My lord."

Lachlan looked over at his now-empty bed, and the woman backing away from it. Her long, pale gold hair had almost dried, and waved around her face like spun sunlight. Her arms and legs trembled, but her gaze remained steady and clear. A rosiness had flooded her pale face, tinting that marvelous skin back to life. Her blue eyes made him think of a loch struck by lightning, but held such terror they tore at his heart.

"Easy, lass." Slowly he stood and held up one hand. "You've naught to fear. You're safe now."

Her lips thinned and her fists curled at her sides as she studied him from boots to brow. That she didn't believe him showed plainly in her narrowed, thunderstruck eyes.

"I am Lachlan McDonnel, Laird of the McDonnel," he said, keeping his voice as low and soft as he would with a spooked mare. "Tonight, on the battlefield, you saved my life. Do you remember it? I was cut off, and surrounded."

Kinley's gaze shifted to Raen.

"My bodyguard, Tharaen Aber." He took a step toward her. "We dinnae mean you harm, Kinley Chandler."

Hearing her name made her stumble backward until her shoulders hit the door. She spun about, fumbling with the latch pull before she wrenched it open and fled.

With a curse, Lachlan ran with Raen after her.

Chapter Four

DOWN IN THE great hall the celebration had reached a noisy pitch, which fell into utter silence as Lachlan came from the tower. Kinley stood by the great hearth and gaped at his clansmen, who looked just as confounded.

"Quiet, and dinnae touch her," Lachlan warned. To her he said, "You've nowhere to run, lass. Come away with me now, and we'll talk."

She skittered away from him and whipped her head around as she sought a new direction.

"Kinley, look at me," Lachlan said and felt a small sense of relief when she gave him her attention. "You're among friends, I swear it."

"Aye, sweetheart," Neac said as he made a quick gesture, and a dozen men silently moved into positions around the hall's exits. "We're none of us blood-suckling bastarts." When she eyed him he bared his teeth and fingered the blunt edges. "You see? No fangs." He lifted his tankard. "We're Scotsmen. We drink *whiskey*. Why, we've a 'stillery on the island that makes such a malt, 'twould curl your hair *and* your toes."

As Neac kept talking to her, Raen and Lachlan approached Kinley from behind, and exchanged a look before the bodyguard made a grab for her. Raen caught only air as she dropped to the ground and rolled over like a dormouse between them. Beyond them she came out of the ball, planted her feet and stood, all in one smooth motion. But as she dodged around the clansman guarding the north hall Lachlan lunged and finally caught her from behind. He clamped her back against him, then picked her up, writhing and screeching.

Tormod Liefson frowned at the laird. "Odin's beard, but she's a noisy one. Shall we fetch a more willing lover for you from among the house wenches, my lord?" He ducked as Kinley tried to kick him in the face. "Or there's always good, strong rope."

Neac slapped the brawny Norseman on the

back of the head. "We're no' thieving, raping, murderous raiders, Tormod. Didnae you hear me before? We're Scotsmen."

Lachlan swore as Kinley latched onto his forearm with her teeth. "Raen. Some help."

"Scotsmen? I'm a Viking." Tormod's expression grew baffled. "And you were painted savages who slaughtered my people, set fire to our settlement, and enslaved me."

"'Twas our facking island first, you sunbleached bawbag," Neac countered.

Raen gripped Kinley's jaw and squeezed it until she released the laird's bleeding forearm, and then grabbed her flailing legs and held them by the ankles.

"Bloodthirsty little wench might as well be undead," Tormod said, sounding almost admiring now. "As for you and yours, Uthar, when you weren't out hunting and eating *Scotsmen*, you were stealing their women and their herds."

"The lasses came willingly," the chieftain said, shaking a thick finger at him. "And we only ever ate their cattle."

"Upstairs," Lachlan told his bodyguard as he backed toward the tower entry. "Easy now, lass."

"I am not a lass, you son of a bitch," Kinley said, her oddly-accented voice echoing through the hall, and silencing the men again. "I'm a captain in the United States Air Force."

As the clan stared at her, Neac screwed up his face. "The United…where the fack is that now?"

"You let me go," she demanded, "or so help me god I will find a way to escape, bring back a bomber wing, and blow this place to kingdom come."

No one understood exactly what she meant, but the clan knew a heartfelt threat when they heard one. The men lifted their tankards and roared their approval.

By the time they carried her back into Lachlan's chambers Kinley had threatened to do all manner of mysterious things. Once they put her on the bed Lachlan was obliged to pin her with his body weight while sending Raen to find some smooth cording that wouldn't tear her flesh.

Kinley turned her face as far away from his as she could and still keep it attached to her neck. "Get off me or I'll–"

"Castrate me with a blunt blade, and shove my bits down my men's throats." That much he'd understood. What Lachlan found fascinating was that Kinley had yet to use her flame-throwing power on him or any of his men. "If I am your enemy, *faodail*, then why would you save me in the grove?"

Her jaw tightened as she glared up at him. "Six on one isn't fair, especially when the six are… whatever they were."

"Undead," he told her. "Creatures of the night that feed on the blood of mortals."

"Jesus," Kinley said and made a disgusted sound. "When do the Nazis and the Spartans show up?"

"If you dinnae believe what you saw," Lachlan said, "then you burned them for naught."

"They were going to kill you." The hard line of her mouth eased a little. "You pushed too far ahead on your own. You should have stayed with your men."

"Aye, but they can be slow, and me impatient." He eased his grip on her wrists. "I thank you for my life, Kinley Chandler."

Suspicion soured her expression. "How do you know my name?"

"'Twas written on the cuff you wore." Lachlan had never heard anyone who had her exotic accent, and the strange words she used made him wonder if English was her natal language. Asking her about her origins, however, might only rile her into another frenzy. "Do you ken this place?"

"No, but I imagine my subconscious is decorating this coma." Her gaze shifted to his chest briefly. "Or I could be having one of those all-night dreams that make you think you're awake. Or it's a very interesting afterlife." She regarded him. "But I'm guessing none of the above."

"This is Dun Aran, our castle on Skye." When he didn't see any change in her expression he added, "Skye is an isle off the coast of Scotland."

"I know. My great-grandparents came from there." She looked all around his chamber again. "I'm from San Diego."

He had no idea where or what that place was. "What brought you here?"

She moved her shoulders. "Maybe I fell down a rabbit hole." She turned her head as Raen came back, and saw the strips of silk in his fist. She glared at Lachlan. "You're tying me up? Is that what you do to all your friends to whom you mean no harm?"

He didn't care to have her bound. No, he

wanted to send his bodyguard away, and strip the semat from Kinley's lovely young body, and caress and kiss her until she begged him to have her. Between them his shaft swelled and stiffened, begging her to have him. From the way her eyes darkened she felt it, too.

"I cannae do as I wish," Lachlan murmured to her. "But, oh, lass, if I could."

"This is crazy," she whispered. "I've known you like five minutes—and you kidnapped me."

"Aye." Lachlan curled his fingers around her wrist, and stretched out her arm so that Raen could bind it to the bed frame's tester. "I cannae have you dashing about the stronghold." As soon as his bodyguard tied her other wrist he forced himself up and off, and covered her with the blanket. "We'll talk more on the morrow. Try to sleep."

Lachlan gestured for Raen to follow him into the hall. "Stay with her, but keep her bound, and tell her nothing."

His bodyguard glanced back at Kinley. "Will you send for the druids, then, my lord?"

He knew he should, and he couldn't think of a reason not to. Only the conclave could fathom something as enormous as Kinley's fiery power, or what her appearance on the battlefield meant. At the same time he felt very protective of his bonny little savior.

"No' yet, lad," Lachlan said finally. "First we'll see if we can tame her."

Chapter Five

IN A REMOTE valley in the north of Scotland a different stronghold lay hidden beneath the earth. Built inside a series of immense limestone caves, the fortress housed the army that had quarried its stone walls, and excavated the miles of tunnels leading to and from it. Animals avoided its cleverly-camouflaged entries, as if they sensed that any living thing dragged into them would never emerge alive. The ruins around it perpetuated legends of entire settlements found deserted for twenty miles in every direction. Elders spun yarns about a merciless legion of invading Romans who had slaughtered the native tribes. But the Romans had been cursed by the ancient druids for their cruelty.

Such were the stories, and stories they

remained. For those who met the pale demons by moonlight never returned to tell their tales.

The sound of boots crushing bones made Prefect Quintus Seneca look up from the old manuscript he studied. The ghastly noise came from one of the lower entry tunnels. Long ago it would have signified some new victory for Emperor Hadrian and Rome. Now, a thousand years later, it meant that some of the men of the Ninth Legion had returned. They had been sent to hunt the McDonnel clan but had to return before the killing rays of the sun found them.

Quintus closed the old, priceless book and handed it to his freedman.

"Orno, put this back with the others in the archive room. Who warms the tribune's bed tonight?"

"One of the wenches taken from the lowland dairy." Orno's round face creased with worry. "She has served him since the scythe moon."

That meant her suffering would end tonight. Quintus disliked the use of females as blood thralls. He'd been raised to respect women. But he had not brought this curse upon the legion, and he could not starve his men or deny them the other needs they suffered.

"Choose the most comely among those untouched for his next."

"Yes, Master." The former slave bowed and retreated.

Before he left his quarters Quintus drained his goblet and took down his mantle from the twelve-pointed antlers Orno had mounted above his pallet. His servant took pleasure in collecting the bones of long-dead lynx, bear and reindeer found in the cave's ancient midden piles, and carving or fashioning them to be useful. To Quintus, they were a silent reminder of what happened to predators when they became the prey.

The sentries on duty snapped to attention as he passed them, and he spared a nod for each before crossing the gallery above the tunnel. Below him he counted nine battered, grim-faced men returning from the hunt. They passed under the rotting remains of dense curtains once used to shield them and their brethren from the sun's lethal rays while they were digging out their lair. At the end of the tunnel they filed in one rank through the new wall of planks Quintus had ordered erected as a more permanent light barrier for the lower levels.

From there the tunnel widened to a large, dark

cavern dimly lit by braziers and torches. Quintus left the gallery to join the legion's commander, Tribune Gaius Lucinius. The most powerful man among the legion sat on a dais perched high above the cave floor on the platform built for his exclusive use. It made the tribune resemble an emperor looking down upon the masses, which was why Quintus had commissioned it.

Since being cursed to exist as an undead blood-drinker, Gaius fancied himself transformed into a god. As that kept the tribune happy, and less inclined to indiscriminately slaughter their men, Quintus did everything he could to cater to his delusions.

Tonight the tribune had taken particular care with his dress. His purple toga and golden laurel crown might shout imperial status, but Gaius had been born *advenae*—the son of freed Hispanic slaves—and everyone in the legion knew it.

"You are very late, Prefect," Gaius said as soon as Quintus joined him. "I begin to think you avoid me."

The shrieks and cries of newly-caught mortals came from the garrison behind them, and echoed around the cave before fading away as their captors fed on them. The metallic stink of their blood sharpened the dank air, making the eyes of all the men on duty glitter with lust.

"Forgive me, Tribune." Quintus knelt on one knee briefly. "Time escaped me while I was reading."

Although the scents and sounds made them shudder with thirst, the mud-spattered soldiers returning from the hunt filed into ranks before the platform. Once the men stood in proper order they bowed their heads and slammed their gauntlets against their chest plates.

"You waste yourself on the words of dead men, Quintus. Better you make tribute to the gods, for only they bestow real wisdom." Gaius regarded the men before him without expression. "This does not appear promising."

"Centurion Brutus Ficini," Quintus said, "Report."

One of the older men stepped forward and extended his arm in a salute. "Our patrols lured the McDonnels away from the village to the appointed place." Ficini paused as his flat, emotionless voice echoed in the silence of the cavern. "Half died before we separated the laird from his men, and summoned the reinforcements.

A female appeared and defended the laird against our efforts."

Quintus moved to stand before the centurion. "A woman defended the McDonnels? How so?"

The older man's face grew bleak. "She burned the execution team with flames that came out of her hands."

Gaius sat up and gripped the golden armrests of his dais. "Ficini, do you mean to say this woman threw fire at them?"

The centurion bowed. "Yes, Tribune."

"Why did you not kill her?" Before Ficini could answer the tribune rose. "Am I to understand that you had the laird, and lost him to a female, and then *retreated*?"

Quintus couldn't help but wince. When their commander grew agitated his voice became shrill. The girlish sound did not instill admiration or respect among the men.

"This woman would have burnt us to ash, had we stayed and fought." The older man stared at the cave floor. "Had we died on the field, you would know nothing of her, Tribune."

"A fine excuse for your cowardice," Gaius spat. He paced back and forth before the dais before he stopped and made an imperious gesture. "Have them whipped," he told Quintus. "Twenty lashes each." With that order he stalked off the platform.

The prefect watched his commander leave the cavern, and only then gave the order to administer the punishment. "Once it is done," Quintus told the whip master, "see to it that they are given enough blood to heal."

Ficini heard this, and bowed to the prefect.

Quintus left to find Gaius, who had retreated to his private chamber. He coughed politely when he saw his commander had his blood thrall naked and braced against a wall, but the tribune only motioned for him to come in.

"Failure again, Quintus," said the tribune. He kicked the cowering female's legs apart. "I vow it shall drive me mad." To the thrall he said, "No weeping this time. It distracts me."

He sank his fangs into the back of her neck. As though he were moving too fast to be seen, the tribune's body vibrated, changing into the woman's, then back to his own, then back again. Long ago the legion had learned that taking the victim's blood caused the transformation, if only briefly. Over the centuries they had learned to control the change, but come the morning they always reverted back to their original bodies.

As Gaius finished drinking, he quickly became himself again. With a quick bite to his own palm, he produced two drops of blood. A careless swipe of his blood across the woman's wounds made the injuries vanish. It would do no good to have her bleed to death or summon the hungry. The tribune hiked up his toga to fist his shaft and rammed it into the slave woman.

Even Quintus's cold heart thawed with a measure of pity for the blood thrall. She tried to weep silently as the tribune's thrusts slammed her into the cave wall again and again.

"Ficini is no coward," Quintus said. "He was correct to retreat and bring news of this woman to us. If she can throw fire, she can kill us."

"Really, Quintus, a *mortal* fire-thrower? What next will Ficini regale us with to explain his failure? Tales of swans and showers of gold turning into horny gods?" Gaius grunted and stiffened as he climaxed, and then withdrew and shoved the woman toward the pallet that served as her bed. Idly he rubbed the scar where his testicles had once been before he straightened his toga. "Never say that you believe him."

"We have served together for centuries, and he has no motive to lie. Some of the men who survived have burns on their limbs." Quintus filled a goblet from a bottle of wine mixed with blood and brought it to his commander. "Tribune, perhaps it is time now for us to seek out a safer territory to inhabit."

Gaius laughed heartily. "We do not leave Scotland until the curse the McDonnels cast over us is broken, and we kill every one of them. Again." He drained the goblet. "Send word to our spy. If this fire-throwing wench is real, I want to know everything about her. Who she is, where she abides, and how we may take her from the fucking highlanders."

Quintus nodded, saluting the tribune before he retreated. But instead of returning to his quarters, he slipped through a passage known only to him. He followed it to the small space he had discovered while looking for a particular observation post. It had taken days of careful drilling to create the spy hole, which permitted him to watch everything Gaius did when he was alone.

Tonight he used the blood thrall's mouth and ass for his pleasure before binding her on the small altar he had erected in the corner of his chamber. There the tribune went down on his knees, spilling wine over her belly and praying to the statue wedged in the wall directly above the mewling woman.

"Father Mars, I entreat thee to look upon thy servant and my offering. I pray that thou shall make me strong and resolute in my command. Take this female whom I have fucked with my sacred phallus and from whom I have taken that which nourishes my spirit." Gaius produced a blade, and rose as he held it over the twisting, screaming wench.

Quintus turned away as Gaius gutted the mortal and began to bathe himself in her blood.

Chapter Six

F ROM THE KEEL-shaped ridges of the Black Cuillin mountains, Evander Talorc strode down toward a broad glen. Before standing first watch at the loch he had gone to the castle's dovecote to send a messenger bird to the druid settlement. The reply had come just before he'd been relieved by the day sentry.

Come to the fairy pool by the old bridge.

He felt no qualms over sending for the druids without consulting the laird. As Dun Aran's seneschal Evander's first responsibility was to the castle and its safety. The female Lachlan had brought back had attacked the laird, which made her no friend of the McDonnel clan. If the fire-tossing harpy did not belong to the druids, they could facking well keep her until they found her people.

If they would not, well, then, she was mortal, and the loch very cold and deep.

The thought of drowning her did give Evander pause. For all that he despised women, he'd never murder one. When had his temper grown so brutish?

Quick to anger, and slow to joy. A man better suited to killing than loving. That was what Baeral had said to him the day before they were supposed to wed. That the whore had given herself to his chieftain's brother that night, and run away to the lowlands with him had made Evander glad, for at least she did it without his name. When the Talorc had forbidden Evander to pursue them or take vengeance, he'd simply laughed. Well rid of Baeral he had been, he assured his leader.

Well rid, but never to forget. The slut had gone to her grave so long ago that surely naught remained of her but dust—and still Evander burned with unspent fury over her betrayal.

A flash of movement and dun-colored fur on the other side of the glen caught his eye. Evander lifted his spear, feeling its weight in his hand. He sighted along the shaft, his cheek next to the mark he'd carved so that all would know who made the kill. Quickly, he spun with the weapon and flung it. The whistling of the shaft through the air made the hare try to hop away. But the shaft skewered it through the neck in mid-air, and it fell dead in the grass.

Evander collected the carcass and tied it to his belt. Mistress Talley would welcome the meat for her morning pottage, and making the kill soothed his pride. Few clansmen still hunted with spears, and none could have hit the hare at such a distance.

Halfway across the glen he came to a small, narrow spring fed by a waterfall. The villagers who dwelled by the island's shore called such places fairy pools, and still left pagan offerings at them for luck, love, and fertility. Several garlands of woven wildflowers had been hung on the rocks at the edge of the water, along with a crude cloth poppet that had been stuffed until its belly bulged.

He picked up the doll, which some female had left doubtless in hopes of conceiving. Tossing it in the water wouldn't drown its maker, but gave him a small measure of satisfaction.

"Have you some pressing need, Seneschal?" a mellow voice asked.

Evander turned with his dagger in hand to see the slender, graceful form of Ovate Cailean Lusk walking out of the trees. The druid looked no older than sixteen, but his youthful appearance had nothing to do with his genuine age. While druids lived mortal lives, when they died their souls reincarnated in the next newborn among their kind. Cailean had already lived many lives. Evander had known him for nigh on six centuries.

The ovate, however, was not the druid Evander wanted to see. Evander lowered his blade.

"I sent word for Bhaltair Flen to attend me. He understands the strain of my duty." And he had complained to him more than once about Lachlan's regular disregard for the security of Dun Aran.

"My master couldnae leave his work. I am sent in his place." Cailean halted at the edge of the spring and glanced down at the poppet slowly sinking to the bottom. "'Twas no' a kindness to do that." He stretched out his hand, murmured some words, and the doll rose from the water to plop on his palm. "Children are a gift," he said quietly, smoothing a thumb over the round of the belly.

Evander scowled at the young man. "What would an ovate ken of it?"

The druid smiled a little sadly. "More than one might think." He placed it atop a sunny stone to dry before his large, serene blue eyes met Evander's gaze. "How may I assist you?"

Druids always made it sound as if they served the clan, when the truth of it was the McDonnels did all the work. "Very well. We've one of your females at the castle. The clan would be obliged if you'd come and take her away."

Cailean's smooth brows rose. "None of our druidesses have been sent to you, Seneschal. What is her name?"

Evander clenched his jaw. "I dinnae ken it. She came to meddle with us at the oak grove in Carstairs Valley, where the tribe's old stones stand."

The druid's eyelids closed as he went still, so that all that moved were the folds of his robe. When he looked at Evander again the dreamy look had vanished from his eyes.

"Take me to her, please."

Cailean remained silent on the walk up into

the ridges. When they reached the castle Evander took him in through a little-used side entry and through a back hall that led to the base of the laird's tower. Halfway up the steps, Raen Aber appeared, stopped, and crossed his huge arms.

"Fair day to you, Master Aber," the druid said politely.

"And you, Ovate Lusk." The bodyguard eyed Cailean before he regarded Evander. "You've been busy."

One day, Evander thought, he and Aber would fight, and he'd teach him just what he could do with a spear. "The ovate has come to see the female," he told Raen flatly. "Step aside."

"I'm told she may be druid kind," the boy said, raising his hands in a peaceful gesture. "I wish only to speak with her a moment, so that I may learn her name, and why she came to you."

The shaggy dark head shook. "She's no' to be disturbed. Laird's orders." When Evander tried to push past him he shifted to block his path. "Remember that beating you gave the lass? I hit much harder, and no' from behind."

Cailean turned to gape at Evander. "You struck this woman?"

"She was attacking the laird, and she can

throw fire from her hands." Evander flung a hand at Raen. "And this one, his own bodyguard, stood there and did naught to stop her."

"She's a woman, Evander," Raen bellowed. "Did your da never teach you that we're supposed to protect them?"

"What was I to do?" he shouted back. "Let her burn off his facking face?"

The druid's gaze bounced between them for a moment, and then grew shuttered. "I think 'tis better I go now. 'Tis likely the female isnae druid kind. Beg your pardon for the trouble, Master Aber. Master Talorc." He nodded to Evander, and before he could stop him hurried back down the steps.

Since indulging his temper would only end in a fight he might not win, Evander tried reason. "That wench cannae stay here. She's an outsider. She's *mortal*."

"Aye, and she can burn up six undead with a gesture. If the laird doesnae want the lass, I may wed her myself." The big man turned and went back upstairs.

Back down in the great hall Neacal Uthar hailed Evander with a loud "good" and a whimpered "morning" before he propped his head between his hands. "Come and break your fast, Seneschal. Meg's making a cannel brew and oat cakes."

Evander sat at the trestle table and watched the tower entry. "Where is the laird?"

"Sleeping in the stables, according to Meg." The bald chieftain cracked open one eye. "That young wand-waver ran out of here at a fast trot. Makes a man wonder what the floor-dusters are plotting now. Might it involve our bastart-burner?"

Even with a sore head Neac saw more than most.

"Cailean claimed she wasnae druid kind," Evander said. "What else could she be but one of theirs? Do you ken a mortal wench with hands of fire?"

"Why do you care what she is? 'Tis the laird's problem." The chieftain sat up as the chatelaine arrived with a tray of cakes and tea. "Ah, here's a fine lady with real magic." He winced as she thumped it down in front of him. "If only you'd wield it a wee bit quieter, lass."

"Ye drink too much whiskey, ye wake with a

pounding pate. After a thousand years ye'd think a man could learn that. Sip the brew slow, or ye'll puke again. And as for ye, Seneschal." Meg poured a mug for Evander and added a dollop of honey to it. "Mayhap this will sweeten yer temper, ye black-hearted woman-beater."

He rose to his feet to tower over the chatelaine. *"I didnae beat her."*

Meg looked up at him, sniffed loudly, and retreated from the hall, her back stiff with disapproval. As soon as she disappeared into the kitchens Evander sat back down and pressed the heels of his hands against his eyes.

"Well done, lad," Neac said. "She'll be spitting in your meals until Lammas." The chieftain drew out a flask, and added a generous measure of whiskey to Evander's brew. "Come now. 'Tis almost certain the wench'll run off herself. She nearly got out last night while we were toasting our victory. I had to distract her with talk so the laird and Raen could snatch her back."

Now Evander felt even angrier. "Why did you stop her?"

Neac shrugged. "The laird wants her, and no' just for those torch-hands of hers. She's as comely as a princess. She has claim on him now, too, and

I've never ken a McDonnel to ignore a life debt. The druids are proof of that, or we'd no' be here in the Black Cuillin."

The potent, cloying taste of the spicy brew made Evander grimace, but he drank it down while he listened to the chieftain's idle speculations. As more Uthars joined them Neac turned his attention to his tribesmen, and what weapons and armor they had that were in need of repair after the battle with the undead.

Evander slipped away unnoticed, and spent some time pacing the long curtain wall walk between the promontory towers. Once he felt he had his temper properly confined, he headed for the stables.

He found Lachlan in a stall with one of the clan's muscular, gray Eriskay pack ponies. He and a mortal stable hand were examining a gash on the mare's right flank. He gritted his teeth as he tried to be polite.

"My lord, a word?"

"Wash it gently, and then use that honey and stanch weed salve," the laird told the mortal. "She's no' to be taken out again until she heals." Lachlan regarded Evander. "Walk with me."

Evander accompanied the laird out of the

stables and down to the loch, where they halted at a spot between two massive tribe stones by the hot spring vent. Standing in the place where their first lives had ended never seemed to disturb Lachlan. He often came to the spot to sit and look out over the dark waters that held so many secrets. Remembering his own brutal death was all that came to Evander here. Although he didn't often agree with the laird, Evander respected the big man.

"I've always wondered," Evander said, "how does a war master like you come to ken so much about healing?"

"As a boy that war master tended to the herds by day," Lachlan said, "and mother and sister by night." Lachlan searched the horizon. "My father had no patience for it, but white plague is maddening. The fevers and coughing never end. By the time they bring up dark blood you're all but half-dead yourself." Absently he ran his fingers along the swirls of the serpent carved in the tribe stone. "Have your word, Seneschal."

"I shouldnae have struck the woman. It grieves you that I did, and for that I am sorry." He watched the laird's expression. "But she can start fires with her hands. That alone makes her dangerous. I am charged with protecting Dun Aran, not only for you, my lord, but for the clan. If she were to set fire to the castle, while everyone was abed…cannae you see? She has to go, and go now."

"If she were a man with the same power, would you wish her gone?" Lachlan held up his hand before Evander could reply. "The truth."

Evander narrowed his eyes, but it was a time for truth. "No, my lord." Insulting the wench would only annoy the laird, so he spoke of what he knew. "Men have discipline, and self-control. We ken our duty and keep our oaths. We are trained for battle. A man could be trusted."

"Women are no' all trollops, Evander," Lachlan told him. "When the lass was lost and terrified and alone, she protected me instead of herself. Without a reason in the world to, for she kens naught of me or the clan. If that matters no' to you, then think on how she killed six undead— by herself—with a single blow. What McDonnel can say the same? No' me or you."

"Then you mean to let her stay."

The prospect made Evander's hands fist.

"We'll keep her close, and learn what we can of her and her power," the laird said, and glanced back at the stronghold. "But if she truly wishes to go, I dinnae think any of us can stop her."

Evander would have to find another way to be rid of the wench. "As you say, my lord."

Chapter Seven

A S LACHLAN STEPPED inside the tower chamber, Raen looked up from the blade hilt he was wrapping.

"She stayed awake until I persuaded her to have some calming brew," his bodyguard said. "It put her to slumber, and she hasnae moved since."

Lachlan nodded as he went to his bed, in which Kinley lay. "Go and get some sleep. I'll stay with her."

When Raen reached the door he hesitated and looked back. "Cailean Lusk came at dawn asking to see her. Evander's doing. I sent him away, but I've a notion he'll be back."

Lachlan had underestimated the seneschal's determination to rid Dun Aran of Kinley. "Put a guard downstairs before you find your bed. No one but you comes up."

"Aye, my lord." Raen glanced at Kinley, shook his head a little and departed.

Lachlan tugged off his shirt, which smelled of the stables, and dragged a hand over his crown. His orders would spawn all manner of new rumors among the clan, most casting Kinley as his bedmate. Yet he had never dallied with any of the serving women at the stronghold. When he needed release he went to one of the villages on the mainland, where he would spend the night with a willing widow. He knew they needed the gold he offered in exchange, and such brief encounters kept his life uncomplicated.

He felt a knot in his groin, and glanced down to see the impressive stoner he'd gotten. He might have to make another trip soon, if he didn't get his lust for Kinley under control.

As he stood over the bed, he realized that Kinley's first sight when she awoke would be his bulge. Gingerly he sat down on the edge of the bed. Sleep had smoothed away the lines of anger and fear from around her eyes and mouth. She looked almost angelic now. If not for the ripe curves of her breasts and hips she might have been a slumbering bairn.

Lachlan glanced at her bonds. The lass had done naught but help him and his, and it wasn't right to bind an ally. He untied the silk strips from the bed. Perhaps it would help her to sleep longer. As if in response, she turned over and a lock of her fine golden hair fell against Lachlan's hand. He caressed the thin, bright strands, and marveled at how silky they felt against his fingertips.

What would it be like, to have such tresses in his hands, or whispering across his chest? His mouth wanted more of hers, and that wild sweetness he'd tasted on the battlefield. Would she make love as ferociously as she fought?

He might blame his rigid cock on the weeks he'd spent celibate while hunting the legion, but it wasn't need for a wench that made him hard. He wanted this strange, fierce lass more than anything in his memory—and not only for her willowy beauty. She had roused something inside him he thought he'd left buried at the bottom of the loch.

Long ago, when the Romans had invaded Caledonia, the Pritani had retreated to their highland settlements. At first it seemed the invaders would not chase them, but the word came that they had begun hunting and killing magic folk. When the druid conclave called upon the McDonnel tribe's war master to help them escape annihilation, Lachlan agreed without hesitation. He appealed to other tribes to stand with him and his men, and so they came together as one great force.

Under the banner of the druid's protective dragon symbol, they carried out raids against the Romans, burning their camps and driving them south. What the invaders never realized was that Lachlan's attacks were made to allow the conclave and the surviving settlements of magic folk to escape Caledonia. The druids left by boat under cover of darkness to sail to Hetlandensis, where they took shelter on one of the unsettled islands.

Luring the Romans to Skye had been a strategic gamble. Lachlan knew the Black Cuillin mountains to be the perfect place for an ambush, but he hadn't counted on the entire Ninth Legion being sent to pursue them. Out-numbered three to one, his men were quickly overrun and captured. The tribune had sneered at his captives.

You were a fool to challenge us.

While the Calendonian slave translated his

words, the Roman tribune surveyed the defeated tribesmen. They knelt bound on the shore of Loch Sìorraidh, as he regarded Lachlan.

Still, I can be generous. He tossed a handful of silver coins on the ground between them. *Tell me where the druids have gone, and I will spare you, and one man out of every ten.*

Lachlan could have told him what he could do with his mercy, but spitting in his face had been far more satisfying. The tribune had ordered him beaten, and then stripped and bound between the tribe's stones.

He hadn't understood why until the executions began.

Lachlan's men had died in silence, each looking at him and nodding their farewells in the moment before they fell beneath Roman blades. Some moved their lips in voiceless prayers to the gods. Many had prayed for him and his sanity, bless their souls.

The centurions ordered the camp slaves to toss the bodies in the loch, until the inlet turned scarlet from their blood. When Lachlan alone remained alive, the tribune came to him and offered him life as a legion slave.

He'd smiled at the Roman, just as he smiled

now, remembering. His last act as a mortal man had been kicking that sadistic facker in the balls with such force that his testicles had ruptured.

The last thing he remembered was a cold-eyed prefect swinging his blade at Lachlan's neck, and then nothingness—until the awakening.

You Pritani went willingly to your death, that we might live, the oldest Druid told Lachlan when he had walked out of the loch. *Now you are reborn and you shall never die.*

Kinley grumbled in her sleep and drew her legs up.

Lachlan stroked her silken hair and watched the gentle rise and fall of her breath, as a peculiar sensation jabbed his chest from within.

Chapter Eight

KINLEY WOKE FEELING as if she'd slept for a thousand years. For a moment she wondered if she had actually come out of the coma, and waited for the pain of her injuries to flare. Nothing but a dull throb at the base of her neck registered. She smelled wood smoke, and herbs, and something like cool, clear water. She felt like she had a headache building on top of the neck pain, but what she mostly felt was wonderfully warm. Slowly she opened her eyes to find a man sitting on her bed.

One thing she knew immediately: she wasn't at the VA hospital anymore.

He wasn't a fellow soldier, not with that long, dark hair. His deep tan hinted he'd been over in

the Sand Pit, but she didn't recognize his handsome face...or did she? She'd seen him somewhere before, in the rain...

A rush of flashing, snapshot memories flooded
Kinley's mind, beginning from the moment she'd
tried to kill herself in Horsethief Canyon, and
ending when she'd fallen asleep while tied to the
laird's bed. She turned her head to see if the
bodyguard (*Rain?*) was around, but it looked as if
they were alone—and someone had untied her
wrists.

With her bare hands she'd burned six men to
death last night, and they'd just tied her up? No,
they were definitely *not* military.

"Dinnae run again, *faodail*," Lachlan said, his
voice rumbling deep. "I'm too jeeked to chase
after you. Go back to sleep."

She should have screamed, jumped from
the bed, yelled for help—something—and she
would have if she were awake. All of her
injuries were gone, which meant she was
dreaming, or still in that coma. Whichever it
was that had landed her in the big highlander's bed, it seemed pretty stupid to fight it.
She might wake up on the psych ward at the
VA hospital with Dr. Stevens hovering and

wanting to know why she'd attempted suicide by cliff.

Or Kinley had gone over the cliff, and this was some kind of very odd afterlife.

"Dinnae be so quiet," Lachlan said softly. "'Tis making me nervous."

Freaking out again would serve no purpose other than getting her tied to the bed again. She also felt none of the terror she had on the battle-field or when she'd tried to escape. On some level being in the big man's bed even felt right. She let her eyes roam over the thick muscles of his broad, bare chest, as well as his chiseled biceps.

She was imagining the whole thing. Had to be that.

"All right," she said, sitting up. "Let's work this out." She arranged her strange shirt as best as she could. "My grandmother was Scottish. You've got to be from one of the stories she told me. That means you're going to, what? Turn into a seal and bite me or drag me into the sea?" That might explain the way he smelled, too.

Now his dark brown eyes regarded her sternly and he frowned. "I'm no' a selkie."

"That's a relief. The seal thing would have been cool, though." He reached to her wrist and began to untie the silk fabric. "So tell me where I am again."

"Dun Aran castle on the isle of Skye." He rubbed a finger gently over a mark the knot had left. "Do you remember my name?"

She frowned. "Ronald MacDonald, lord of something."

"Lachlan McDonnel, laird of the McDonnel clan," he corrected.

"That's it," she said, as her gaze shifted to the tattoo of a snake's head on his right shoulder. It stretched across his upper torso to end with a tail that curled just above his left forearm. "I've never seen tribal ink like this." Which suggested she hadn't dreamed up the dream man. She lightly ran her fingertip over the tattoo, and was rewarded with a twitch of the big man's pec. "Why did you go for the giant snake?"

"As a lad I grew too fast," he said. "My size made me clumsy, and it angered my Da. When my Choosing Day came, I asked for a serpent, that I might be as one."

She recalled how fluidly he moved, particularly in battle. "Worked like a charm."

"'Tis no' a charm," Lachlan assured her, very gravely, as if what she'd said meant something else to him. "I offered myself to the serpent spirit, and it chose to join with me. It doesnae always happen. Some ask too much, or they're found unworthy." He hesitated before he said, "You are no' Pritani."

"My grandmother raised me Protestant, but I stopped going to church after she died. Kind of hard to thank god for killing off all your family." He had no clue what that meant, Kinley realized, any more than she had about what he was saying. "Let's try something easier. What day is it?"

He thought for a moment. "Washday, I think, or baking day, mayhap."

"Okay." So he wasn't big on calendars. Neither was she. "Do you know what year it is?"

"By mortal reckoning, ah...thirteen fourteen." He paused. "Why do you laugh now?"

It took her another moment to get her hilarity under control. "Okay. You're telling me that I'm in the fourteenth century, on an island off the coast of Scotland, in the bed of a clan laird chosen by the snake spirit to fight vampires— sorry, the undead—and let's not forget that I can throw fire out of my hands." Yeah, she was definitely dreaming.

"The serpent gifted me only my ability. I

chose to fight the undead." Lachlan studied her face. "But for the rest, aye, you've the right of it."

"Could be worse, I guess. I could be trapped serving pitchers in an endless beer commercial." She stared up at the rough ceiling beams, which had been carved with more primitive symbols. "Maybe I saw all this on the History Channel. Gran loved watching shows about old Scotland. She never got to visit, you know?"

His brows drew together as if he were trying to work out what she meant. "You dinnae believe me."

"Oh, no, I do," she countered. "Why wouldn't I? I invented you and this place." She grimaced. "Didn't you leave me with a bigger guy last night? I mean, after I interrupted all those men drinking in that cathedral? Where's Lightning Face?"

"I'm real, Kinley," he said and took her hand. "Flesh, blood, bone, and no' of your imagining."

"It's so authentic, the way you talk. I love the no' thing." She patted his cheek. "All you need is a kilt, and you'll be the perfect highlander."

He caught her hand and held it against his face. "What's a kilt, then?"

Kinley felt another, more serious tremor of doubt. "A guy skirt. Oh, but since this is the middle ages, they're not fashionable yet." She tried to remember what Bridget had told her about Scotland, but his warm hand over hers was distracting. "Maybe we should, ah, get up."

"I'm up already." As his dark eyes searched her face, a shaft of sunlight poured in from the window, gilding them both. "Kinley."

From the way he stared at her mouth she could guess what was about to happen. Then she saw how the light revealed all the colors of October in his eyes, from the amber starbursts around his pupils to the deep, rich bronze of his outer irises. His hair glinted as he bent down to her, falling in a dark curtain around her face.

His breath whispered across her lips, and then the touch of his mouth made it all real. His lips felt firm and soft all at once, and caressed hers until she opened for him. His hand slid under the back of her skull as he slanted his mouth over hers, and gave her his tongue.

Her imaginary Scottish laird tasted of cinnamon and herbs, and the way he kissed made everything from her collarbones to her thighs go liquid. When she kissed him back, he easily drew her onto his lap, and she straddled his massive thighs. She could feel his muscles tightening, and her own hips pulsed forward. The scent of cool water grew so intense it seemed to stream through her now. He moved, and the hard ridge of his erection fit against her, long and thick.

Man, could she dream, or what?

He caught her lower lip between his teeth, slowly releasing it to end the kiss.

"What?" she breathed.

He buried his face in her hair, inhaling deeply, and then moved to do the same thing to her neck. Finally he met her gaze. "The smell of your hair, your skin. 'Tis like you've been bathed in sunlight."

Kinley touched his mouth with her fingertips. "You like it?"

Lachlan dragged her up with him until they knelt together on the bed. The small gap between their bodies disappeared as he splayed his big hands over her back and urged her closer for another kiss. She ran her palms up his chest and clung to his shoulders, her fingernails digging in to his resilient flesh as their mouths grew hungrier.

Yep. He liked it all right.

If she could just kiss him like this for the rest of eternity, it would be enough. But no, in another moment she'd be tearing off whatever he'd dressed her in and offering him whatever he wanted. Because suddenly it wasn't enough.

A hammering knock startled them apart, and the door to the chamber swung open as a very large, broad man came in.

"My lord, Mistress Tally asks if she should…" The brawny man stopped in his tracks to stare at Kinley. "You're Pritani?"

She knew he was looking at the tattoo on her thigh, which the shirt didn't quite cover. "No, sorry, Protestant. Who are you?"

"Tormod Liefson, our land scout and map maker," Lachlan said as he covered her bare legs with the blanket and climbed off the bed. "Tormod, meet Kinley Chandler, of San Diego."

The scout grunted and inclined his head as he stepped closer. "You fight well for a candle-making wench from Hispania."

"Thanks," Kinley said but felt as if she'd dropped down a second rabbit hole. Tormod had white-blonde hair, icy blue eyes, and tattoos of his own. Scars slashed across his skin as if someone had tried to hack him to pieces with a hatchet. "I bet you fight well, too."

Chapter Nine

J UST OUTSIDE THE sleepy mortal village Quintus reined in his horse, dismounted and hobbled his mount in a grassy field. Once he had donned a long, hooded cloak to conceal his pale skin and field armor, he approached the cluster of cottages. When he had first come to this barbaric land the tribes used slaves to work their farms and fields. Over the centuries the mortals had formed clans. Now powerful lairds ruled most of the country, and commanded the service of kin related by blood or marriage. Quintus often wondered if the cotters ever realized that they were still slaves, bound by a name instead of shackles.

And what am I, if not bound by my oath?

Bitterly he looked toward the east, where the

sun he could never see again would rise in a few hours. Beyond the stand of pine and alder lay the sea he would have to cross, and so too Belgica and Germania, before he could reach his homeland. Even if Quintus found some manner in which he could travel solely by night, he had no reason to make the journey. The Rome he had known had long ago been overrun and conquered. The Emperor he had served, the Imperial Legate, his wife and children, and every other soul he had known had been dead for over a thousand years.

All Quintus had left to live for was the Ninth Legion.

He made his way through the shadows to the back of the cottage where he was to meet the legion's spy. He could hear two voices speaking from within, however, and positioned himself by the open window to listen in.

❦

"THE LAIRD IS A FOOL," Evander muttered as he watched Fiona Marphee refill his goblet with dark wine. "He hasnae a thought for what I must do to keep the clan safe."

Fiona sat on the planked floor by his feet, and

rested her chin on his knee as she gazed up at him, her heart-shaped face wistful. "You are the strongest man I ken, Master Talorc." She curled her hand around his calf. "I ken you will manage this strange outsider wench who plagues you. I only wish I might give you some ease from your burdens tonight."

"That you will, my lass," Evander said.

He absently stroked her hair as he admired the bountiful curves swelling from her loosely-laced bodice.

A talented weaver, Fiona spent most of her day indoors at her loom, which kept her skin milk-white. Her paleness made her amber-green eyes and russet curls striking. Yet her gentle, quiet nature pleased Evander just as much as her womanly curves.

The first time he had seen Fiona buying fleeces at a crossroads market he'd been riveted by her beauty. He'd followed her back to her village to see her enter a modest, well-kept cottage surrounded by flowers and berry bushes. He'd watched for a husband or father for hours, convinced that such a lovely woman could not be unattached, but no one else came to the cottage. Each time he came to the village after that, he saw

her in the street, or in the little yard outside her
cottage, or delivering her wovens to the other
villagers.

Finding out who she was proved simple.
Evander questioned a pair of plowmen drinking
after their long day in the fields, and they'd
explained much about the wench in their thick
country brogues.

"Tha' cottage belongs to Dougal Marphee, a
weaver come from tha' lowlands ten year back.
No sons, poor devil, for tha' wife died bearing
their one bairn, Fiona. Dougal taught tha' lassie
all he knew before plague took him. You'd never
ken it for looking at her." The peasant cupped his
hands against his chest to suggest Fiona's large
breasts. "But she's a finer hand than her Da."

For a moment Evander thought of her small,
pretty hands working on something other than a
shuttle and loom. "Why does she live alone?"

"No man wants tha' cow," the other plowmen
said, and spat on the ground. "Too facking proud,
tha' one."

"Och, you're a'ways flapping about Fiona
since she wouldnae have you," his companion
said, and rolled his eyes at Evander. "Plenty of
lads would wed her, but she willnae have them.

Some reckon she fears birthing, the way it ended her ma."

Meeting Fiona was even simpler, as the McDonnels raised their own wool but sent it out to be woven. He had his shearers dye and send their finest fleeces to Fiona to have her weave tartans for the clan. When she sent word they were ready, Evander went in person to collect them. That went on for several weeks as he came to know her, and felt sure his other offer would not be rejected.

"'Tis too much, Master Talorc," she'd said when he'd come after sunset, and paid her twice her price. "I cannae accept."

"Half for the weaving," he told her, "and the rest for a night in your bed."

Instead of slapping him or having hysterics Fiona had blushed and said, "I am no hoor, sir. In truth I've no' yet lain with a man."

Evander silently cursed himself. Of course she'd be a virgin. At least she'd proven to be as modest as her manner. "Then keep it for your dowry."

Her russet curls danced as she shook her head. "I cannae marry. The midwife told me that bearing a bairn would kill me, as it did my Mam."

She handed him back half the coin, and looked up at him with tears in her eyes. "But if I could be with a man, Master, I would choose you."

He could have walked away from her, and left her to live her lonely, chaste, little life. But he wanted her more than breathing, and he knew himself to be the perfect lover for her.

"I am no' like other men, Fiona. The magic folk changed me." He reached out and took her hands in his. "They gave me many gifts, but took from me in turn. I cannae ever again sire a bairn."

Her eyes went wide, and then the loveliest smile he'd ever seen lit up her sweet face. "Keep your coin, Master." She brought his hands up to her face, and kissed each one. "Stay the night, and make me yours."

Evander had intended to spend only one night with her, to rid himself of his inconvenient lust. But Fiona had been fashioned for a man's pleasure, and her shy responses fueled his desire for more. He stayed away from her for three weeks, and when he could bear no more he went to her in the middle of the night. He woke her, expecting tears or sulks, but Fiona had simply pulled off her nightdress and opened her arms.

Evander taught her how to please him with every part of her body, and Fiona took to bed play as if she'd been born to be a courtesan. For the next year he stole away as often as he could to be with his mortal mistress, who surrendered herself to his desires completely, and yet asked nothing in return.

Now as he looked down at Fiona, Evander felt the last of his ire evaporate. "Come here, lass. Your laces want untangling."

Her cheeks pinked adorably as she rose and perched herself on his strong thighs. As he slowly drew open her bodice, her large, ruddy nipples swelled around the hard nub, where she was especially sensitive. Evander watched her face as he fondled her, squeezing and stroking her ripe mounds until she uttered a helpless moan.

"Oh, Master, oh, please."

She wriggled on his lap, agitated and eager, and squeaked when he lifted her in his strong arms and carried her over to her standing loom. Pushing her over the narrow, high bench where she sat to work, Evander lifted her skirts up over her broad, curvy buttocks, which were bare. He caressed her flank.

"Where are your drawers, you wanton?"

"I left them off today, Master," she said as he reached between her thighs. "'Twas too hot."

"Or you were," Evander said and worked his fingers against her soft, slick folds, circling her small, throbbing pearl. "Did you touch yourself today, wench? Is that why you're so tender and wet?"

"'Tis you, sir," Fiona said, and moaned as he penetrated her with one long finger. "I've but to see you and I drench myself."

"You wicked little wench."

Evander took his hand from her to tear open his breeches and guide his thick, stiff penis to press against her. The first touch of her nether honey on his cockhead sent a surge of heat down his shaft, and he notched himself in her before he gripped her hips.

She enveloped him with her heat and his balls tightened as the urge to thrust became unbearable. Crouching over her, he worked his cock deeper and reached for her soft, full breasts.

"A man cannae resist such temptation. 'Tis time you learned that, wench." He plowed deep, and Fiona pressed her mouth against the bench to muffle a cry. "And I shall teach you."

Evander grunted as he buried himself to his

root in her, and then drew out to pump into her again. She tightened around him, and the bewitching clasp of her cunt drove him to madness. Beneath him her body shook with his powerful thrusts, and little whimpers escaped her lips as he tugged and gripped her bouncing tits. He could smell her sweetness now as she saturated his cock with her honey, and he played her nipples until she stiffened and cried out.

The feel of Fiona's fluttering pleasure on his cock nearly made Evander jet, but he tightened his jaw and held back, allowing her to know her full bliss before he drew out of her.

"Attend me," he said and held his glistening shaft as he watched her turn and drop down on her knees. "Open that pretty mouth for me, sweet wanton."

Fiona pushed back her hair, her bare breasts heaving as she looked up at him, her face flushed and her eyes drowsy with delight. Slowly she parted her lips, showing him the tip of her pink tongue.

Evander moved so that his engorged cockhead shadowed her face. "I'll have your mouth on me now, wench." He adored the way her eyelashes shyly fluttered as she pressed her lips to the flaring ridge. "Open wider. Wider." When she obeyed him he skewered her with his glistening dome, pressing in to slide against her tongue and into the satiny heat of her mouth. "'Tis good, aye. Suck my cock, and make me forget that facking Kinley Chandler."

Fiona closed her lips around him as he gripped a handful of her hair, and sucked lightly as he thrust deeper. He watched every flicker of emotion that crossed her face, and knew it excited her as much as him. She loved to be made helpless by him, and it brought out his dark desire to master her entirely. He knew she could taste herself on his cock as it stroked in and out, and seeing her suck him turned his need to come into a battle he always lost. Soon he was guiding her head, pushing her onto him as he went deeper and harder into her mouth, compelling her to take every inch.

Evander felt the pressure building in his balls, but this time could not hold back the explosion of ecstasy. His body went rigid and jerked as the hard, fast spurts of his seed jetted past Fiona's lips, filling her mouth. She swallowed and purred, sucking at him until he had no more to give her, and then caressed him with her tongue as she let him slide from her lips.

When he felt sure of his legs, he scooped her up from the floor and kissed her lips, savoring the taste of his cream on her until he tasted salt and drew back to see the gleaming trails on her cheeks.

"Why do you weep?"

"'Tis so good to be yours, Master," she said, and quickly swiped at her tears. "But I am selfish, and what hours we have seem so meager." She rested her cheek against his shoulder and closed her eyes, her voice slurring. "If only every day and night I could be with you, in your bed, and slumber in your arms."

Bitterly he thought of Lachlan forbidding the clan to bring women outside the ranks of their trusted retainers to Dun Aran. Yet the laird had brought Kinley in without hesitation.

"What we can have is only this," he said quietly, "and only here."

Evander carried her into her bed, and lay holding her until she fell asleep. Leaving her tore at him, but he had already stayed too long. When he glanced back at his sleeping mistress, he felt the coldness in his heart return. He had accepted that he could never again take Fiona, or any woman, as wife. For the McDonnel women were a fleeting, temporary pleasure.

The laird needed to be reminded of that.

❧

QUINTUS LOOKED up as someone came out of the back of the cottage, and stepped away from the window and into the moonlight. "You've kept me waiting for an hour. Although I suppose watching you fucking was amusing."

"I'm glad you were entertained," the legion's spy said. "Now, shall we speak of Kinley Chandler?"

Chapter Ten

I T TOOK A week at Dun Aran for Kinley
to give up waiting to wake up back in the
hospital. She'd thought up and discarded a
hundred other theories about why she had landed
in fourteenth century Scotland. She'd even entertained the idea that she'd actually traveled back in
time, but if she had, how could falling out of her
wheelchair send her back eight centuries to
another country? Shouldn't there have been some
kind of time machine involved?

Whatever had happened to her, it seemed she
would be stuck here for a while.

Most nights when she slept—assuming she
was actually sleeping—she dreamed of standing
surrounded by the ancient stones in the oak grove.
She'd watch the carvings on them glow with light,

and wake up feeling vaguely frustrated, as if she was supposed to know or remember something, and couldn't.

Walking around whole and healed, on the other hand, felt amazing. She didn't want that to end, and if that made her selfish and delusional, fine.

The heavily-fortified castle appeared to be authentic, and from what she could see through the narrow windows, had been built in some sort of crater beside an enormous lake. In keeping with the era there was no electricity or running water, and what passed for lavatories made field latrines seem luxurious. Yet something warmed the hard stone floors, and took the chill out of the air even in the great hall. When the maid brought up washing water for her every evening, it was steaming hot.

"How do they heat the water?" Kinley finally asked Raen.

His smile bent the jagged lines of the gray lightning tattoos that covered half his face. He pointed down.

"Beneath are hot springs that warm the castle. The maids draw buckets from the cellar wells we dug, where the water is close to boiling."

Meals were basic, yet well-prepared and, strangely, pretty healthy. For their mid-morning breakfast the cook served huge platters of oatcakes, vats of porridge and a thick, delicious soup called pottage. The second, bigger meal came in the afternoon, and included fresh fish, smoked or salted meats, vegetables, cheese and whole-grain breads, all skillfully flavored with herbs and sometimes garlic. The clan seemed to drink only whiskey, cider, or a very sweet beer they called mead, and had no idea what coffee or real tea was. Kinley stuck with the herbal brews the maids brought her, which seemed innocuous enough, or milk, which was so rich and heavy with cream that shaking it a few times would probably turn it into butter.

The laird kept her in his tower chamber for several days, always guarded by Raen or Tormod, and casually questioned her several times about herself, her life, and how she came to Scotland. Since he wouldn't believe her answers, Kinley remained vague or claimed she couldn't remember. She could tell by the way he looked at her that he felt alternately frustrated and suspicious, but there was nothing she could do about that. He had to make up his mind whether to trust her or not.

Although Kinley was tempted, she didn't try to escape again. Through casual conversations with Raen and Tormod about the island, she learned that there were only a few villages on Skye, and all of them were loyal to Lachlan. Transportation was scarce, and evidently only fisherman ferried people to and from the mainland. She also had to assume the entire world was also in the fourteenth century, with nice things like rampant disease, famine and political revolts. If she were to steal a boat, she was fairly sure she wouldn't know how to sail it. Even on the chance that she could figure it out, once she reached the mainland, where would she go? A woman alone without money or contacts wouldn't get very far.

Making the best of the situation seemed her only recourse. She did ask Raen if he would take her for a walk outside, but he told her she had to dress for that.

Clothing turned out to be her biggest problem.

All Kinley had brought with her was her hospital gown, under which she'd been naked. Lachlan had been giving her some of his shirts to wear, which were so large they reached down to her knees. When she asked for some clothes of her own, both the laird and his bodyguard had gone off to consult with the castle's chatelaine, Meg Talley, who sent back a pile.

Kinley sorted through two floor-length dresses with wide, flowing sleeves, a knee-length shirt, a primitive corset, a wide belt and several undergarments so bizarre-looking that she wasn't sure where they went or how to keep them there. There was also a long drape that went with a circular band for her head, and a huge, heavy tartan to be belted on top of everything.

"Sorry, but none of this works for me," Kinley told Lachlan as she handed back the huge pile of garments. "Women in my, ah, homeland have been liberated." At his blank look she added, "We don't dress like nuns anymore."

Raen looked slightly appalled. "They made you dress like nuns?"

"It's a figure of speech." She patted Lachlan's shoulder. "Find me a shirt and some pants. Socks and boots would be nice, too. My feet are freezing."

The laird frowned. "Why would you wish to dress like a man?"

She pointed at the clothes. "Try those on and you'll find out."

The next day Lachlan returned with a smaller version of a clansman's tunic and trousers, knitted knee-length stockings, and some soft, fur-lined boots. Kinley could see they were brand-new, and so small they had obviously been made for her, so she took them into the adjoining dressing room and put them on. The boots were a little big, and the trousers on the snug side, but when she walked out Lachlan and Raen both smiled, which she took as approval.

Until they began to laugh.

"Stop being jerks," she told them flatly, and planted her hands on her hips as she looked down at herself. "Okay, what did I do wrong?"

Lachlan came over and tugged at the laces at her waist. "You've put your trews on backward, lass." He cocked his head as he surveyed her other side. "Although on you it works better that way." When he looked at her again his eyes had darkened, and he brought up his hand to her waist. "But you'll no' pass as a man."

Each day he found some excuse to touch her, and the feel of his big hands on her body made Kinley's skin judder with nerves. "I don't want to."

His fingers skimmed over her hip before he took his hand away. "Mayhap you should."

Raen broke the spell by bringing over one of the laird's tartans and draping it over her shoulder. "You'll want it for your walk outside," he told her when she began to protest. "'Tis windy and cold." His gaze shifted to Lachlan. "This time of day, the view from the back curtain wall is best."

Lachlan escorted her on the walk, for which he took her out through the back of the castle and then up some cobweb-draped stairs. "You should see our loch from the center of the wall," he told her as he helped her up through the narrow opening at the top of the steps. "'Tis bonny with the sunlight shining on it."

Kinley suspected seeing the water view also kept her away from the clan, who usually congregated this time of morning for their main meal of the day. As she stepped to the wall to look out on the shimmering lake, she said, "You're going to have to let them see me eventually, McDonnel. I promise, this time I'll behave myself."

"'Tis no' you who worries me." He came to stand beside her. "We have a rule about outsiders in the stronghold. They're no' permitted."

"So the guys will, what? Kick me out into the moat?" She glanced down and for the first time saw the deep, black trench that surrounded the base of the castle. "Make that the bottomless pit. Holy cow. I think I will stay in the tower."

"If you're to stay, lass, we'll have to get around more than the trench." He turned toward her. "You told me you have no family. What of a lover, or a husband? Bairns?"

"No, no, and if you mean kids, no and can't." She leaned against the edge of the rampart to look out at the horizon. "I wanted to fall in love, once, but I never had the time. In the end I was sorry about that, too."

"The end of what?" he prompted.

"Never mind." When she turned away from the wall he caught her arm, and she looked up at him. "Uh, this didn't work out so well for you the last time, remember?"

"My apologies," Lachlan said, and turned his grip on her into a caressing stroke. "Was there ever a man who held your heart?"

Kinley shook her head. "I had too much responsibility with my job, and too much stress, and then the world exploded and I lost everything that mattered." She knew she wasn't making any sense, but she had the feeling he understood. "I have to stay, McDonnel, mainly because I have nothing to go back to."

"Lass." He tilted up her chin and looked into her eyes. "Once I lost everything that mattered, and I thought it ended me. In too many ways it did. But if you prove your worth, sometimes you're given a second chance."

The moment stretched out in a kind of electric silence that crackled unheard all around them. It scared her a little, because Kinley could sense what was waiting behind that careful, guarded expression. Something he held on a short, tight leash, she suspected. He had no clue about her, though, and she wanted to keep it that way.

"I'm not like you, Lachlan," she told him, her voice tight. "I'm damaged, and sometimes, I'm dangerous. If I ever lose it, the way I did at the battle, you need to knock me out. I'm not kidding. Hit me the way Evander did, just not so hard."

He touched her cheek. "I dinnae think I can ever do that, lass."

Someone cleared their throat, and Kinley looked over to see Raen hovering a few yards away. "Hey, big guy. Come and see the view.

Super bonny. The sunlight is shining on the water and everything."

"Forgive the intrusion, Kinley." He turned to the laird. "We've reports come in that you should read now, my lord."

Reports were always coming in, usually about the undead. The McDonnels seemed to be collectively an on-call, vampire-slaying army who sent out on a constant basis large contingents to track and intercept their enemy. Kinley had been able to glean a bit more about the mysterious Roman soldiers from listening to the laird's conversations with his bodyguard, but she knew she was missing most of the big picture.

This time when she accompanied the laird to his tower, she didn't go to take a nap but went to his map table and stood watching as he marked several areas. "They come after the villagers by night, right?"

Lachlan made a vague affirmative sound as he began drawing lines between the marks.

"The undead hunt only by night," Raen said as he took her tartan and hung it neatly in the big armoire. "Sunlight turns them to ash. They must hide from it by day."

She watched the laird finish working on the

map. "Are you trying to figure out where they're hiding?" At his surprised look she added, "I was a soldier in my, ah, homeland. I know how to use maps and incident locations to extrapolate positions."

"You were a soldier?" Raen asked, sounding incredulous, at the same time Lachlan said, "Show me this extrapolate positions you do."

Kinley shook her head at the quill pen he offered, and went over to the hearth to retrieve a small piece of charred wood. "What I wouldn't give for a good old number two." Using the blackened sliver like a pencil, she dotted the locations. "Okay. These are where the attacks occurred. Since the undead can't tolerate daylight, they have about twelve hours to leave and return to their base camp. Do they travel by foot, or on horseback?"

"We think they ride in close, and hide their horses before they attack," Raen said.

"So that would give them a range of about twenty to thirty miles." She turned to Lachlan and pointed at two dots that were the closest to each other. "What's the distance between these two villages?"

"I dinnae ken miles." The laird studied the map. "Mayhap five leagues."

"Right, we have different measurement systems." She rubbed her forehead. "We'll have to use travel time. How long does it take to ride from one village to the other?" When he told her, she used that as her measurement key for the rest of the map, and carefully drew a light line around her dots. "The undead are camped somewhere inside this circle, so that's where you should look. The perimeter is as far as they can go in twelve hours from any of these locations."

Both men stared at each other and then her.

"Hey, you can keep chasing them all over Scotland if you want," Kinley said, stepping back from the table. "But if you find their camp, and destroy it, they'll have nowhere to run to when the sun rises. Good-bye, soulless creatures of the night."

Lachlan rolled up the map and handed it to his bodyguard. "Raen, find Tormod and have him make copies, if you would. I want one made for every chieftain."

"Aye, my lord." The big man winked at Kinley before he left.

When they were alone the laird moved to

tower over her. "You're a clever one." He took out a square of linen and wiped her brow with it, steadying her with his other hand as if she were a child. "But you need a wash."

"Oh," she said when she saw the dark smudge on the cloth and looked at her blackened fingers. "Next time I'll use the quill."

Lachlan studied her face. "Come with me."

Kinley followed him out of the chamber and down the hall to another door. "Am I in trouble or something?"

"No, lass." He opened the door and gestured for her to go inside.

The chamber contained a carved oak bed draped with woven curtains and made up with embroidered linens, all in shades of cream and brownish-green. There were also two cushioned chairs, a small washstand with a porcelain jug and basin, a small armoire and a trunk bound with iron straps. Everything looked new or newly-made, but seemed to be scaled down from the huge furnishings Lachlan and his men used.

"This is nice," she said and ran a hand over the top of the trunk. "I'll guess this isn't Raen's room. He'd never fit in that bed."

"'Tis your chamber, Kinley," Lachlan said and

opened the armoire to reveal stacks of neatly-folded clothing on the inner shelves. "There are kirtles, mantles and slippers as well as more semats and trews. Wear what pleases you."

The odd, ever-present tension between them jumped up a notch, and she glanced at the door.

"There's no lock."

"I saw no reason for one," he said as he leaned back against the wall. "If you meant to run, you'd be gone already, and you ken we would no' hurt you."

"You've certainly had plenty of chances." Despite all he'd done to make her comfortable, she sensed he wasn't happy about this move. "Why are you really kicking me out of your room?"

Lachlan straightened, and came to her. "To get you out of my bed," he said, touching a strand of her hair before letting it slip from his fingers. "Stay in it, and you'll have your answer, lass."

"I think I've got it now." So the crazy needy wanting she couldn't shake was mutual. In a weird way knowing that made her feel a little better. "Do I have permission to move about the castle freely, sir?"

"Aye, if you've Raen or Tormod with you, but

go easy, Kinley," he warned her. "Dun Aran isnae San Diego, and my clan are accustomed to unliberated females."

"Where are their families?" she couldn't help asking. "I mean, the only women in the castle are servants, and I haven't seen any children at all."

"The servants keep their families in the village," Lachlan said, his voice going flat as he went to the door. "The clan doesnae have wives or bairns. We cannae."

Kinley felt stunned. "Why not?"

He glanced back at her. "The McDonnels are no' mortal, lass."

Chapter Eleven

THOUGH KINLEY DID not try to run, Lachlan rarely found her in her room. At first she wandered the stronghold from roof to cellar.

"She questions everything," Tormod complained to him. "And no' like any wench I've ken. Naught about fripperies or sewing or cooking. She wants to ken how many in a warband, and the manner of weapons we carry, and even how the undead might get into the stronghold. I had to walk her through every tower. She'd shame a siege master the night before a battle."

Lachlan allowed Kinley to have her "look around" as she put it, but once she had inspected the whole of Dun Aran she went about finding ways to be useful.

"Yesterday the stable master had her mucking out stalls," Raen reported before he relieved Tormod from escort duty. "I watched her. I'll reckon she's never used a pitchfork in her life, but the lass kept at it until she learnt. Then she had him show her how to groom the nags before she put them back."

"She's no' afraid to work," Lachlan said. He had heard similar reports from his dairy manager, the shepherds and his cook. "Where does she go today?"

"She asked if she could watch the men sparring in the lists." His bodyguard grimaced. "I tried to explain that females are a distraction, but you ken how she is when you remind her she's a lass. Like a pine marten in a rabbit snare."

"Take her to the armory," he suggested. "She can watch from the crosswalk outside Neac's work room."

As laird Lachlan had many daily responsibilities, ranging from meeting with his chieftains to sorting out plans and grievances to seeing that the stronghold remained well-supplied and secure. He also liked to ride out every week to inspect their herds, and every month to the village to check on the welfare of their mortal neighbors and his servants' families.

Lachlan had intended to visit the village today, and stop by the old lodge he had built for himself to check how the roof had fared through the winter. His claymores wanted honing, however, and he felt curious about Kinley's interest in his clan's battle practice. Once he finished his meeting with the chieftains he made his way to the crosswalk above the lists, where he found Raen and Neac flanking Kinley as they watched a bout.

"See, that's what I mean," she said, pointing to the clansmen who had locked blades and were grappling for the upper hand. "They're wasting time and energy that way."

"Aye, but they're enjoying it," Neac told her. "Especially Fadar there. Naught he loves more than a hard wrestle."

"Do you spar?" Lachlan asked, startling her.

"Ah, not like that." Kinley glanced down at the fighters. "I've never used a sword. But hand-to-hand combat, fighting with just your body, sure."

"You are a woman, Kinley," Raen chided.

"You couldnae match a man bare-handed. And if you could prevail, well, I'd eat my horse."

Lachlan expected her to take offense, but instead she chuckled and shook her head. "Come down to the lists," he told her. "Neac will spar with you, so you can show us your ways."

"I will?" the bald chieftain said, and then caught the look Raen gave him. "Och, of course, lass. I'd be honored. Your bones dinnae snap easily, do they?"

Lachlan escorted her down, and called on the men to step back as he led Kinley to the center of the hard-packed dirt training yard. He noted that most of the clansmen looked at her with visible unease, and wondered if he'd made a mistake. Then Kinley took off her boots and stockings, drawing a few lecherous whistles before she planted her bare feet and faced Neac.

"We fight until only one is left standing," the chieftain said and gave her an uncertain smile. "Or you say to stop. I'll try no' to hurt you, lass."

"Same here."

She bent her knees slightly, and shook her arms before nodding to him.

Neac circled around her, not attempting to strike but moving in close enough to grab her by the waist and drop her to the ground. Kinley turned as he did, never permitting him to get behind her, and then moved around him. With an exasperated sound Neac snatched at her.

Lachlan blinked, and his chieftain was on the ground with Kinley's foot pressed against his wide neck. None of the clan moved or spoke. Neac looked up at her and made a choking sound, while Raen's jaw became unhinged.

"Sorry," Kinley said and reached down to help the sword master to his feet. "Do you want to go again?"

"Aye, once more," Neac said. He backed away from her, and all the indulgent humor left his expression. "Attack me this time, you wily wench."

Kinley grinned, and when he nodded she ran straight at the chieftain. This time Lachlan saw how at the very last moment she spun out of reach of his hands, hooked his leg from behind, and drove her elbow into the bend of his spine.

A heartbeat later Neac was on his back again, staring up at her. Low, shocked murmurs spread through the watching men as Kinley moved back from the chieftain.

Lachlan clapped his gaping bodyguard on the

shoulder. "You never liked that horse anyway, lad."

After seeing their chieftain taken down twice by a female, a dozen of the Uthars stepped forward to challenge her. One by one Kinley sparred with them, using techniques to defeat them that Lachlan had never seen. What amazed him even more was how she showed her moves again to her opponents after they'd lost, in a slower fashion so they could see what she'd done.

When the clan called on Raen, he stepped in front of Kinley. The zig-zag lines of his gray facial tattoo caught the light.

"You cannae defeat me, lass," he said as he moved to flank her. "So now we'll see how well you lose."

"You never know," she told him as she mirrored his movements, and then ducked to avoid the sweep of one of his massive arms. "I might be faster."

"Likely no'," he assured her, and watched as she came around to drive her bare foot into the side of his knee. "That also willnae work on me."

She limped backward. "Ow. No kidding."

"Dinnae hurt yourself now." The bodyguard moved like lightning as he grabbed her, hoisted her off her feet, and tucked her against his side. While she struggled and pummeled him he sighed and looked at Lachlan. "She's quick, and uses leverage like a weapon." He knelt on the ground and gently placed her on her back, holding her down with one hand as she tried to get back up. "Lass, you're clever, and nimble as a dormouse, but there's a reason I guard the laird. No one has ever prevailed over me, here or in battle."

"Fine, I concede," she grumbled, and when he released her she smacked his arm. Instantly she made a face and shook her hand. "It's like you're made out of solid iron. How do you move that fast?"

"'Tis what Tharaen is," a harsh voice said. "A Pritani warrior, like us all. You'll no' see any helpless wenches on our battlefields."

Lachlan looked over as Evander pushed his way through the men. "I think we're done now. Raen, help Kinley up."

She was already on her feet by the time the seneschal reached her. "I'm fine, and FYI, not all wenches are helpless. Some of us are actually good fighters."

Evander's upper lip curled. "You've no place here, you brazen trollop. Go back and warm the

laird's bed." He bent down to look in her face.
"It's the only worth you have at Dun Aran."

"I don't think so," Kinley said, as much to the
seneschal as to Raen and Lachlan when they
would have stepped in. "You're the one who hit
me from behind, right? Evander Talorc." After he
glowered at her she cocked her head. "Yeah, you
seem like the type to jump a girl from behind.
Think you can knock me out while I'm looking
at you?"

The men hooted as they shuffled back to give
them more room.

When Lachlan would have snatched her away
from the seneschal Neac put a big hand on his
arm. "No' yet, Laird," the chieftain warned.
"Respect cannae be ordered. It comes by earning.
Let the lass have her go at him."

He wanted to clout Neac, but he knew he was
right. "No weapons or injuring," he told the
seneschal. "Sparring moves only."

Evander unbelted his tartan and took off his
tunic, revealing the hard-muscled grace of his
long-limbed body, as well as his tattoo. Two large,
tattooed discs with scrollwork were connected by a
wide bar across his chest. But through the bar ran
a diagonal line that was part of a giant backward

'Z' that overlay the whole design. One end of the Z was tipped with a point.

Once Kinley had moved into position, the big man barreled directly at her. Lachlan's hands balled into fists but Kinley landed a kick to the seneschal's side that sent him staggering.

"Evander was no' watching her before this," Raen muttered.

It took all of Lachlan's self-control to resist the urge to jump in and beat the seneschal into the ground. The Talorc tribe had always been the most devious and unrelenting of fighters, and Evander a legendary champion even during his mortal life. Kinley quickly learned this, taking several hard punches in the process, and had to rely on her more elusive moves to remain standing.

"Do we fight, or do we dance?" Evander taunted as he struck a glancing blow to her shoulder.

"Personally, I don't dance with jerks," Kinley assured him, dropping to avoid another punch and spinning around the seneschal. "Even when they're pretty damn good-looking. You should walk around without a shirt all the time. All that eye candy makes up for your crappy personality."

He turned and grunted as he took a kick to the knee. "You sluts are good for only one thing."

Tormod huffed out a rude sound. "You're thinking with your cock again, Talorc. Try employing the bigger head."

As the seneschal glared at the Norseman, Kinley took advantage of the distraction. She skittered around him, jumped on his back and locked her legs around his torso and her arms around his neck.

"Why don't you take a nap now?" she said through gritted teeth as she cut off his air. "You might be nicer when you wake up."

Evander choked and shook like a wet dog, but Kinley held on, and Lachlan saw how the match would end. If Kinley prevailed over the proud seneschal, he would never forgive her for humiliating him in front of the clan. That could lead to a much more lethal bout.

"Choke holds are no' sparring moves," Lachlan said as he wrenched Kinley off the seneschal's back and handed her to Raen. As Evander bent over and gasped for air, he grabbed the front of his tunic and jerked him upright. "'Tis the last time you put hands on her, Talorc. Do you understand me, man?"

The seneschal coughed before he replied. "I'd rather fack a diseased cow than touch that—"

His head snapped back as Lachlan's fist plowed into his jaw, and his body followed as he dropped like a stone.

All of the men fell silent as they looked from Kinley to Evander to their laird.

"Kinley is a warrior in her homeland," Lachlan told his clan. "She has methods of fighting that we dinnae ken, but she is mortal, so she will spar only with Raen. Learn from her, show her our ways, but remember this." He bent and hefted Evander over his shoulder. "She is under my protection."

As he carried the seneschal into the castle, Lachlan heard Kinley ask, "What does that mean, 'under his protection?'"

Neac was the one to answer her. "Any insult or harm to you will be answered directly by the laird. He's declaring that you're his woman now, lass."

Chapter Twelve

"THERE YE ARE, milady," Meg said as she carried a heavily-laden tray into the map room, where Kinley sat at the surveyor's desk. "What do ye there now?"

Kinley glanced down at the notes she had made while comparing the map scrolls of the region. That she had to do it with a feather on the thinly-scraped animal hide they called parchment mildly disgusted her.

"Just writing up some things for the laird."

After two weeks at Dun Aran, Kinley had mostly settled into her new reality, which had proven surprisingly satisfying. Daily life in the fourteenth century required plenty of work from every member of the clan as well as their household staff, so she did her part by pitching in whenever and wherever she could. As for the modern conveniences she had always taken for granted, she didn't miss much from her time. Now and then she thought she might kill for a cup of coffee, or a decent bottle of moisturizer, but that was all.

The biggest step she'd taken to adjust was deciding that she couldn't be dreaming or comatose. There were too many things at the castle that she'd never seen and couldn't have imagined on her own, like the carved puzzle stones the clansmen used for some kind of speed-solving game, or how everyone seemed to know what *faodail* meant, except for her. She'd finally asked Meg why Lachlan would call her 'foot-ill', only to learn it meant something like a waif or a foundling or maybe a lucky find.

Then there'd been the medieval version of a tooth brush.

"We dinnae have such brushes," Raen had told Kinley when she'd asked for one.

He gave her instead a wide strip of rough cloth and a small box filled with a mixture of ashes, salt crystals and ground mint leaves.

"What am I supposed to do with these?" she asked perplexed.

"You clean your teeth."

He sprinkled some of the mixture in the center of the cloth, tied it into a bundle, dampened it and used it in a scrubbing motion in front of his teeth.

She tried it, surprised by how well it worked. "What are the ashes made from?"

"Burnt rosemary stalks," Raen told her. "Sage works as well, but I cannae abide the taste."

Kinley had always assumed most medieval people had rotten teeth due to poor dental hygiene. Judging by the healthy smiles she saw around the stronghold, the reality was the exact opposite. Not knowing that simple fact ruled out dreaming or a coma, since both presented alternate realities based on her subconscious and memories.

Then there was Lachlan, and the strange connection she felt to him. The laird was unlike any man she'd ever known, hands down. Whatever was going on between them had an almost magical feel to it, as if some mystical force was trying to shove them together. In her other life Kinley had been a pragmatist: clear-eyed, hardheaded and with both feet firmly planted on the ground. She had never believed in magic, and had always felt amused by anyone who did.

Sometimes Kinley still wondered if she had died, and this was her afterlife. She wouldn't have ever guessed that heaven would be a medieval castle filled with huge, inhumanly strong highland warriors. Even if she'd been a believer, she wouldn't have fulfilled the entry requirements. She considered reincarnation, but if her soul had been reborn, why hadn't she woken up in the future, or in a different body?

"The laird said to tell ye to eat this," the chatelaine said as she set down the tray, "or he'll have the Viking spoon-feed ye."

"Thanks, Meg," Kinley said as she glanced at the amount of food on the tray, which was rather more than she could eat in a week. "Tormod, you hungry?"

"I'm a man. I'm never no' hungry." The brawny Norseman emerged from the racks containing hundreds of scrolls, clay tablets and etched hides, but when he spotted the dishes on the tray he scowled. "You're feeding us flowers, Chatelaine?"

"Fresh cider, bannocks with cloudberries, honey cakes, and my very best prymerose pudding." Meg gave him an evil look. "'Tis for milady, no' ye."

Kinley suppressed a sigh.

Tormod plucked a primrose from the gooey sweet and sniffed it. "Gods forbid you bring her a tankard of ale and a trencher of rare beef." He dropped the bloom as Meg curtseyed to Kinley and stomped out. "You've conquered another heart. The stingy old wench never makes such puddings for us."

"Meg thinks I'm too skinny. Fattening me up is her new mission in life. Unfortunately, I have the metabolism of a greyhound on crack." Kinley rolled up the scrolls and secured them with their ribbons before returning them to the racks. "All right, so if everything we've looked at is accurate, then at this point our undead search grid is about the size of Vermont. We don't want to go there." She saw his expression and added, "That means it's way too big. We need more intel—reports— about their attacks to narrow it down to a more manageable area."

"Mortals keep silent because they fear the vengeance of the legion," the Norseman told her. "The undead are vicious when someone tries to stand against them. They torture them and their families in front of their entire village. Then they drag off the rest to serve as blood thralls, who are imprisoned and slowly drained until they die of it."

"If they're all about payback, then why aren't they force-projecting on you guys?"

The Norseman yawned until his jaw cracked. "Your words confound me again, wench."

"Sorry," she said, thinking of how to translate her slang into his medieval-speak. "If the legion is so vengeful, then why aren't they on the island and sieging the castle?"

"That you must ask the laird," Tormod said and handed her a mug of cider. "Now drink, and eat, or Mistress Talley shall put fish bones and vetch in my pottage for the next moon." He eyed the prymerose pudding. "Do you really no' want that?"

After Kinley returned the tray to the kitchen, she and Tormod went up to the laird's tower with her notes to report to Lachlan. They found him talking with Neac, Raen and Seoc Talorc, the stable master.

"Kinley," Lachlan said and came to inspect her from head to toe before eyeing the roll of parchment she carried. "How do you fare with the new quill I cut for you?"

"Better. I didn't get any ink on my fingers this time."

She could smell him now, and felt a zing of desire ricochet through her lower belly. All she had to do was get within touching range and that delicious, cool water scent of his nailed her. They'd also both been implicitly avoiding each other since he'd moved her out of his chamber, which only seemed to make her more painfully aware of him when they did meet.

She glanced at Neac, Raen, and Seoc. "Are we interrupting?"

"No' at all, my lady," Seoc said. Tall and lanky like his cousin, the stable master was much more charming, and always made a point to smile before he bowed to her. "We were just speaking of you."

"Aye, that's all anyone does when you're no' here," Neac assured her. "'Tis Kinley this and Kinley that, from sunup to twilight. Where is she, what is she doing, can anyone make out what she says today? We've given up warbanding for gossiping on you, wench."

"This wouldn't be because my idea to use two bellows instead of one to make your forge fire get hotter faster actually worked, would it?" When he grumbled something at his boots she grinned. "You're welcome."

"'Twas a sensible notion," the chieftain admitted. He crossed his arms, making his huge hammer tattoos look as though they were stacked. Then he glared at Tormod and Raen. "That doesnae mean I'll be having the wee lass hammering iron in my armory. Look at her. My cross-peen weighs more."

"Dinnae be fooled by the fairy lass she appears," Raen put in as he went to open the big cabinet where the laird stored his weapons. "She can carry two water buckets from the cistern to the stables without spilling a drop."

As the men debated Kinley's potential as a smith's apprentice, Lachlan asked her, "Do you ride horseback?"

"It's been a while, but I think I can manage." She handed him her notes. "I'll have to translate these for you, but basically if we don't somehow reduce the search area, we'll be looking for the undead for years. So where are we riding?"

"Out to the glen. Red deer of late have been pillaging the villagers' gardens, and since they belong to me, I must act." He carefully tucked her notes into one of his hanging satchels. "Do you hunt as well as you fight, lass?"

Kinley thought of how many times she'd watched *Bambi* as a girl, and her heart sank. "Probably not." She looked up at him. "Can I maybe just watch while you and Raen hunt?"

"You might, if he were riding with us." Lachlan tossed his tartan over one broad shoulder and tucked the ends under his belt. "Today 'twill be just we two."

❦

KINLEY TOOK the reins in her hands and squirmed a little in the four-horned saddle. Seoc had padded it until it felt comfortable.

"Tama's sweet-tempered," Seoc said, as he stroked the sturdy brown mare's nose, "and kens glen paths like an island-bred palfrey." He glanced over at Lachlan, who had mounted a much larger, muscular gray stallion. "And she doesnae rile Selon. He's the laird's war horse, and a bit of an ill-tempered bugger, that one."

Kinley had never ridden without stirrups, but after a little practice walking her mount inside the stable, she felt more confident. The saddle clung to the mare's broad back as if molded to it, and was flexible without having too much give where she didn't need it.

"Does she spook easily?" she asked.

"No' ever, my lady," Seoc said and patted the mare's neck. "We took her from the undead, and if there's one thing those evil bastarts ken, 'tis how to train out the skittish from a mount."

"Great, I'm riding the *vampire* horse," Kinley muttered as she walked Tama out to where Lachlan was waiting. "I hope we're not going to head down the side of this mountain. I do better riding slowly, and horizontally."

He grinned. "We've fashioned many trails to and from Dun Aran. Or you could leave Tama and ride pillion with me."

Riding while pressed up against all that hard, beautiful muscle, and smelling him to boot? Kinley suspected she'd melt into a big puddle of prymerose pudding.

"Thanks, but I'm good."

Lachlan held Selon to a slow walk as he led Kinley to the trail down from the mountain. From what she could see it appeared as if it had been chiseled directly out of the rock, and was wide enough to accommodate several riders. Since the

McDonnels had only the most basic of hand tools, she marveled at the amount of sheer brute strength it must have taken to cut the trail.

Upslope in the distance, a small grove of ancient oaks spread their green canopy. In their midst stood weathered rock sentinels, half-buried in the ground. Though Kinley couldn't tell at this distance they seemed to form some sort of ring. Was it like the one on the mainland?

That reminded Kinley of the question Tormod had dodged. He implied that the undead didn't come after the McDonnels, but wouldn't tell her why. She looked down at the trail again. It had been cut so deeply that the walls of rock on either side of them likely hid them from view. Just like the towering walls of the volcanic crater in which Dun Aran sat probably kept it out of sight from anyone traversing the ridges of the Black Cuillin.

In Afghanistan the insurgents had used the extensive cave systems as base camps and supply caches. The natural cover had been so effective that not even the Russians had been able to find them while searching for more than a decade.

"You are thinking so hard I can hear it," Lachlan said, startling her. "Tormod and Raen have said you have many questions. Ask me what you will."

As they emerged from the trail into the upper slopes of the glen, she turned slightly to look back. "You can't see the entrance to the trail at all, even from here." Finally she put it all together. "It isn't that the undead don't come after you. It's that they can't. They don't know where you are."

The laird reined in his stallion to look out over the brilliant green grasses carpeting the island's rugged coast.

"'Twas why the McDonnels came here to build our stronghold. Skye was home to many of our tribes, including my own. The people here are loyal to us because the Pritani are their ancestors, and we care for them. Some of their families have served my clan for more than a thousand years."

He was trying to tell her something in a roundabout way, and Kinley felt as if she were on the brink of understanding.

"We didn't come on this ride to hunt, did we?"

"'Twould be a shame if we didnae," Lachlan said and nodded toward a large herd of red-brown deer that were grazing through a broad field of grain stalks. He touched his heels to the stallion's sides and took off at a fast run.

Kinley followed at a slower lope for a few minutes, and then relaxed the reins to give the mare her head. Tama shot off after Lachlan and Selon, her shorter legs eating up the distance between them. The herd reacted by uttering calls that sounded like long, stuttering belches before rocketing off en masse toward the protection at the edge of the glen, where the trees, rocks and slopes formed a natural barrier.

Lachlan drove the deer into the trees and went in after them, whistling as he did. Suddenly men stood up from grass blinds and released a hail of arrows. Deer began dropping as the remainder of the herd scrabbled up the slopes and poured into a narrow pass between two ridges.

Kinley reined in Tama as she saw Lachlan dismount and pull a long, wide lattice made of branches out of the brush, which he used to block the pass. The men all around her shouldered their bows and took out clubs as they went to inspect the fallen deer.

Kinley rode past them to Lachlan, who caught Tama's bridle as he looked up at her.

"I thought we were doing the hunting," she said.

"An island has only so much graze. The herd needed thinning, else they'd starve," he told her, and lifted her off the mare to set her on her feet. "We've livestock enough to keep the castle's larders filled for years, but the villagers dinnae have a tenth so much. These men's families will be glad of the meat."

He'd said the clan cared for the island's families, and now the hunt made more sense. "You're really a neat laird, you know that?"

One of the villagers shouted as a huge stag scrambled to its feet, an arrow piercing the side of his neck. The animal kicked away the hunter and bellowed with fury before lowering its long, many-pointed antlers. It charged straight at Kinley and the laird.

Lachlan ran toward the wounded stag, catching it around the neck and dragging it to the ground. A long blade flashed in his hand before he buried it in the thrashing animal's chest, and the huge furry body went limp.

Kinley felt horrified as she rushed over to the laird, who staggered to his feet and pulled a broken section of antler out of his left shoulder.

Blood from three large puncture wounds soaked the front of his tunic.

"Lachlan."

"I couldnae let him at you, lass." He caught her with his arm and tugged her against his uninjured side before addressing the villagers gathering around them. "My lady and I must be off now, else someone mistakes me for a fresh haunch. Get to it, lads."

The men seemed remarkably unconcerned as they tugged on their caps and forelocks before turning their attention to the carcasses. As Lachlan took Kinley back to the horses she wriggled free and blocked his path.

"What the hell are you doing?" she demanded. "You can't ride anywhere like that. You're losing too much blood." She pressed a hand to her forehead as she looked around them. "We have to get you to the village doctor, or healer, or whatever you call the guy who sews up antler holes in men who wrestle deer."

"They sew wounds in San Diego, do they?" He gripped his saddle and jumped up onto Selon with one smooth motion. "Sounds painful." He reached down to her, and when she took his hand he hauled her up and held her as he walked his charger over to Tama. "Swing on, that's a good lass." Once she had clambered onto the mare he nodded toward the ridge. "We'll ride to the loch and have a soak. Can you swim?"

She gaped at him. "Have you completely lost your mind?"

He grinned and tapped his temple. "Doesnae sound like it." He made a clicking sound to Selon, who trotted away with him.

Kinley caught up and paced him, expecting the laird to keel over and fall off the big stallion at any moment. Lachlan instead kept his seat, pointed out some crofts they passed and told her of the families working them, and generally behaved as if he hadn't been impaled by the stag. By the time they reached the loch Kinley was almost frantic, especially when he helped her down and she saw he was still bleeding.

"Okay, you've impressed me with your awesome highlander stoicism," she told him as he drew her down to the edge of the water. "Now we need to get you back to the castle, so I can–" She gaped as he removed his tunic. "What are you doing?"

"Having a soak," he said and eyed the blood-stained shirt before tossing it to the ground and reaching for his trouser laces. "If you cannae swim you should stay on the bank. 'Tis deep here, and the loch's currents can be devious."

Seeing the wounds in his shoulder made her feel sick. "Lachlan, you're badly hurt. Now is not the time to take a dip. Please."

He removed his boots and dropped his trousers. "'Tis the best time, lass."

Kinley tried not to stare, but the laird had the most perfectly ripped body she'd ever seen: a huge muscular chest beneath his giant snake tat, abs so hard and defined they'd have made body builders weep in defeat, and lean hips above long, strong legs with large, high-arched feet. Even with his skin streaked with blood, Kinley wanted nothing more than to jump on him and drag him to the ground. But something else gave her pause: namely, the thick, long column of his penis, which was all serious business. Framed by a thatch of dark body hair, and swelling bigger with every moment that passed, it looked hell-yeah ready to make her acquaintance.

Lachlan glanced down at his erection and then at her. "You're no' screeching."

"I'm too busy losing my mind," she told him.

"Don't you dare go in that water. I mean it, Lachlan. If it doesn't kill you, I will."

"Trust me, lass." He waded in and dove under
the surface.

Kinley shouted his name as she waded in after
him, splashing wildly as she went and desperately
peering into the dark waters of the loch. He might
be bold and built and beautiful, but if she didn't
get him out of the damn lake he might finish
bleeding to death in it, and then what would she
do? Tell the clan their laird was a reckless moron
who thought swimming in ice-cold water was the
way to treat deep animal puncture wounds?

All around her the water took on a subtle
glow, and she felt every inch of her skin tingle as
if in response. Something was happening beneath
the surface of the loch. Lachlan's scent—the smell
of cool, clear water—rose to fill her head as something whirled around her legs. The man himself
suddenly emerged, scooping her up in his arms
and carrying her back to shore. She looked at his
injured shoulder and saw nothing but three faint
pink marks and unbroken skin.

"You're healed," she said and touched one of
the marks. "Lachlan, what happened to your
wounds?"

"The loch's waters heal me and my clan." He set her down on her feet and rolled his head from side to side.

"Water heals you. Ah, no." She shook her head. "Water is just water."

"No' here, lass." He dragged his hair back from his face. "And no' for the clan."

Kinley peered at him as one of her grand-mother's stories emerged from her memory. "Are you and the clan kelpies?"

"Have you seen us turn into horses and eat mortals?" Curling up his arm, he tested the shoulder and nodded as if satisfied. "No' even a twinge left. Now, would you like to—"

Kinley slapped his face as hard as she could, throwing all her weight behind the blow. He barely blinked, so she thumped him on the chest, kicked his shin and released a screech of fury.

"How could you do that to me?" she demanded. "Do you have any idea how scared I was? That I'd have to go and tell the clan you were dead? And then Evander would blame me and kill me for sure?"

"Raen would keep Evander from killing you," Lachlan said and tried to put his dripping arms around her. He sighed as she eluded him. "Kinley, I told you, we are no' mortal."

"I thought you were joking." Dazed now, she sank down onto the bank and stared at the jagged silhouette of the opposite ridge. "You're not undead. I've seen you eat food, and walk around in the sunlight."

His mouth hitched. "I'm no' undead."

Kinley turned her head as he sat down beside her, and for the first time saw the faint marks of the scars on his body. A few had been covered by the snake ink, but dozens of others appeared all over his chest, arms and legs, as if he'd been stabbed hundreds of times. The most ominous scar was a thin line that completely encircled his neck. She couldn't believe she'd missed them, until she recalled the piss-poor lighting inside the castle.

"Why does the lake heal you?" Kinley demanded.

He laced his fingers through hers, and drew her to her feet. "I will tell you, my lady, but first you must take an oath of loyalty to me and mine."

Kinley understood what he was asking. She'd sworn an oath when she'd enlisted in the Air Force. She didn't know why he wanted her to, but he probably wouldn't tell her anything until she did.

"All right," she agreed. "What do I say?"

Lachlan reached for his belt, and removed a small knife. Instead of cutting himself or her, he wrapped her hand around the hilt. Then he folded his hand on top of hers and used an old piece of cord to bind her wrist to his.

"Say thus: I pledge myself to Lachlan McDonnel, laird of the McDonnels, and his clan. Ever when they call on me, I am theirs to command. Their battles are mine, and their secrets I keep. This I swear on my soul and my life."

As she repeated the powerful words, she watched the laird's dark eyes, and how suddenly ancient they seemed. When she'd finished her oath, she asked, "Why does the water heal you?"

"'Tis where the clan and I were slaughtered by the Romans." Lachlan's gaze grew distant as he looked out over the loch. "And where we awakened as immortals."

Chapter Thirteen

L ACHLAN TOOK KINLEY back to the stronghold, where they looked after the horses before retreating to his tower. Word must have gotten around that the laird wanted some alone time with her, for the great hall was deserted, as was Lachlan's chamber. She saw that Raen had left out a bottle and two cups for them, as if he'd known they would need a drink.

Kinley didn't want whiskey. She wanted answers, and to get them she needed a clear head.

"You said you weren't a selkie or a kelpie, and I know you're not the Loch Ness monster, so how does a big, cold lake bring you back from the dead?"

Lachlan peered at her. "There's a monster in Loch Ness?"

"Probably not," she admitted, shivering. "Forget I said that. Tell me about *this* loch."

Lachlan leaned against a wall and watched her as she crouched down to feed some splits to the fire.

"It happened when the Roman legions first came to our lands," he said. "I will tell you, but first give us a taste of that bottle, lass."

Kinley poured some whiskey for him, and then perched on the chair by the fire.

The laird described the Roman invasion of Scotland, then known as Caledonia. Ruthless and unstoppable, the legions had quickly conquered Britannia and marched north to claim the highlands. They called Lachlan and his people "Picts" for their tattoos, which the invaders considered barbaric and uncivilized.

"They sneered at us when our ancestors came here from an ancient land of powerful, learned peoples," Lachlan said. "In the time before the Great Flood, the Pritani ruled half the world, long before Rome was so much as a croft by a river."

Kinley felt enchanted now. "Half the world.

Impressive. So did you teach the Romans not to sneer?"

His smile faded. "Naught could stop that, or them." He told her how the southern tribes had marauded the Romans with blitz attacks on their columns by day, and stealthy raids on their encampments by night. "They did well," he said, "but the legion had no' come for the Pritani. They hunted the magic folk called druids."

An odd chapter in a history textbook from school came back to Kinley, probably because she'd always loved telling her grandmother whatever she learned about Scotland. During their invasion the Romans had gone after the druids, as they were believed to be bloodthirsty primitives who performed human sacrifice. One of the Roman Emperors had even ordered that the entire druid race be wiped off the face of the earth. His legions did their best by attacking any druid settlement they found, massacring the inhabitants, and burning their homes and fields.

"Were the druids members of your tribes?" she asked.

He shook his head. "They lived among us, and traded with us, but they were no' like the Pritani. Druids didnae believe in fighting, and refused to use their powerful magics against others. They go a different way, and I admire that. They couldnae defend themselves against so many. I summoned the war masters of all the other Pritani tribes, and convinced them to help me hide them away from the Romans. When I had gathered two thousand warriors, we began to raid the legion's camps. That allowed the Druids to escape." He took a swallow from his cup. "I should have ended it there, but I wanted them gone from our lands, so I lured them here, to Skye."

The rasp of pain in his voice made Kinley reach out to touch his arm. "Listen, we don't have to talk about this tonight."

"'Twill always be the wound that cannae be healed." Lachlan folded his hand over hers. "I thought we could prevail on our own land, but I had never fought against a legion. They came and came and kept coming, Kinley, as if the world were filled with naught but Romans. So many of them landed their boats and marched on Skye that we soon saw how it would be."

She rubbed her thumb against his palm in a soothing caress. "I'm guessing you didn't run."

He smiled a little. "Pritani warriors dinnae

run or surrender. We fight until we prevail, or we die. It didnae take long for them to overrun our front lines, and swarm over us like hungry rats. They bound us, and dragged us to the loch, and offered us freedom if we would tell them where to find the druids. No' a single man would betray our friends, so there we died. They tossed our bodies in the water."

If any other man had told her such a story Kinley wouldn't have believed it. But she'd seen his wounds vanish.

"So being in the water brought you and the clan back from the dead?"

"No, *faodail*. After the Romans left the island, the druids came back." Absently he rubbed the thin scar around his neck. "When they knew what we had done, they surrounded the loch, and cast a spell to awaken us, and change us. When we came out of the waters, we were whole and healed. Since that day of awakening we dinnae age or suffer sickness. We cannae die as mortal men do. But being reborn in the loch gave us more than eternal life. The magic bonded our spirits to its water. It heals us, and protects us, and takes us wherever we wish."

"That must have been some spell," she said,

and saw his shoulders stiffen. "Did something else happen to you?"

"No' to the clan." He finished his whiskey. "When the druids awakened us back to life, they cast our deaths on the legion. The conclave intended the curse to change them into living corpses, the undead, so they would all burn like torches at daybreak. But as soon as the Romans learned that sunlight would kill them, somehow they found a place to hide from it. They learned to live by night, drinking the blood of mortals."

"Gruesome bastards," Kinley muttered, and then scowled. "Didn't the druids know that cursing six thousand, highly-adaptable men might not turn out so well?"

"They do now," he said and started to say something else. But then he shook his head and went to his wash basin, where he tugged off his damp tunic. "You should go to bed. 'Tis late."

She got up and started for the door, and then stopped. Since moving into her own room Kinley hadn't slept very well at all. Even when she worked herself to exhaustion during the day, she usually spent half the night staring at the curving ceiling above her bed while she thought about

Lachlan, and what he was doing, and if he lay awake thinking about her.

Kinley had been trained to evaluate and solve crisis situations. Lachlan might be big, strong, handsome, and tempting as all hell, but he was still an unknown. Unsure what to make of his history, and concealing from him her own, didn't put much in the Let's Do This column. Oh, she wanted him— wanted him until it gnawed at her insides with hot, sharp teeth—but sex rarely made things *less* complicated. Since she'd pledged her loyalty to the clan, in a sense that made him her commanding officer. It was never a good idea to sleep with the brass.

No, she had plenty of good reasons not to do this. Yet the one thing she couldn't get out of her head was that moment on the battlefield, and what he'd said just before snatching her up in his arms: *Come here to me.*

She had come here to him. It didn't feel accidental. Everything about him made her hot and crazy and almost tearful, especially now that she knew what he'd gone through on the other side of becoming immortal. Could he really be twelve hundred years old? Did it matter?

He wanted her, she wanted him. That was

what mattered. She bent down to remove her boots.

As if he knew what she was thinking, the laird stopped splashing his face with water and turned around.

"I'm no' sleeping in the hayloft again, Kinley lass."

"Yeah, you told me that." She reached to unlace her trousers.

He came to her so fast she jumped under the hands he put on her shoulders. "My own bed isnae all I want." He looked over her head, as if meeting her gaze might be too much for him. "If you stay, I'll have you."

Kinley glanced down. The bulge in his pants suggested magnitude on an astronomical scale. There was a slight tremor in both of his hands. When she looked up she saw that his eyes had gone as dark as ink, and glittered with something about to snap its leash.

"Well, then." She skimmed her hand up his chest and pressed it against his lean, hard cheek. "I think we should get to it."

Lachlan turned his head into Kinley's hand, pressing his mouth against her palm as he reached between them. She felt him tug loose her laces before he slid her trousers down over her bottom to her knees. He knelt to remove them, and then remained on his knees as he pressed his face against her belly and nuzzled her.

Threading her fingers through his thick, heavy mane, she drew his hair back so she could see his mouth on her skin. He looked up at her while he grazed the edge of her navel with his teeth. She felt the curve of his smile before he laved her there with his tongue. Had she ever thought of her stomach as an erogenous zone? What he was doing to her set off little quakes of sensation that shot through her like crackling sparks, and made her go completely, utterly wet between her thighs.

"My knees are turning to prymerose pudding," she told him.

Lachlan made a tortured sound and stood, his hands catching the edge of her shirt and tugging it up over her head. The last of her clothing went sailing behind him to float down onto the floor. Then he held her at arm's length, not inspecting or ogling, but admiring her.

His silence unnerved her a little. "Stop staring. I know you've already seen all the goodies."

"Aye, but you've no' goodies," he said, his voice so deep now it seemed to pour through her like dark honey. "You've lovelies." His fingertips trailed over the contours of her breast, the touch whispering all her nerves to life. The sensation felt so exquisite a rush of reaction flashed through her, saturating her flesh with aching heat. He pressed the backs of his fingers against her swelling curves. "And they blush for me."

"That's because you're teasing them," Kinley said and pushed one puckered nipple against his palm. "I'm not a virgin, Lachlan. I know that's an issue in this, ah, culture, but…does it count that you're making me feel like one?"

"This is *our* first time," he said, and circled her peak with the pad of his thumb. "So you are maiden to me."

Without warning he grabbed her and dropped with her on the bed, his mouth muffling the low cry she released.

His scent rolled over her, cool and crisp despite his intense body heat. *Like the loch where he died.* Finally making the connection made Kinley dizzy on top of what he was doing to her. It was as if she were back in the oak grove, back in the rain, helpless as he thrilled and terrified her. There was so much of him, erasing every space, every gap, and Kinley struggled not to panic. As if he knew how she felt he rolled away from her and stood by the bed.

"If you've doubt, Kinley," he warned as he unfastened his trousers, "say to me now, for when I am naked with you I fear I willnae hear it."

The man had a Mt. Everest erection, a chest silvered by sweat, and every muscle on him looked knotted. And yet still he was offering her an out. If she didn't take it now, she'd have no right to bitch later.

Kinley let her desire for him crush her fear into dust. Feeling like a real woman for the first time in years, she stretched her arms up to make her breasts lift higher, and parted her legs just enough for him to see what she had waiting for him.

"No doubt," she said, "but lots of aching, and wanting, and needing. Help me out with them?"

Lachlan was naked and on top of her a heartbeat later, his big body dwarfing hers again, his mouth hard and hungry as he kissed her breathless. He tasted of whiskey and man, a combination that made Kinley feel drunk and soft and almost helpless. She braced herself as he clamped one hand around her wrists to pin them over her head. He wedged his hips between her thighs, but he didn't penetrate her. Instead Lachlan nestled against her, notching his hard shaft like an arrow in the ellipse of her folds.

"I'm your man now, my lass." He moved his hips, rubbing his length against her so gently that she could feel the veins lacing the heavy column of his cock. "All night, every night." He lowered his mouth to hers again.

His ravishing kisses and the maddening friction between her thighs went on until Kinley's thoughts dwindled away. She gave herself over to what he was doing to her mouth and her pussy.

Slowly Lachlan raised his head, watching her eyes as he shifted, and pressed the satin-smooth dome of his penis against the pulsing nub of her clit.

"So sweet you are, all spiced apples and warm cream and new clover flower." He nudged her clit, smiling a little as she shivered, and reached down to fist his shaft and work the flared ridge of his glans against her bared nub. "Shhh," he said as she whimpered in protest. "Does that no' please you, my golden goddess?"

"I think you like to tease rather than please," Kinley said and curled her leg around his. She tilted her hips so that his cockhead slid down into the drenched seam of her sex. "Come inside me, my beautiful man, before you make me scream and the guards break down the door."

Lachlan worked an arm under her, and closed his eyes briefly before he began to press in. His broad girth stretched Kinley to the brink of pain, but she was so aroused her wetness soon engulfed him. She could feel every inch of him sinking deep inside her, so thick and hard he felt like satin-wrapped iron. Then their body hair tangled, and the root of his shaft sealed him inside her. His cool scent blended with her heat, swamping her as if they were swimming in a lake of light. Time went away with the rest of the world. All Kinley knew was him, inside her and holding her, and looking at her with the same stunned wonder she felt.

"You are…" Lachlan's chest heaved and his shoulders shook as he bowed his head, and touched his brow to hers. "Gods, Kinley."

"Yeah. You, too," she managed to say as she squeezed him with her inner muscles. She worked them around his shaft until he groaned something in Pritani. "What does that mean?"

"This. I must. Kinley." He drew out of her,

almost completely, and then plowed back in as he gave her a hard, deep fucking.

He'd been holding back for her, but no longer. Kinley cried out, her body writhing beneath his as he plunged into her, his cock filling her and stroking her and destroying her. She'd never been invaded so deeply. She could feel his cockhead colliding with her cervix over and over, relentless and unstoppable.

Could she bear much more of this?

Something bloomed inside her, a dark and fiery answer that exploded through her as she flung her arms around him and dragged his head to her breast. She needed to feel him on her there, and then he was sucking her, his hot mouth almost brutal as he clamped on and lashed her with his tongue.

The bed began thudding against the wall. She could hear it and yet she didn't care, she couldn't care. All that mattered was Lachlan and this maddening, boiling wanting that was going to scald her from the inside out.

The laird wrenched his mouth from her breast and stared down at her, his eyes narrow and intent as he pounded his cock into her pussy.

"Your pleasure, Kinley. Give it to me. I want

it. I want to feel it when I spill in you. Give it, lass."

Darkness crowded in on her, and then splintered as Kinley arched under him, wailing wildly as she came. Lachlan kept stroking in and out of her, riding her through the incredible, soul-shaking bliss, his cock drawing it out until she thought the pleasure would drown her. Then she felt him go deep with one final, impossibly powerful stroke, and a low, animal grunt escaped him. Inside her his cock swelled and erupted, pumping his come into her. It went on for so long she felt it crest around his shaft and flow out of her.

Lachlan kept himself braced above her, his lips parted and his eyes half-closed as he jerked through the last of his pulsing jets. He almost collapsed on her as he bent to kiss her lips, and then rolled until he was on his back and she lay draped over him.

"Dinnae move," he whispered. His big hands splayed over her bottom, holding her so their bodies remained joined. "Never move again. Die with me thus."

"I'll die but, sorry, you're immortal." She found a comfortable spot for her cheek on his shoulder, but she didn't feel tired at all. If anything she felt dazzled, a little bewildered, and brimming with so much energy she could run five miles double-time. "Is it always like this for you?" His chest lifted and fell as he made a growling sound. "Yeah, me neither."

She couldn't resist running her hand over the expanse of his chest to feel the contours of his muscles. But as she did she felt something ripple under her touch. She pushed herself up, and thought she saw his ink actually moving. He was flexing his muscles to make the serpent move.

"Nice trick—" Suddenly his shaft swelled again inside her. "*Oh*."

❦

LACHLAN HAD ALWAYS BEEN gentle with women. A man of his size and strength had to be, or risk injuring instead of pleasuring. He'd meant to be the same with Kinley. She might be a quick, clever fighter but her slender limbs and soft skin were not fashioned for rough play. Yet the moment he'd pushed full into her, and felt the clasp of her on him, he'd lost himself and all notion of tenderness. A ravening madness followed, a beastly claiming and ravaging that she'd somehow endured.

And now this. She'd moved. Not only moved, but come astride him, driving him deeper into her tight, wet quim. He gripped her hips as his cock hardened inside her, watching her lovely face as she felt him grow.

"Be still, lass."

"I don't think I can," she said, and rolled her hips, just enough to caress him from within.

Lachlan felt a familiar burn of power across his chest and shoulders. Any challenge stirred his serpent spirit, and since it was joined with him it felt the same desires. He groaned as it moved inside him, as hungry for her as he was.

"No, Kinley, no."

Quickly he lifted her off his shaft and put her beside him. Seeing the state of his glistening, rampant penis decided it. He would have to leave her or risk—

"Mmmm," she hummed.

Golden hair brushed his belly as she curled her fingers around his thick root. Then she pressed her lips to his engorged head, as bold as a king's courtesan.

"Lass," he hissed. He gripped the linens

beneath him as she tasted him with her tongue. Sweat beaded above his lip and brow as he watched her, and fabric tore when she wrapped her lips around his cockhead. "You need no' do this. 'Tis unseemly."

She ignored him as she sucked lightly, bobbing her head as she took more and more of him into her mouth. Seeing her lips on his shaft and feeling the working of her tongue made Lachlan groan. It also pleased the serpent, now fully awake and slipping down from his ink into his groin.

Neglecting his own needs had become habit, and now Lachlan was about to pay for them. But so was his adorable, unknowing lover.

"Please," he groaned. "I beg you, stop."

Kinley released him, and frowned. "Don't you like it?" Before he could answer her eyes went wide. "Lachlan, your tattoo. It's– Oh my god."

"The serpent desires you," Lachlan said through clenched teeth. "It wants to take you." The ink moved across his belly to wrap itself around his shaft. "You should go to your room now. You should run."

"You know, I'd rather stay." A tenderness softened her eyes. She gently touched the ink as it crested on his penis, tracing the serpent's scales with her fingertip. "I want all of you, Lachlan."

Her hand stroked him and the serpent as she leaned over him and kissed the hard line of his mouth.

He could hold it off no more, and seized her, dragging her over onto her belly and yanking her hips up in the air. Kneeling behind her, he watched as the serpent found her clenching opening with his cock, its ink lines shimmering with power as it entered her. He wrapped his arms around her writhing body as he impaled her, his hips churning as the serpent used him to fill her. His thoughts tangled with the spirit's, and spilled from him, raw and hungry and desperate.

"So long I have wanted to touch you." He punctuated the words with heavy, powerful thrusts. "And come into you." He drove himself and the serpent deeper into her clenching soft-ness. "And fack your lovely golden quim. Your pretty lips parted for my tongue. Your tits ached for my hands." He slid his fingers to her bobbing breasts, capturing them and squeezing them as he plunged in and out. "Never again will you sleep without my seed painting your thighs."

Lachlan pulled out of her, flipping her onto

her back. As he shouldered her legs, the serpent guided him back to her. Now when he stroked into her he could see her face, and all the emotions that danced over it. Her gasping mouth and darkened eyes told him that he possessed her completely. The hard beads of her nipples and the clutch of her hands assured him that she wanted what he did to her.

"I can never have enough of you," he said, his voice rasping out the words. "Part your legs and I am there. My cock inside you. My hands on you. My mouth catching your cries."

Kinley's back bowed, her willowy form shaking as she came on him, and Lachlan felt the serpent coil and stretch as it thrashed with bliss. He needed to mark her now, mark her in the way of the tribe, as a man taking a woman on her maiden night. When he felt his balls tighten, he jerked out of her, spattering her belly and folds with the long, thick spurts of his seed.

But on her hip, where they had been no ink, a new design sizzled to life beneath his cream. His fingers shook as he smoothed it away to reveal a small serpent tattoo that was an echo of his own.

"You are truly my woman now, Kinley Chandler."

When he dropped down beside her his ink slithered from his cock across his torso and draped itself over his shoulders and chest, wriggling back into place.

Lachlan stared up at the roof beams, his body still shuddering from the intense sensations, and his heart shriveling to a husk. He had facked his woman as if she were a Pritani wife, open and understanding of her husband's wants. Only tribeswomen could call a man's ink spirit into his cock. Yet he had done this to Kinley without warning or explanation.

But she was not Pritani. She would be outraged, or frightened, or repulsed. She would never forgive him. She would certainly never bed him again—and that alone made him want to howl like a beaten dog.

Kinley raised her head and looked at her new skinwork. "Oh," she gasped between heaving breaths. "A snake." Her head flopped back down to the pillow. "Matching tattoos. That's nice." When he didn't reply, she turned to look at him, her face flushed and her eyes slumberous. "You all right?"

"I didnae mean to—" he said but stopped, furious with himself for even beginning such a lie.

"I did mean to do that, but no' our first night together. No' until you knew before what would happen."

"Did I just have sex with you *and* your tattoo?" When he nodded she clambered onto him and pressed her lips to his ink before she rested her chin on his chest. "How does your ink do that?"

She was not screaming, or running away, or even frowning.

"As mortals the spirit of our skinwork could compel us," he said, feeling bemused now as he stroked his hand over her rumpled hair. "We would be driven to great courage, or fierce passion. Since the immortal awakening, the spirits somehow came alive within us. When they are stirred now they join with us to share what we ken, mark our mates, and move on our skins."

"Okay," Kinley said quietly and smiled a little. "Just in case we don't work out, I'm never going to bed with Neac."

Lachlan laughed.

Chapter Fourteen

KINLEY WOKE AT dawn, wrapped in a tangle of heavy limbs and shredded bed linens. Lachlan had her gathered against him, with one arm around her shoulders and one long leg thrown over hers. It felt odd to see his face so close to hers. She'd never slept with any of her past lovers, but sex in a war zone tended to be quick and furtive and almost impersonal.

Last night had been anything but that.

Watching Lachlan sleep gave her some time to contemplate what had happened between them in bed. She'd expected it to be good, but from the delicious foreplay to the serpent spirit stepping in it had been like the sexiest, wettest dream she'd never had. She'd also never be able look at his ink again without getting hot and bothered. Even now she wanted to give it another kiss.

The laird opened his eyes. "Dinnae wake the snake."

Kinley suppressed a smile as she glanced down at his morning erection. "Too late for that. It's good to be the snake. I like the snake."

"You are too tender to take us again," he chided, and climbed out of the bed to pull on a robe and open the curtains.

Kinley was sore, but that was to be expected after spending most of the night under and on top of the man, taking his inexhaustible cock in her hungry little pussy and partying with his tattoo, which was just as earthy and lusty and kind of kinky, too. She wasn't lying about her new affection for his snake, either. The snake could come out and play *any* time it wanted.

It perplexed her, however. If all the clansmen were like Lachlan—which they were—then they should have been beating the women away. Instead they had maybe a couple dozen female retainers, most of whom were married or old enough to be grandmothers.

As Lachlan returned with one of his shirts for her, Kinley suddenly understood.

"It's because you're immortal," she said, taking the shirt from him. "That's why you don't have wives or children. You'd outlive them."

"In the first years, we didnae ken how greatly we were changed," he said, and idly stroked his hand over her hair. "Some of the clan went back to their families for a time. But the Pritani tribes remained mortal, and the clan couldnae sire new bairns. They suffered as they watched grow old and die their wives, and the sons and daughters sired before the awakening. We couldnae tell our people what had happened—we promised the druids we wouldnae—and so when we didnae age, some called us demons and tried to kill us."

Kinley winced. "Which only made matters worse when you didn't die."

He nodded. "In time all the tribes drove away my clansmen. 'Tis why we came back to Skye, and built Dun Aran."

"I always thought immortality would be amazing," Kinley said, frowning. "I never considered the cost of outliving everyone else."

"To live forever seems like a boon beyond

imagining, but after a thousand and two hundred years the clan has begun to lose heart. If not for fighting the undead, we would have nothing but an empty eternity of watching everyone and everything we love die again and again. 'Tis why we dinnae take wives." He hesitated before he added, "And why some of my men are ending their lives."

She sat up. "You mean there's a way you can be killed?"

"Aye, more than one," he said nodding. "It can be done in battle, but 'tis difficult." He drew her hand to the back of his head, pressing her fingers against the top of his spine. "A sword thrust here, or burning our bodies to ash, or giving ourselves to the loch, and we are no more."

She gripped his strong neck. "That's why the undead were going to stab you from behind. They know how to kill you and the clan." Shaking now, she folded her arms around him to hold him close. "Oh, Lachlan. Those assholes."

"Fast as Raen is, he couldnae have reached me in time. So now you see, you truly did save my life that night." He drew back a little to study her face. "What is it?"

Kinley could do some of the math. She was a combat search and rescue officer who just *happened* to drop into the middle of a battle where the McDonnel laird would have been killed. Then she had been changed into a living flame-thrower. Fate covered a lot, but not that much. She'd been brought here for this man. She'd swear to it.

"Lass?"

"Sorry." Although he'd been completely candid with her, Kinley wasn't yet ready to tell him her story. "This is why you had me take the oath."

"All mortals entrusted with our secrets do, or they cannae share them." He tipped up her chin. "Do you regret it now?"

"No, and even if I hadn't, I wouldn't tell anyone about the clan." She heard a knock on the door and quickly pulled his shirt over her head as Raen came in with a tray, followed by Evander.

"My lord," Evander said, "we have received word that—" The seneschal went silent and still as he saw Kinley.

She almost felt like shimmying her boobs at him, trollop that she was, but instead she settled for a nice, though slightly snide smile. "Morning."

His composure held, just barely, but his dark green eyes flared with ire. "I will return later."

Evander slammed the door on his way out,

while Raen handed her a mug of Meg's morning brew. "Will you teach me how you do that, Kinley?"

"It's easy." She glanced at the door. "Just change into a woman and breathe."

Chapter Fifteen

E VANDER WAITED UNTIL nightfall
before he left the stronghold for the
mainland. Once away from the clan he
no longer had to feign indifference to the other
men's sly looks and half-muttered remarks.

She's spent the night in his bed.

'Tis why he kept her at the castle, I knew it.

*You've seen his rod. Och, wee thing will want a month
to recover.*

*Talorc must have shouted with joy to see the little
wench warming Lachlan's blankets.*

If he hadn't seen it with his own eyes Evander
would have dismissed it as idle gossip. But burned
in his memory lay the image of Kinley Chandler,
her hair mussed and her lips swollen, whisker

burn patching her long, lying throat, perched on Lachlan's bed as if it were her new throne.

And the way she'd smiled at him.

So Lachlan had finally facked the little hoor. Why did it stick in his craw like a jagged fishbone? Hadn't he predicted as much after Lachlan had brought her to Dun Aran? She'd likely plotted worming her way into the laird's tartan trousers from the moment she'd interfered in their battle with the undead.

Three messages of warning Evander had already sent to the druids, all unanswered still. That the magic folk seemed supremely unconcerned about Kinley Chandler only piled more knotwood on his anger's pyre. It was plague enough that the haughty, unnatural wench had spent weeks strutting about dressed as a man, meddled in clan affairs, and seduced the wits from every careless fool who cast an eye on her. Now she had set her cap on the laird. By month's end she'd be calling herself queen of the McDonnels or some other such nonsense.

Walking into the loch, Evander thought of a remote brook on the mainland, and felt the light swallow him as the water bubbled around him. Then everything blurred as he gave himself over to the bond of magic that made his body go liquid. Moving through water usually made him feel better, but what he suffered was not a physical injury. The loch could not repair the damage done to him this time.

Once he emerged from the brook, Evander walked without noticing where he went, crossing pastures and croplands as he wandered, in search of some haven where he might fume in peace. When his legs stopped he found himself standing outside Fiona Marphee's cottage. He had no business here, not with bitterness swelling hot and sour in his gullet. He needed to leave his mistress be tonight, and find a brothel, where he might release his darker demons.

The door opened, and Fiona smiled up at him. "Milord, I didnae hear you."

She did not listen for him. Lachlan remained deaf to his warnings. Not even the facking druids paid him heed. Did he have no voice? Were his words unclear?

Evander bent down, flinging Fiona over his shoulder as he came in and slammed shut the door. He carried her into her little bed chamber, where he tossed her on the coverlet and stood over her, his hands clenched to keep from touching her again. He knew he should leave her, but the rush of hot blood to his head made it impossible to listen to his own sense.

"Oh, milord, forgive me," Fiona implored and sat up, arranging herself in a penitent pose. "I was carding wool, and dreaming as I do, so I didnae hear your knock."

Evander stared down at her, and once again saw Kinley in the laird's bed. The golden-haired slut had been fair glowing with sunlight, as bright and lovely as a pale fire. He'd hated her on first sight, but seeing her thus, and then the smile she'd given him… If he hadn't walked out, he would have lunged at her.

"What did you say to me?" Evander asked his mistress.

She ducked her head, and twisted her hands together in her lap. "Please, dinnae be angry with me, milord."

The vision of Kinley changed back into that of his dark-haired, white-skinned mistress. Fiona liked to play such games with him, pretending to be at fault when she had done naught wrong. He knew she did it so he could use her roughly, something she craved more than any kind of bed play. On another night Evander would have indulged her desires, for they pleased him as well. Now they just drove home the fact that all women, his mistress among them, were devious, scheming liars.

"Stop simpering and look at me." He had to make her do that, and felt furious when he saw mock tears gleaming in her eyes. "You are naught but a slut, like all the rest. I care naught for you. What I come to do here is fack you. Always. Only. What do you say to that?"

Yearning flickered across her face. "Whatever I am, I am yours. Do with me as you want."

"You think I jest?" He dragged her half-off the bed, shoving her face-down as he ripped her skirt from her waist. He swore at her as he held her by the nape, and bared her curvy white arse. Then he plied his palm against her ripe cheeks, slapping her over and over until her flesh splotched bright pink, and his hand went numb.

Fiona sobbed into the mattress, her pitiful cries like the mewling of a kitten, but when he touched her between her legs she slicked his fingers with her wet heat.

Evander gently stroked her quim. His cock felt ready to burst through his trews, but plowing her now seemed worse than the skelpin he'd given her. "What have I made of you, lass?"

He brought her to climax by rubbing her pearl, and then gathered her up and held her as she shuddered through the last of her delight. She wouldn't look at him, her eyes closed tightly, and yet she clutched at his tunic as if she meant never to let him go. Finally she pressed her face against her sleeve, using it to mop up her tears before she slipped out of his arms and picked up her ruined skirt.

"I've been with no man but you, milord," she said, her voice more flat and harsh than he'd ever heard. "When you are done with me, I'll have no other. For me 'tis only ever you." She regarded him as she folded the torn garment over her arm. "Now call me slut, and fack me, or no', and be on your way. It doesnae change me. I cannae be made anything but what I am: yours."

She shamed him more surely than Kinley Chandler ever could. He took the skirt from her, and put it aside, and drew her back to the bed. This time he made his touch as gentle as it had been their first time together while he undressed her, and lifted her onto the bed linens. She pillowed her face with an arm to watch as he stripped to his skin, and reached for him when he stretched out beside her. Her fingers drew four unseen lines from one shoulder to the other, and then plied the muscles of his upper arm.

Evander drew her thigh over his hip, opening her for the nudge of his cockhead. Her lashes fluttered as he worked into her sweet, pleasure-soaked quim, and when he had skewered her with every inch, he held himself still and reached around to gently caress her abused arse. He wanted to beg her forgiveness, and tell her that she was his, now and forever, but his pride would not allow the first, and the awakening made the second impossible.

He felt her shiver under his stroking fingers, and wondered how much more undeserved pain he would inflict on her. "You will want a cushion for your weaving bench these next days."

"I like the ache of you on me. It feels as if you still touch me, in secret." She brought his hand up to her lips, and down to her breast. "It makes me dream of the time when you next will again. 'Tis all I have of you sometimes."

Evander tugged her over atop him, guiding her to move herself on the ferocious spike of his cock. Fiona did so slowly, her head flung back and her full breasts swaying, and the close clasp of her massaging his shaft. When he was close he clamped his hands on her buttocks, squeezing them just enough to make her moan and shake. Inside her body her softness tightened, and milked the seed from his throbbing length.

She fell onto him, her limbs quaking and her skin hot. "Now I will need a cushion," she said, gasping against his neck.

Evander held her as she drifted off, his lust sated but his thoughts ensnaring him again. He could not bring Fiona to Dun Aran, or even to the village on Skye where their servants kept their families. Because she was not clan, or tribe, she could never share his days or his bed. He could not even explain to her why she could not, for that, too, was forbidden. When Fiona began to grow old, he would have to put her aside altogether, else she might question why he didn't age like her.

Lachlan had no such burden on him. He had brought his hoor into the castle. He would share his bed with her as long as he wished. He was the laird, the head of the clan, and none but the druid conclave could overrule him. Even on those rare occasions, the magic folk had to have very good reason…

Evander went still. Such as when a mortal grievance caused by the clan was brought before them.

Carefully Evander disengaged their bodies, covering Fiona with her blanket before rising from the bed and pulling on his clothes. He would need to borrow a mount from the village stables, and ride until dawn to reach the druid settlement where the conclave dwelled. Cailean Lusk would be there to bear witness. All Evander had to do was tell the truth.

Kinley Chandler had been brought to Dun Aran against her will, and had been held captive there for nigh on a moon. She was mortal, an outsider, but had done no wrong.

It was time she was set free.

Bluebells gently swayed on their bowed stalks as Cailean Lusk walked through the glen, his steps stirring the tiny trumpet blooms carpeting the highland glen. Beyond the slopes lay his home in a secret valley, which in another life he had protected with charms that clouded the eyes of mortals. There his small village of the magic folk dwelled for a thousand and two hundred years, practicing arts much older than their settlement. From the rich, black soil in which they grew their spell gardens to the mist-veiled groves where they honored their gods, the druids walked the path of the immortal within the mortal.

Cailean stopped and watched Bhaltair Flen climb a hilly slope to stand before a weathered stone altar. There the stout, gray-haired druid carefully placed wood wands around a basket of fruit, nuts and bread. Everything had been arranged in triple clusters, as was proper to honor the Goddess of the Three Faces. He lifted his hands up in entreaty as he recited the ritual spell that had been taught to him and his bloodline for one hundred and forty generations.

"You, lady, who walked widdershins thrice around the Well of Segais, and for your pride lost your thigh, hand, and eye to the waves of the Boyne born," Bhaltair Flen intoned, "accept these humble gifts as comfort, and healing. We see you whole and well among us, Very Shining One, and hope you grant us your favor."

Cailean remained at a respectful distance,

observing while silently repeating the ritual words. It had taken many incarnations before he had finally risen to the rank of Ovate, a spell-caster and ritual holder, and he had memorized all of the enchantments known by his master, Bhaltair Flen. He had not yet rid himself of his novice desire to practice, but he did not consider that a hindrance.

Bhaltair completed the spell by kneeling and touching his forehead to the base of the altar, and then came down the hill, his black eyes searching Cailean's face. "Strife, this early? 'Tis barely dawn. I've no' even had my morning brew."

"The McDonnel seneschal is arrived and seeks petition. He claims grievance." He plucked from his sleeve band the three messages he had received from Evander Talorc. "Again."

"Oh, that woman the laird brought to the castle," Bhaltair said. "I remember now." His round face wrinkled with displeasure. "I shall see Lachlan about the matter, and examine the female myself to assure she's no threat. The laird has needs, and rarely indulges them. Mayhap they went to his head. "

"The seneschal comes to us on her behalf," Cailean said. "He claims the laird abducted her and now keeps her at Dun Aran. Since she is mortal, and an outsider—"

"I ken clan law, Ovate. Lachlan and I wrote it." His master made a dismissive gesture. "Come. I remember his seneschal as a proud one."

As they walked together back to the settlement Cailean related what he had found at the oak grove where the woman had been taken. "The rains washed away any trail she might have left, but I found a strange mark on one of the standing stones."

Bhaltair came to an abrupt stop. "What manner of mark?"

"'Twas silver and green, and shaped as a winged Pritani serpent." He murmured a light spell and used the magic to draw the image in the air between them. "It had been burned into the stone with great power. The mark felt as smooth as glass."

"That is no' the work of the Pritani." His master's lips pressed so tightly together they went white. "Did you look at the trees?"

Cailean nodded. "There were new roots everywhere in the grasses. But master, none of us have used that grove since we resettled."

"'Twas no' our doing." Bhaltair paced for a

moment in a tight circle, and muttered invoca-
tions under his breath before he stopped. "I will
seek counsel with the conclave, but until they can
be convened, we must attend to this female.
Today."

Cailean wanted to ask why, but the look in the
other man's eyes held his tongue. When they
reached the settlement, and entered the meeting
house, they found Evander Talorc pacing with
impatience.

"Master Flen," the seneschal said. He bowed
to Bhaltair, and gave Cailean a surly look. "Ovate
Lusk. I am come with grievance against the Laird
Lachlan McDonnel–"

Bhaltair held up his big hands. "As Cailean
has already told me, my son. We will travel with
you this day to Dun Aran, and speak to your laird
about the female outsider."

Evander's expression tightened with suspicion.
"Talk does naught. You must remove her from the
stronghold."

Bhaltair slipped his hands into the ends of his
robe's flowing sleeves. "Do you mean to
command a member of the conclave, Seneschal?"

The highlander held his hands up palm-out.
"I overstep," he said, his voice gruff. "My apolo-

gies. 'Tis my duty to protect the castle and the clan that compels my urgency."

Cailean felt the dark emotions tainting Evander's aura. They had always been present, for the past haunted the man, but now they had grown enormous. Whatever ate at him, it had driven him here.

"Master Talorc," Cailean said, "what has changed with the woman since last we met?"

Evander gave him a barely-veiled look of contempt. "Come and see for yourself, Ovate."

Chapter Sixteen

❧❧❧

ENTERING THE GREAT hall of Dun Aran always gave Cailean pause, and not merely to soak in the power and magnificence of the place. Here was a perpetual reminder of his own people's power, embodied in the fierce, brawny men of the clan. Even the ancient Pritani blades and axes that adorned the walls of their stronghold was a reminder of it. But it also represented their greatest failure, that which was the dark side of the gift they had bestowed on the brave warriors.

Had they not made the McDonnels, the undead would not exist.

The moment they came into the castle, however, their presence sent servants fleeing and clansmen into the hall. A conclavist like Bhaltair

Flen rarely came to call on the McDonnels, but when he did it meant grave matters were at hand.

Lachlan McDonnel came out of his tower to greet them, which he did with visible respect and obvious wariness. "Master Flen. Ovate Lusk. 'Tis good to see you both."

That, Cailean thought, was an interesting lie. The laird's aura radiated displeasure, although it seemed not directed at them. "My master and I would speak to you, my lord. May we find a quiet spot to do so?"

Lachlan took them out to the thriving kitchen garden, where he sent away a pair of maids gathering cooking herbs. In the center of the garden sat stone benches around a large catch basin used to collect rain for watering. A few sparrows perched on the edge, dipping their diminutive beaks to drink.

Cailean smiled his thanks to the laird. Druids felt most comfortable being out of doors and surrounded by nature. By bringing them here he meant to put them at ease.

As they sat down, Lachlan remained standing. "I reckon my seneschal summoned you here."

"We came of our own accord," Bhaltair corrected him, and grim lines deepened around his mouth. "Tell me of this mortal female you discovered in the oak grove."

"Her name is Kinley Chandler, and she is from a far-off land called San Diego." The laird told them how she had saved his life during the battle. "She has no living kin here or back in her homeland. Since I owe her a life-debt, I have taken her under my protection."

"She works for you now, mayhap as a maid servant?" Cailean asked.

Lachlan smiled a little. "She is my lover, and gave her vow of loyalty to me last night. I expect Talorc didnae mention the latter."

Bhaltair rubbed his face with his hands, sighing into them before he slapped them against his heavy thighs. "I will say this to you now because this female is dangerous to you and your clan. She is no' from a far-off place. She was brought here from another time."

The laird frowned. "Another time? There is no other time but this."

Cailean cringed a little. Of course he would think that. The Pritani lived completely in the now. Even after twelve hundred years of existence they had no understanding of the fluidity of time, or how the druids could use it.

"My lord," Cailean said, "there are infinite times existing all around us. The past, the present, the future are but separated and held apart by the gods, and their apotheoses on this…" He stopped himself and turned to his master. "Master Flen, she couldnae have used the grove, and if we didnae—"

"Aye, and that path will be traveled later," Bhaltair warned him before he regarded the laird. "Cailean went to the oak grove where this woman first appeared. He found spellmark left by that which dragged her to our time."

"Dragged?" Lachlan said sounding alarmed. "She didnae come willingly?"

The old druid pursed his lips and tried to out-stare the laird. Finally he said, "Spellmark, such as was left where the female appeared, cannae be made by any magic of ours. It must be the work of the grove itself. It took her from her time, and brought her to ours. She doesnae belong here."

"'Tis very rare for such a thing to happen," Cailean put in hastily. "That grove hasnae been used since the awakening, so the magic absorbed by the soil must have leeched into the oaks themselves—"

"Cailean, close your mouth now," Bhaltair

said, "or I shall remove it from your face." He stood. "Lachlan, I must consult with my fellows in the conclave to determine why this female was thrust upon us. Until we have more knowledge of that, you must imprison her."

The laird loomed over the old druid. "I shall do no such thing. You will take Kinley Chandler back to that damned grove, and return her to her own time. *Today*."

Chapter Seventeen

KINLEY WALKED BLINDLY away from the kitchen garden, entering the stronghold through the scullery door. Fury pounded away at the inside of her skull, as if it had made a hammer of what she had overheard in the kitchen garden.

You will take Kinley Chandler back to that damned grove—

"Mistress, come and have a sit," Meg said. The chatelaine wiped her hands on her apron as she bustled over to her. "I've a nice new press of cider—"

"Not now, Meg."

Kinley gritted her teeth to keep from snarling as she went around her and strode into the back passage.

Return her to her own time–

"Kinley, there you are," Raen said. His huge form loomed in front of her. "I've time for a bout, if you've a mind to bruise yourself–"

"Already did," she said curtly. She dodged him. "I'm really tired, Raen. I'll be in the tower, taking a long nap."

Today.

Raen must have believed her, for he didn't follow her to the map room. There she found Tormod examining a moldy piece of parchment he'd unearthed from the archives. For a moment she thought she might upend the table in front of him and kick it across the room.

It wouldn't be enough. She felt ready to explode.

"The Caledonians were idiots," the tall Norseman told her as he spread out the crude drawing. "You see thus? They think Germania and Abyssinia were giant islands floating around Norrvegr and Svitjod. They must have been drunk when they drew this. 'Tis why Scotsman are such ninnies. All that drink diluted their bloodlines and addled their brains. Why do you look as if you wish to eat my nose?"

"Do we have a map of that oak grove where I

saved the laird's life?" she demanded. "You know, right before I punched him in the face?"

"Aye." His eyes went wary as he glanced at a shelf by the wall. "Why do you need it?"

Reining in her temper took all her self-control. "I want to see where I was in relation to our search grid," she lied. "If it's central, we might set some pit traps in it."

Tormod retrieved the scroll, and pointed out a small, leafy circle on the mainland. "'Tis no' far from the center, but the undead avoid the groves. We'd do better to dig traps around it, but you are lying to me, so there will be none. If you try to eat my nose, Kinley, I will call for Evander."

"I'd love that, if I had a blow-torch and a shovel. As for the traps, you never know. The laird might grow a brain in another century or two and think of it himself. You know, after he kicks me out of the castle. That's happening today, by the way." She closed her eyes and took in a deep breath. "I have to get out of here and find some answers on my own."

"And that is truth." His expression softened a few degrees. "Is it the laird? What has he done? Taken away your pitchfork? Demanded you dress like a lass?"

She eyed him.

Tormod heaved a sigh. "If you go down to the village, one of the fisherman will take you across to the port. You'll need a horse to reach the grove before dark. Ask Jens in the Red Ox Stables to give you my white gelding. Say I will kill him if he doesnae."

Now it was her turn to be suspicious. "Why are you helping me?"

"I didnae help you," Tormod said. "You held a blade to my neck, you vicious wench, and forced my counsel." He put the map room key, his belt sheath and his purse in her hands. "Then you stole my coin and my favorite dagger, and left me locked in here." He scrubbed the back of his neck. "I think you bashed me over the head, too. That is why I didnae cry out for help."

She tucked away his gifts and rolled up the map. "How long before you're missed?"

"Sunset, when I dinnae report for guard duty." He studied her face. "Kinley."

"He doesn't want me here. He told the druids to send me back to San Diego. Right now." She would not start crying in front of the damnably helpful Viking. "So I'll save him the trouble of whatever that takes." She held out her arm, which he clasped in a warrior's hold. "Keep working on narrowing the grid, and you'll find the undead nest. I'd burn it at high noon. That way any that try to escape get torched by the sun."

"You'll always be a bloodthirsty wench," he said, and smiled a little. "Walk with the gods' eyes at your back."

Taking Tama from the stables to ride to the village was easy. Seoc liked to flirt with the girls in the kitchen, and telling him the prettiest one had asked for him sent him hurrying off. She saddled the mare and rode her out to the entrance of the trail, which her mount could probably traverse blindfolded. Once she reached the glen she loped Tama across the fields to the little village by the fishing docks.

Kinley left her mount with the village stable master, asking him to keep her overnight before returning her to the stronghold. Since he had been one of the men who had seen her on the red deer hunt with Lachlan, he didn't even question her instructions. From there she walked down and picked the sturdiest-looking boat, and asked its owner to take her to the mainland. The coin she pressed in the fisherman's callused fingers convinced him to agree in a heartbeat.

Since she was a kid Kinley had always been steady on boats, but the farther they sailed away from Skye the sicker she felt. It served her right for eavesdropping on Lachlan and the druids, but if she hadn't, she wouldn't know how little her lover cared about her. Could she even call him that when they'd been together less than twenty-four hours?

One-night stand Lachlan. She'd never have imagined it would be nothing but that.

Of course it was her fault. She'd fallen for him last night, him and his damn snake, and this morning woke up feeling like she'd finally found her reason for living again. How could she be so naïve? This wasn't her first rodeo. She'd had flings in the military with guys who were one-nighters. As soon as they thought she was asleep they'd sneak off, and the next day act like strangers. Kinley had kept her game face on, but it had always hurt. Lachlan had actually been crueler. He'd lured her out of her emotional shell when all the while he'd just wanted to get laid. Was his heart made of ice? Did he even have one?

Jesus. Her life had turned into a bad young adult romance novel.

The port on the mainland proved to be busy

enough that no one noticed her, but Kinley kept her cloak hood pulled forward and her head down as she searched for Tormod's stable, which she found marked by a rickety wood sign painted with a crude red cow.

"Aye, I've Tormod Liefson's nag," said Jens, a much older Norseman with a crooked shoulder, showing her all four of his remaining teeth. "Stingy whoreson owes me for three months stabling and feed. I mean to stab him in the heart, next I lay eyes on him. What of it?"

"I'm borrowing the horse, and a saddle." Kinley handed him enough coins to make his eyes widen. "Unless you want Tormod to come here and kill you, in which case, give me my money back."

"What do you mean, woman? Tormod is an auld, dear friend." Jens fisted the coins, turned and hobbled off, and a few minutes later led out the Norseman's huge white gelding.

Kinley's jaw dropped. "Holy crap."

"You're too wee to ride this behemoth." His jaw sagged as she swung onto the gelding and scooped up the reins. "Right, then I'm abed at midnight."

"Sweet dreams," Kinley said as she guided the

horse out of the open stable doors, and walked him down the busy road. Once she reached the outskirts she took out her map and studied it for a moment. "Well, No Balls, we've got to cover about ten miles, but if I let you gallop, you can't toss me into the dirt."

The gelding turned its big head to eye her.

"You're right, that's a terrible idea and a nasty nickname. We'll try a nice trot first, Snowball." She situated herself in the too-big saddle and gave the reins some slack.

The horse started forward, his long legs smartly clopping, and when she leaned forward began to pick up his pace. By the time they covered the first mile he was loping with a rock-ing-chair gait that made Kinley appreciate the extra room in the four-horned saddle.

No one crossed their path on the way to the grove, but Kinley knew from history that the common people in medieval times generally stayed within the confines of the village. Some never left it until they were buried. If she ran into anyone they were likely brigands or highwaymen, or whatever they called the muggers of the era. She had Tormod's dagger, but hoped she wouldn't have to defend herself. In the state she was in any kind of a fight would probably shove her over the edge into a full-blown breakdown.

"I'll tell you what, Snowball," she said to the horse as she slowed him to a walk to give him a breather. "I might not go back to San Diego. I might set up a medieval counseling business, so I can warn all the wenches around here to steer clear of Lachlan Heartless User Bastard McDonnel. Or maybe I'll just invent moisturizer." She blinked hard to keep the tears at bay. "Oil of Kinley. Chandler's Cream. No, they'll probably think it's candlewax-based."

The sun dropped behind the tree line when Kinley found the scrolling dirt road that led directly to the entrance of the oak grove. She dismounted by the stream running parallel, where she let the horse drink.

"We made good time." The longer she stared at the road, the less she wanted to get back on the gelding. "What do you think will happen if I go back? Will I arrive barely alive? Or will I still be healed?" If she was like this she could go on another tour. Maybe this time she'd have the good sense not to survive it. "Great, I'm suicidal again."

Snowball lifted his head and shook it, splattering her with some water drops.

"We'll take a look and then we'll decide," she assured him. With the twilight rising now, she'd have to move fast.

"Help me."

Kinley turned around to see a skinny adolescent boy standing at the edge of the tree line. Blood streaked the front of his tunic from a deep neck wound, and he held onto a tree trunk as if ready to collapse. She tethered the horse to a branch and took off running. As soon as she reached the boy he fell to his knees.

Slipping into rescue mode, Kinley quickly checked the surroundings—all clear.

"What happened?" she asked, as she examined his neck wound. Two puncture wounds were bleeding freely.

"The undead," he gasped. He looked up at her, his blue eyes swimming with tears. "They came and took my mam. I fought them but..." He clutched at her, his small hands tight with desperation. "Please, Mistress, we have to get my mam!"

"I need to see to your wound first," she told him, and tore the sleeve from her tunic, wrapping it around his neck to staunch the bleeding. "You saw the vamp...the undead take your mother?"

When he nodded she peered into the forest. "You live back in there?"

He shook his head and tried to swallow. "I followed them. There's a cave." His voice broke on the last words. "Oh, please, Mistress," he cried, grabbing her arm. "They'll kill her!"

His shrill voice pierced the air, and suddenly Kinley remembered a very different child. On the outskirts of a dusty desert village, another boy had shrieked for her help in a language she didn't know. He'd grabbed her arm and pointed at one of the houses, but she'd been ordered back to the bird. The rest of her team was already gone. The orders for evacuation came through her comm unit, loud and clear. Then they came again, the pilot screaming her name. She pried the boy's little fingers loose and ran, but couldn't help but look over her shoulder. The hopeless look on his face was burned into her memory.

"Please!" the injured boy screamed as he shook her. "My mam!"

She blinked at him and stared at his terrified, tear-streaked face.

Screw the orders.

"Can you walk?" she said. When he nodded, Kinley helped him to his feet. "Take me to her."

The boy staggered as he led her through the woods, following a newly-churned path through the moss and dead leaves that carpeted the soil. In the growing darkness, he lurched forward toward a dim light. Next to a recess in the side of a slope was a flaming torch that had been rammed into the earth. He collapsed to his knees and pointed, his hand trembling with the effort.

"In there," he gasped. "He took her in there. Please. Hurry."

Kinley drew her dagger as she peered into a dark tunnel, but when she glanced back at the boy, the light from the torch shone on his neck. Her makeshift bandage had loosened, and the bleeding wound had vanished. He smiled at her.

"Let me guess," Kinley said, backing away. "Your mother isn't in there."

"No, but I ate one earlier," he said and two long, sharp white fangs extended down from his gums. "And her son."

He flew forward, almost too fast to see, and tackled her against the tunnel wall. As the air left her lungs in a whoosh, her hand hit the rock and the dagger dropped. With a cold, merciless grip he took her by the throat and hair and dragged her deeper into the cave. As she fought to free herself she saw his clothing and body blurring and changing, reshaping into a tall, lean man with short-cropped brown hair and bloodless white skin. The undead Roman hauled her up against his chest as he crushed her arms against her sides.

"My men and I have been waiting here for you for weeks. Our prefect thought you might return, but I doubted him. I shall have to apologize when I am done with you."

More undead emerged from the shadows, their black eyes gleaming with hunger as they trailed after Kinley and her captor. To conserve her energy she stopped resisting, and instead studied the walls of the cave around her. She saw no other tunnels but the one he was carrying her through, and from the look of this one it had been recently dug out. No one but Tormod knew where she was going, and he was probably still locked in the map room.

She was going to die here.

Panic gnawed its way from her belly to her lungs, making it difficult to breathe. She had to focus.

"Why would you wait...for me?" she managed to get out. "I'm nobody."

"You butchered six of our hunters," the

Roman corrected her, and slammed her against two wooden posts nailed together with a cross beam. "For that I would permit my men to fuck you to death, but you have knowledge I must possess." He leaned in, close enough for her to smell the stink of blood on his breath. "Once I have it, then I will give you to them, and watch."

Kinley twisted her arms when he tried to lash them to the beam, and her face exploded with pain as he backhanded her. Another Roman came to help him, and the two of them bound her wrists, waist and ankles, immobilizing her.

"Now," her captor said as he backed away. He reached out to catch a coil of braided leather that one of his men tossed to him. He shook out the whip, snapping it as he did, and Kinley saw that it had been studded with huge, thick thorns. "Where did the McDonnels take you after the battle?"

She gulped in enough air to say, "Candyland."

The Roman moved, and pain slashed across her from shoulder to hip, tearing at her tunic and flesh.

Kinley tried to scream, but her throat tightened, and all that came out was a garbled wheeze.

"We know you were taken to their castle and

kept there for weeks." He cracked the whip in front of her nose, flinging drops of blood against her face. "Where is it located?"

Kinley panted through the needling pain, watching his eyes as she forced her lips to smile.

"Rome."

She knew he would whip her again, this time in the face, and squeezed her eyes shut. The leather blazed a white-hot path across her forehead and nose and cheek, thorns tearing at her skin.

But the pain tore her away from the tunnel, dragging her through the sandy dirt. The downwash from the bird sprayed small pebbles in her face. Her body was riddled with bullets, and her face was a smashed ruin. She couldn't breathe. *She was choking to death.*

"No more," Kinley muttered through a clenched jaw. "*No more of this.*"

Power rammed through the pain, blazing out from the cold core of rage burning inside her. The white-faced torturer dropped his whip and spun around, shouting to the others. Little thuds made her look down at the scorched cords that had fallen from her wrists and ankles to the tunnel floor. Flames danced over her bloody skin, sealing the ugly weals. As she stepped away from the burning posts, she turned toward the pale men.

"Hello, boys."

She'd been trained to deal with capture and interrogation, but had the insurgents been trained to deal with her? Time to find out.

Orbs of pure blue-white heat floated around her hands, shrinking smaller as they glowed brighter and hotter. The only sleeve left on her uniform charred and fell away. She looked at the fire, mildly surprised that she felt no heat at all from it on her skin. But then flames had always moved away from her, even when she was a kid. Now fire loved her, it caressed her, it adored her. On some level she knew it wanted to fight for her.

And fire was *pissed*.

Kinley tossed the orbs from one hand to the other, testing her ability to control them. They were so much cooler than an M16A2. And no ammo to run out of, or a semi-auto to jam, two huge pluses. But what was this? Her captors were starting to run away, the cowardly assholes.

Flinging the orbs at the fleeing men, she smiled and watched as they enveloped them. They screamed as their bodies withered and blackened, and fell in curtains of powdery ash to the ground.

Kinley studied the little gray piles. Instant cremation. She could work with that.

Surrounded by the dust of his men, her captor stood, whole and unmarked, his insectile eyes glittering as he watched her walk toward him.

"We will find them, and come for you," he promised her. "Nothing can stop the Ninth. And when that day comes, you will–"

"Oh, shut up," Kinley said and impaled him with a stream of fire, twisting it as she watched his white face melt, and then his body, until nothing remained of him but another little heap of ash.

Somewhere inside her something small and helpless wailed without sound, but Kinley had no more time for that soft, silly, little bitch. As the silence of the night drifted into the tunnel, she bent down and scooped up a handful of what had been a man, and let it sift through her cold fingers.

"These things we do, that others may live. It's not just a tattoo anymore, pal. I can back it up."

She straightened, and looked around her. She didn't recognize the territory, but it was obvious that she had landed behind enemy lines. Her camo had been badly singed, and she didn't have any equipment. The tunnel around her appeared unstable, so she wouldn't hunker down here. She'd have to scout the surrounding area to find suitable shelter for the night.

And if anyone got in her way, she would do those things again.

Chapter Eighteen

"**S**HE WHAT?" LACHLAN bellowed, his voice echoing in the great hall.

His men had searched the entire stronghold, from his own bed to the dungeons, and from the ramparts to the kitchen. Even the scullery maids and druids had been enlisted. But now the rushing to and fro came to an abrupt stop as Lachlan glared at Raen, Tormod, and Seoc.

"Aye, my lord," Raen said, his voice tight. He dragged Seoc forward by the shoulder. "The stable master was the last to see the lass."

Lachlan's hands clenched into fists. "When?"

The shorter man flinched and looked away. "I reckon late afternoon, my lord."

Lachlan took a step closer. "And you just let her take a horse?"

"I...I..." Seoc swallowed hard. "I wasn't there, my lord."

"The fack you say?" Lachlan said through clenched teeth.

Raen pulled the man back and pushed the Viking forward. "There's more, my lord."

Lachlan scowled at Tormod. "What have you to do with this?" As the Viking related his conversation with Kinley, Lachlan could scarce believe his ears. "The mainland?" he demanded. "Where?"

"The lass didnae say," he replied evenly, matching Lachlan's stare. "Only that she meant to leave the castle before you forced her out."

"Forced her out?" Lachlan growled, grabbing the front of Tormod's tunic. "Are you daft?"

"My lord," Cailean said calmly, resting a hand on his arm. "Our conversation." Though Lachlan could have pummeled the viking into the ground, he forced himself to look at the druid. "Regarding Kinley," the smaller man said quietly.

Lachlan recalled their talk of the grove and how it had brought Kinley from the future—unwillingly. He'd ordered them to send her back to her own time.

He glowered at Bhaltair Flen. "Is this druid doing?"

Flen puffed himself up. "The lass left of her own accord." But then he cleared his throat. "Though mayhap she has returned to the grove."

Lachlan thrust Tormod away from him and stormed from the hall.

❧

As KINLEY MADE her way through cover, she decided that Robert Frost would have loved the woods outside the insurgents' dugout: dark and deep, and silent with heavy air that seemed a bit on the frosty side for Afghanistan. She must have bailed out over a northern province, which meant she'd be all right. All the real fighting was to the south, where the insurgents protected their poppy farmers and ammo dumps.

She'd always hated the sand pit, but there wasn't any sand to speak of here. Lots of green-ery, and a fast-flowing stream where she found a massive white horse left by some local. The saddle on it made her stifle a giggle. Jesus Christ Almighty, it had four horns, and no stirrups. But the horse seemed placid enough. She used a big rock to mount the gelding. His coat made her think of the white hydrangea bushes her grandmother had called snowballs.

"You think you can find me an Air Force base, Snowy?" she asked the horse as she walked him back along the dirt road north. He answered her with a snort. "Yeah, I'm thinking no, too. Maybe there's a combat outpost somewhere. I'll settle for a farmhouse or a barn or even a tool shed."

Kinley didn't find any of those, but she did spot an orchard of apples, which made her empty belly rumble. Dismounting nearly put her on her ass, thanks to the crap saddle, but the gelding didn't spook.

"I like you, Snowy. You may not have any balls, but I don't think you actually need them."

She led him to a tree on the perimeter where she tethered him so he could feast on the apples while she made camp. Gathering dead wood to make a fire gave her time to think. Her memories of Kandahar seemed weirdly fuzzy, and she couldn't remember what had happened to her rescue bird or her air crew. Every time she tried to think of the assignment they'd been sent on, her head started to pound. She was probably in shock, which was okay. She'd survived some pretty nasty torture.

Whips with thorns. The guys back at the base wouldn't believe it.

Slowly she lugged the armful of wood she'd gathered to a clear spot, dumped it, and crouched down to stack it properly. She'd have to sleep on the ground, but she'd been there, done that, too many times to count. If she covered herself with some of the dead leaves heaped around the trees, she'd stay warm, and blend in with the ground if the insurgent boys had friends.

The tree behind her rustled, and she glanced over her shoulder to see Snowy rooting through the branches for more apples.

"Don't be greedy," she told him.

She flicked flames from her fingers onto the wood. It blazed up instantly, and she settled back on her haunches. The fire would do nicely.

"Witch."

The whispered word brought Kinley to her feet. She whirled, squinting in the dark to see who had come for her.

"You get away from me," she told the darkness. "Get away, or I'll send you straight to Hell, too."

Something came flying out of the trees, striking her in the head. She staggered, almost falling into the campfire, and dropped to her knees. Blood dripped onto the back of her hand, and she frowned at the big stone by her fire. They were throwing rocks at her? Had to be villagers or farmers. The insurgents always stripped them of their weapons.

They weren't vampires, so she couldn't kill them. That wouldn't be very Air Force of her.

"Okay, now," she said and pushed herself upright. She held up her hands. "I'm not going to hurt anyone. I'm a Joe, all right? I had to bail from my bird. I just need to find the nearest base. The COP, you know? Where the other Joes are?"

Another rock came whizzing straight at her, and she blocked it with her arm, hissing with pain as it bounced off her forearm.

"We saw you, witch," said a plump woman dressed in a bizarre peasant costume and holding a bigger stone in her hand. "We saw you cast fire with your hand."

"We cannae burn one such as she," a male voice growled. "It will have to be the loch."

Why were they all talking like her grandmother? "Excuse me?"

"Never," the woman said, and flung her rock.

It hit Kinley in the temple, knocking her down
again. This time she didn't get up. This time, she
bailed.

Chapter Nineteen

"I SHALL TAKE great pleasure in killing that facking Viking," Lachlan told Raen as they finished searching the oak grove and walked back to their horses. "It will take time, but I shall enjoy that as well."

"Kinley would have found a way off the island without his help," his bodyguard said. "Tormod but saw to it that she went safely. And Neac wishes to kill him first." He saw something on the ground and crouched down to hold the torch closer. "There are fresh tracks here, from small boots and a large mount." He stood and walked a short distance before returning. "She went north."

"Good. She would have needed shelter for the night, and there's a croft of orcharders two leagues from here." Lachlan mounted and waited for Raen to do the same before riding off toward the village.

As they left the place where Kinley had first appeared, he remembered the words of the two druids. Cailean had said that magic had been absorbed by the soil of the grove. Bhaltair claimed it was no magic of theirs, but had stopped Cailean from saying more. The magic folk brooked no outside interference with their kin, or matters relating to them. Could Kinley be druid kind? No matter their looks, the druids were ancient. They were born into one life after another. Could it be that Kinley was a druid reborn from this time, and that the grove brought her back to rejoin her people?

And why did that make him even angrier?

At the village, Lachlan expected to find the mortals asleep, but all of the cottages around the apple orchards stood empty. Tormod's big white gelding had been left tied outside a barn, sooty handprints on his neck. Lachlan scanned the area before spotting torchlight by the small loch just beyond the trees, and pointed it out to his bodyguard.

"There."

Raen's expression emptied, and he took off at

a fast gallop, shouting over his shoulder, "Quickly, my lord."

Lachlan saw the reason for his man's urgency when they came within sight of the loch. The crofters stood assembled with hatchets, pitchforks and shovels around a woman and two men, who held another, slender woman who sagged unconscious between them. They were dragging her toward the water as the others shrieked their hatred.

"Douse the witch."

"Use the poles to keep her on the bottom."

"Drown that evil filth."

Lachlan leapt down from his horse as Raen forced his way through the throng to reach the trio and their prisoner. The big man put himself between them and the water.

"You superstitious bastarts," Raen said, his voice so cold it made all the mortals take a step back. "Give her to me."

The plump woman scowled at him. "She's a witch, Master. We saw her cast fire spell with our own eyes. We must douse her, else she torch our homes and crops."

"Do you ken who we are?" Lachlan asked, and saw recognition on the faces that turned to look at him. "This is our clanswoman, no' a witch. You will hand her to my man, or *I* will burn this place until naught is left but scorched earth."

Raen shoved the woman aside and lifted Kinley in his arms, bringing her to Lachlan. When he saw her head injury he grew worried, but the marks on her face and torso made his gut clench.

After handing her over as gently as he could, Raen carefully plucked a thorn from her cheek. Tossing it away, he looked up at the sky, his face a grim mask of rage.

"Facking undead bastarts whipped her."

"Find a place where we may tend to her," Lachlan said, barely able to form the words.

His bodyguard trotted ahead to the croft, where he took charge of the largest cottage and cleared out the occupants. When Lachlan carried her inside, Raen spread a sheet over a large table and brought a brimming wash basin.

"Bring clean cloth," his bodyguard ordered the mortal couple who came in behind them. To Lachlan he said, "Did they drain her?"

"No' that I can see."

He inspected the gash in her scalp, which was

fresh, before he cut open her tunic to see the full extent of her lash marks.

Kinley snatched the blade from his hand before she rolled off the table and backed away, stumbling as she did.

"So you stone women before you rape them, huh? Takes the fight out of them?" She took in her surroundings before she stared at Lachlan. "Lay another finger on me and I'll cut it off, along with your dick. Or maybe I'll roast it. You want well-done penis? Take another step."

Lachlan saw the same wildness in her eyes that he'd witnessed on the battlefield. She behaved as if she didn't recognize him.

"Kinley, we are your friends," Lachlan said calmly. "Do you ken where you are?"

"Idiot farmers jumped me," she said and blinked as blood dripped into her eye. "Who taught you to talk Scots? Did you catch some of the U.N. troops? Torture them, too?" Her gaze shifted to Raen, who was inching forward. "You. Jag Face. Back off." When he kept coming she slashed the air between them with the dagger. "I'll slice you to ribbons, I swear to—" She ended with a scream as Raen slapped the blade from her hand and seized her, clamping her against his chest.

"She'll do herself harm," the big man said, grimacing as she kneed him in the groin. "I'll put her out, then?"

Seeing her like this made Lachlan feel sick. "Gently," he told his bodyguard, who gripped the side of her neck.

"Let me go," she said and twisted against the arm holding her, but her struggles slowed and her eyes grew dazed. "Can't. Die. Not…like… this…please…"

The moment she lost consciousness Raen released her throat and carried her back to the table. Lachlan wasted no time cleaning her wounds, and used the cloth the crofter woman brought to him to bind her head. Finally he tore off his own tunic to wrap around and cover the ruins of hers.

"We'll tie her to the back of the gelding," Raen said and saw Lachlan's expression and his own turned bleak. "My lord, we cannae ken if she will wake herself. Clever as she is at escaping, 'tis too risky."

"Aye, but you'll tie her to me," Lachlan said

and looked at the crofter couple. "Bring me rope. Now."

Outside the cottage Lachlan mounted his horse, and took Kinley from Raen as he lifted her to sit on his thighs facing him. She slumped against his chest, and looked so pitiful the laird rested his cheek atop her head. His bodyguard quickly bound her wrists behind Lachlan's back, and secured her ankles to the saddle straps.

When he would have tied a gag over her mouth, Lachlan shook his head. "'Tis enough to bind her."

"Watch her teeth, my lord," Raen said and swung up on his own mount, tying the reins for Tormod's gelding to his saddle, and then looked at the faces of the fearful mortals around them. "Naught ever changes with you ignorant fools. She comes here hurt and alone, and in need, and you try to kill her. 'Tis you who are evil."

One of the oldest men lifted a torch to him. "Do I not ken you?" he said, squinting at him. But then his eyes went wide. "Aye. You came when I was a boy. But…"

He backed away, stumbled and almost fell, then hurried off.

"You'll murder no more women," Lachlan

ordered the crowd, "whatever you think they are. If I learn you've done this again, I'll come back with my men, and we will name each of you witches, and drown you in that loch."

Neither he nor Raen waited for their reaction but headed their horses back south. Raen didn't speak until they had ridden several miles.

"That old man did ken me," he said. "He was Bradana's youngest brother."

"That was her family's croft?" Lachlan said. When his bodyguard nodded Lachlan sighed. "You should have said."

The big man glanced at Kinley. "I still cannae speak her name so easily."

Fifty years ago Raen had fallen in love with Bradana, a mortal woman he'd met on the mainland. Because she was an outsider he'd married her in secret, and visited her when he could. When Bradana's family discovered she was consorting with Raen they'd assumed he was a demon, and subjected her to a witch test by dousing. Unable to swim, she'd proven her innocence by drowning.

Lachlan had never understood the mortal penchant to blame their woes on those innocent and helpless. The Pritani had always been fiercely protective of their women and children. He also hated that Raen had been reminded of his worst loss.

"I'm sorry, lad."

"As am I," he said. He nodded at Kinley. "I should be carrying her, my lord. When she wakes, she may take fright again and burn you."

"She didnae in the grove, or when we first brought her to Dun Aran, when she knew naught of me." Lachlan tucked her head under his chin. "I think the undead somehow awakened her power. Mayhap that is why the grove stole her from her time, and brought her to us."

"I pray 'tis so," Raen said, and looked out into the night. "They are turning more mortals every season, while the clan cannae sire new warriors to replace the fallen. Already our numbers are too few against so many, and if they find Dun Aran…"

"They will kill us all," Lachlan said, and suddenly understood the lash marks on Kinley's body. "And 'tis why they tortured her."

Chapter Twenty

QUINTUS DISMOUNTED FROM his horse, and handed the reins to his aid before he made his way to the great cavern. There Gaius had stationed his guards around the platform and reclined on his dais while he watched two naked mortal men fighting with spiked staffs on the steps.

"Prefect, you are just in time for the night's games." He stood and gestured to the guards, who seized the fighters. "They are terrible gladiators. Kill them, and bring the wenches."

Mounting the steps, Quintus avoided the splatters of blood as he joined the tribune. "The men watching the grove are dead. I found their remains in the dugout."

"Replace them. She will return."

"I fear she did." Now came the unpleasant part. "Our men were burned to ash."

The tribune sat upright. "You warned them about her power."

Quintus nodded. "They took the proper precautions. She…overcame them."

The guards dragged two young, naked mortal women to the base of the steps. Both were given daggers and pushed toward each other. They stood sobbing noisily as they stared at the blades in their hands.

"Excuse me for a moment," the tribune said. He stood and clapped his hands. "Attend me now, mortals. Yes, I speak to you. You are to fight each other. The first to cut off a breast from the other will win her freedom." He waved his hand for them to begin, and then sat back down with a heavy sigh as one of the women stabbed herself in the chest. "Guard, get another wench."

"Tribune, we must rethink our strategy," Quintus suggested carefully. "Attempting to capture this one female is not working. I think we must use the spy now."

"Whatever you think is best, Prefect," Gaius said and perked up as his guards dragged in a woman with large breasts. "Oh, I do hope this one is a fighter."

Quintus bowed and left the cavern for his chambers, which he found empty. He did not mind removing his own armor, but as soon as he had changed he went in search of his manservant. An uneasy feeling came over him as he checked the bone pits and the servants' caves, and then went to the guards stationed outside the Temple of Mars.

"Have you seen Orno?" he asked one of the men, whose expression turned grim.

Inside the tribune's temple the cages of the sacrificial victims stood empty. More bodies had been tossed into the charnel pit. The great altar Gaius had built for his offerings to Mars gleamed with blood mixed with ash. As Quintus walked up to it he saw the gold ring he had given his former slave to mark him protected. It gleamed dully from a pile of ash.

"Mars demands much from us, my friend," said Gaius from behind him. "But when we sacrifice those we hold in great esteem, he showers us with gifts." The tribune took the ring from the altar and offered it to him. "You should be proud. He was very brave, and hardly screamed at all."

Quintus closed his eyes briefly. "Am I to thank you for this, Tribune?"

"Oh, come now, Prefect. Do not be shrewish. He was a slave." Gaius pressed the ring into his hand. "You weren't fucking him, I hope. There are much better-looking men in the pens."

In that moment Quintus nearly reached for his dagger. They were alone in the temple. He could say that the tribune had become suddenly despondent and sacrificed himself to Mars for the good of the legion. The men would likely celebrate for weeks. But he knew the tribune, knew his wily ways, his paranoia, and suspected this was but another of his endless loyalty tests. He could also smell pitch burning somewhere close.

"I do thank you, Tribune, for so honoring my servant." He let his hand drop from his blade as he bowed. "I feel certain that Mars will bring us victory over our enemies."

Gaius studied his face as he called out, "Show yourselves." A dozen archers emerged from hiding, and lowered bows notched with the flaming arrows. "Victory is all I wish. All I have ever wished, Quintus." He grinned like a boy. "Now that we have settled that matter, let us discuss this plot of yours, to use the spy."

Chapter Twenty-One

WHEN LACHLAN AND Raen reached the port town they left the horses with Jens. Before the clan could afford to stable horses on this side of the water, the men had trained their mounts to accompany them through it. Though it was troublesome to get the great beasts to stand for it, Lachlan considered doing so again. Perhaps without the gelding, Kinley wouldn't have got as far as she had. But when he looked down at her, he grimaced, knowing that wasn't true. She'd have found a way.

As Jens came out and lifted his lantern, he was wise enough not to grumble about the late hour.

"You'll no' find a fisher to take you back before dawn," the old Norseman warned as he watched Raen untie Kinley and lift her down. "McEwan has a shed aback his place. He locks up the drunken for the town."

"She's hurt, no' drunk," Lachlan said as he dismounted. He took her from his bodyguard. "No' a word of this to anyone."

"Aye, or Tormod'll end me, I ken it." Jens nodded at Kinley. "She's a brave one, my lord. Never once gave pause, or looked back." He hobbled off with the gelding.

From the Red Ox, Lachlan and Raen walked to the river that provided fresh water for the town. Kinley stirred as Lachlan gently placed her on the bank. He knelt beside her, watching her face as his bodyguard scouted the immediate area. Using water to cross any distance was one of the clan's most closely-guarded secrets, one that Lachlan could not afford to let the undead discover.

"We're alone, my lord," Raen said when he returned, and glanced down. "She may wake this time."

"Then we'll be quick about it," Lachlan said and brushed her tangled, soot-blackened hair back from her pale face. "Hold on, lass. We're almost home."

Raen stepped into the river and crossed his

arms over his chest as light shimmered around his hips, and glowed in the lines of his Pritani tattoos. As he sank down into the water and vanished, Lachlan picked up Kinley and carried her into the rushing current.

In his mind Lachlan saw Loch Sìorraidh, and as soon as he sank in the river with Kinley he clasped her to him with his thoughts as well as his arms. Light fountained around them as his form changed from man to spirit, and a torrent of bubbles swirled around them. From there the water around them blurred as they were swept off, pouring through the currents as effortlessly as two beams of light. When Lachlan's feet once more touched bottom he walked up out of the calm waters to stand in the shadow of Dun Aran.

Kinley sputtered and blinked, lifting her hand to her wet face, and then saw him looking down at her. Her bewilderment changed to horror and fury as she writhed against his hold.

"Get your hands off me."

The laird's jaw tightened as he carried her into the castle, where Raen was ordering the men to clear a path. Meg took one look at Kinley and fled into the kitchens, while Neac trotted over to the laird and paced him as he headed for his tower.

"Those filthy scunners got hold of her," the chieftain said as soon as he saw Kinley's wounds. When she shrieked at him he met Lachlan's gaze. "She's gone crazed again. She must have battle madness."

Lachlan scowled at him. "She's no' a man, Neac."

"She fights like one," the shorter man said and waved away the guard and followed him up into the tower. "She said wenches in her homeland can be warriors, like us, and go to battle. If she spoke the truth, then they must also share in a warrior's afflictions. Did she ken you or Raen when you found her?"

The laird shook his head, grimacing as Kinley clawed at his neck. In his chamber, he had Neac help him tie her to his bed, and then stood back to watch her fight her bonds.

"She's no' the same," the chieftain muttered. "See her eyes? They've too much black. This is far worse than the last bout. Poor wee thing." He reached as if to touch her hair, and snatched his hand away when she snapped at his fingers.

"What are you looking at?" she shouted at

Neac. "You think I'm afraid of you? I'll burn your face off, you bald little troll."

Knowing she would only spew more of the same, Lachlan drew Neac out into the corridor. "I dinnae ken how to help her. My father chained men with battle madness to god stones, and had their wives and bairns pray for healing. If the afflicted didnae regain their mind after a moon, he opened their neck veins."

"Aye, my tribe did much the same," Neac admitted, and winced as he heard Lachlan's bed thump against the wall. "'Twas that or be killed by them."

"What of the druids?" Lachlan said.

"I told them we'd send word when we found the lass," the chieftain told him. "And I will, when I've time for it. I'm so busy in the armory now, and I think some of the birds are sick, too. Aye, they should rest a bit." A furious screech from the chamber made Neac cringe. "You'll no' open her neck veins?"

"Never," Lachlan said but felt like slamming his head against the wall. "But I must manage something to calm her."

The chieftain thought for a moment. "When you first brought the lass to us, you kept her close, and gentled her with kindness. Mayhap 'twill work again."

"I cannae bar my chamber door for days on end," Lachlan said. "The clan willnae stand for it. And Evander." He shook his head.

"Then take her to a quiet spot, where you can be alone with her," the chieftain told him. "Raen and I can manage while you're gone."

Lachlan thought of his old lodge on the other side of the ridge. "I ken just the place."

⁂

BEING HELD CAPTIVE SUCKED, Kinley thought as she watched the leader of the insurgents preparing for her next interrogation. He hadn't resorted to torture yet, but his mind-boggling imitation of a Scotsmen needled her like a shiv. He even dressed in some Dark Ages outfit in an attempt to fool her, but she wasn't buying his story.

She had to hold it together. No one was coming to save her. She had to do that herself.

"Hey, Snake Guy," she called out to him from where she sat tied to a roof support post. "Why did you drag me up to this old drug shack anyway? You plan on dosing me with poppy juice so I'll talk? Just so you know, I'm allergic. That means you feed me that poison, I die on you."

He didn't reply, but he didn't say much anyway. He knew her name, and he kept telling her that his was Lachlan McDonnel and that he was a friendly. Right. Because friendlies kept you tied up while asking you nonsense questions to screw with your head.

She'd tried to bring on the fire, but it didn't seem interested in the guy. Or maybe it was the way he smelled, like cold, sweet water. In any case, every time she tried to make her hands flame they simply went numb.

He finally came over and crouched down, just out of her reach. "I've made a meal for you."

"Not hungry," she said. She was, so much so that she felt hollow, but eating would be cooperating—and making herself available to drug. The last thing she wanted was to be high around Snake Guy. "But thanks for the humane treatment. I'll be sure to mention it at the war trial."

"Kinley, you've no' eaten in two days," he chided. "You'll have some, or I'll take your clothes."

She glanced down at the ridiculous dress he'd

put her in, which made her look like a milkmaid with a lousy seamstress. "Oh, please. Take them, and give me back my flight suit. And my rifle. I'd really like my rifle."

He sat back on his haunches. "If you eat, I'll leave you untied."

Idiot, idiot, idiot. She gave him her sweetest smile. "Wow, suddenly I'm starving. Where's the chow?"

He untied her from the post, but once he marched her over to the table he tied her to the chair, the careful bastard. On the table sat two plates of smoked fish, a pile of greens and bread so dark it bordered on black.

Her stomach rumbled, and she had to swallow hard. Of course it smelled delicious. All part of his plan to get the drugs in her, no doubt.

"Who'd you steal the salmon from?" she asked as he poured a mug of cloudy-looking juice for her. "An outpost? Is there one near here? What, no comment at all? Come on. I'm asking nicely."

He broke off a chunk of the fish and held it up to her lips. "Eat."

She sniffed the piece before she reluctantly parted her lips and let him place it in her mouth. The salty, smoky flavor of the salmon spread over her tongue, making her suppress a moan as she chewed it slowly. She didn't taste any bitterness from drugs in the fish or the juice he gave her to sip, which turned out to be a strong apple cider.

Kinley was pretty sure he didn't use eating utensils because he thought she'd try to steal them. Of course he'd be absolutely right if he did. But the guy really knew how to eat with his hands, so maybe not. She'd noted the people in the serious backwater provinces regularly ate with their fingers. They had the same competent, almost elegant way about them, as if they'd had to go without knives, forks and spoons since birth.

"So what's the name of your village?" she asked him casually. She'd been trying like hell to glean enough information to narrow down her position, but the idiot kept telling her she was on the Isle of Skye in Scotland. "Do your people herd for the local fighters? Maybe goats? Goats are nice. I guess. Their eyes freak me out a little."

"We've sheep and cattle," he said as he fed her a pinch of the greens, which tasted like sweet onions. "The village is called the village. We are fighters, Kinley, but we're on the same side. You're pledged to my clan."

She sat back in her chair. This was new.

"And yet I don't remember, which is so strange. I remember when I took my oath for the Air Force to serve my country. They don't make you guys do that, huh? Even when I wanted nothing more than to break it, I held fast and toed the line. Before that I pledged Allegiance to the United States in school, hand over my heart, one nation, under God, the works. Hell, when my grandmother put me in Girl Scouts, I even made their three-fingered wimpass pledge, too. Do you know what all that means?"

He took a drink of his cider. "You've a loyal heart."

"Oh, yeah, I do." She leaned forward to look directly in his eyes. "I'm so loyal, in fact, that I'd rather cut my tongue out than pledge myself to a bunch of outlaw jerkoffs like you."

As soon as she said that she silently cursed herself. She didn't have to feed the guy ideas on how to torture her.

All he did was nod. "Why did you wish to break your military oath?"

Kinley averted her face. She hadn't seen any kids around here or the big Taj Mahal he'd taken her from, and she was glad. She could dance with the insurgents all the livelong day, but she couldn't stand seeing how they treated their kids.

"Kinley?"

"I got an order I didn't want to follow," she said, and then forced a smile. "You probably get those all the time, too, like 'Be nice to the American captive' and 'No raping the prisoner until we get the intel we want out of her.' Can I have some more fish, or are we done with today's mind game lunch session?" When he didn't say anything her temper snapped. "What, is it time for the video-taped beheading already? And me without my infidel confession."

"Tell me why you didn't agree with the order you were given," he countered, "and I will give you the rest of the food."

He really was a completely worthless interrogator. "I was told to return to base before I could secure a position." She saw his blank expression and sighed. "We went out to a village to recover some injured troops who were defending the locals. You know, those innocent people you keep killing? Most of them and the civvies were dead by the time we got there. Once we loaded the wounded on board, I saw some other survivors. My pilot ordered me to close the hatch, I did, and we took off without them. End of story."

"I doubt that," he said and studied her face. "Why did you want to save them?"

"They were just kids," Kinley said. She could see every one of their faces, too, including the one who'd gripped her arm. "Three boys and a little girl, running across a field toward us. We had room on the bird for them. I told the pilot that. There was no enemy fire. He said they were probably cubs of the caliphate—suicide bombers— sent to blow us up, and told me to shut the door. I didn't agree. Those kids were terrified, and it was for real. But the pilot was a major, and I had no choice but to follow orders. I went back as soon as I could."

He gave her another sip of cider, and wiped something from her face. "Did you find them?"

"Their bodies, yeah. They hung all four of them in a tree in the center of town. Even though the vultures had been nibbling on them, I recognized them. They'd been beaten so badly that most of their bones were broken or crushed, but they never touched their faces. Unless you want vomit for dessert, I'm done eating now. Can you tie me back up, or cut off my head, or whatever?"

He rose and went around to untie her, but instead of hauling her back to the post he took her by the hand and led her out of the lodge.

"We'll walk to the cliffs," he told her. "There's something I want to show you."

Probably her last view of the world before he pushed her over the edge, Kinley thought, but went along with him. This part of Afghanistan was unbelievably green, and the trees so huge she felt like a midget by comparison. The path they followed looked very old, but it ran alongside a river that seemed to be much wider and deeper than it should have been for this part of the country.

Her interrogator—Lachlan, that was what he kept calling himself—held onto her hand, but didn't try to restrain her. Anyone looking at them would think they were a couple, just out for a stroll.

Thinking that way made her head hurt again. Better to watch for a chance to run. But then they reached the end of the river trail at the cliffs.

Kinley stared at the dark sapphire sea. She blinked several times, but it didn't go away. Had he gotten some poppy juice in her after all? No, she wasn't seeing things. She could smell the salt in the air.

"What the hell is this?"

"The ocean, and the fall to freedom." He guided her closer to the edge so she could see the river spilling over the cliff to fall hundreds of feet down to the sea. "My tribe has always lived on the island, since the time our ancestors escaped the Great Flood to come here and make new lives."

Kinley listened as he told her about the hardships the Pritani had endured while claiming the uninhabited island, and turning it into their personal paradise. Everything he said should have been nonsense, but the sea spreading out in front of them told her it wasn't.

Afghanistan was many things, but it didn't have a seaside coast. The country was entirely land-locked. This man was not an insurgent playing a Scotsman. He *was* a Scotsman. She was on the Isle of Skye.

No, there had to be another explanation.

"Why are you boring me with the ancient history lesson?" she demanded.

"It will come to you, lass. Just as the first raiders came from the north to our island. When they landed my father named me war master, so that I might lead the men in battle. 'Twas the first test of my courage." He turned and pointed to a nearby crest, on which stood a line of short stone pillars. "That is where we took our prisoners after we prevailed. The prisoners my father ordered me to execute."

"I don't want to hear this." She tried to walk away from him, but he caught her.

"I didnae obey him. I was young and full of myself, and it didnae seem sporting to me. I offered the prisoners a chance to win back their lives by swimming the fall." Lachlan gestured toward the river pouring over the cliff. "If they survived the plunge, I told them, they would be released and permitted to return to their homeland. I called it the fall to freedom."

Kinley marched over and looked down at the waterfall. If the impact hadn't killed them, the jagged rocks at the base of the cliff must have.

"How many survived?"

"One," he said and came to stand beside her. "My father made me honor my word to him. That was our way. I nursed him until he was well enough to travel, and then gave him my own boat to sail back to his people. Even then I was no' concerned. I thought, what can a Viking with two shattered legs do?"

She shuddered. "Plenty, if you let him live."

"Aye. You see? You are younger than I was, and still wiser." His mouth twisted. "No' long after that the Viking's sons returned seeking vengeance, and brought with them ten longboats of warriors. Their father had told them everything about our defenses and our numbers. Half the men of my tribe were injured or killed fighting them off. All because I disobeyed my father's orders."

"You couldn't have known that would happen," Kinley assured him, and then saw the reason behind the story. "It's not the same thing." She reached up and touched his hair. "It's not a wig. There is no sea in Afghanistan." Waves of dizzying pain poured through her head. "I've been here before, haven't I?"

"No' here, but on the island, aye." He put his arm around her waist to support her. "Mayhap we've walked too far. We'll go back."

"Wait, please."

She turned to him and clutched the front of his costume—his tunic—to help keep her on her feet.

Gingerly, she felt the lump on her temple. A stone had struck her there. Her nose filled with the smoke of the fire she had lit in the orchard. She could hear the horse chomping apples. Darkness, pain, terror, fire. Then everything went backward, from the gelding and the grove to Jens and sailing from the village. Stealing the horse. Taking the map and the things Tormod had given her. Listening to Lachlan tell the two robed men to send her back to her time.

Kinley looked up at the man whom she had thought had used her, and didn't want her, and knew she had made a terrible mistake.

"Lachlan."

He smiled slowly. "There you are, lass."

Chapter Twenty-Two

B
EFORE RETURNING TO Dun Aran, Lachlan asked Kinley to accompany him to Loch Sìorraidh. "I ken you've lost the battle madness, and regained your memories, but there is something that I need to do with you there."

She hoped it wasn't taking a swim, as the loch was bitterly cold. And she was still feeling a bit wobbly after spending too much time as PTSD Kinley. On the other hand, the man had dragged her out of the abyss, and kept her from hurting anyone until he could talk her down. Yeah, she'd pretty much do anything for him. Even wear pantyhose, as soon as they were invented.

"Okay."

Lachlan rode Selon without his saddle so she

could sit pillion, and took her to a sheltered cove on the side opposite the castle. Once there he put the stallion in a fenced meadow and walked down to the bank with Kinley.

"Hot stuff," she said, watching wisps of steam skate across the rippling surface.

But on the path just ahead, something glinted in the dirt. She bent down to pick up an old silver coin stamped with the head of a chinless woman encircled by letters.

"Eye vee Ulia Maesa vee cee," she read and handed it to Lachlan. "Doesn't look Scottish."

"Roman," he said. Instead of keeping it, or tossing it in the lake, he dropped it and ground it into the dirt with his heel. "'Tis where they brought us after we were beaten and captured. They offered me their pretty coin, and freedom for me and some of my men, if I would betray the magic folk."

Kinley looked out over the loch at the forbidding towers of the castle. "And you said no."

"I spit in the tribune's face," he said and glanced at her. "'Twas the finest moment of my mortal life. Or the second finest. I kicked him in the bawbag just before I died."

She laughed, but caught herself. "I'm sorry. I

know it's not funny. But holy cow. What a great way to check out."

He began stripping out of his clothes. "Would you care to test the waters with me, lass?"

A minute later she'd stripped as well, and he held her hand as he waded into the depths. She trailed behind him into the very warm cove, until the steaming surface covered her shoulders. Lachlan held her at arm's length as he scooped up a handful of water, and poured it over her head.

Kinley smiled and blinked the water from her eyes. "Mind telling me what you're doing?"

"Washing away your sorrows," he said and repeated the drenching move until her hair flattened against her scalp and water beaded on her lashes. "The loch saved us to become the clan. It gave us immortal life. Now I wish it to protect and heal you. By bathing you in these waters, I entreat the gods to favor me and make this so."

"Too bad it can't do that for my battle madness."

Her temple suddenly itched, as did the whip marks on her face and body. When she tentatively touched the stoning wound, it seemed a little smaller, and felt a lot better.

"You are healing," he told her, sounding a little smug now.

She looked down at the water, and saw the lash mark disappearing from her torso.

"Why me? I'm not an immortal or a McDonnel."

"But you are one of us," he said and brought her hand up to his chest. "You pledged yourself to me and the clan. The gods ken your heart. They favor the valiant, Kinley lass."

"Sounds good to me," she said with a little smile. That he still had faith after what he'd been through impressed her. "But if that's how you really feel, then why did you tell the druids to send me back to my own time?"

"You were listening to us," he muttered, and looked to the sky. "Now I ken why you left." Lachlan touched her cheek. "You heard them tell me that you had been brought here against your will. That explained so much of your fear and anger, and shamed me for no' seeing it. I realized I had seduced you without once asking if you wished to stay with me. I ken naught of your trials. In that moment, I never hated myself so much."

Kinley suppressed a smile. "Actually, I have to

cop to the seducing part. I knew what would happen, and I stayed in your bed chamber any way." She tapped her cheek with her finger. "I also didn't tell you I was from the future, not even after you spilled the beans about being an immortal and all. So I think it's on both of us."

"I confess, I am curious," he said, tracing the line of her upper lip. "How far did you travel?"

"More than eight hundred years. I was born in the year nineteen eight-nine." She nodded as his brows arched. "My world is very different, very advanced. We have machines and gadgets for everything. Guns instead of swords. Cars instead of horses. War is still the same, but we got better at it—and worse."

Kinley described San Diego for him, and all the things she loved about it: the seaside, the canyons, and her grandmother's house.

"But as much as I miss double cheeseburgers, dark roast coffee, and unscented skin lotion, I don't want to go back to the twenty-first century. I was badly injured during my last tour in Afghanistan, and I was close to dying from my wounds when I crossed over into your time. Coming through the grove completely healed me. I don't even have scars." She pressed her hand against his chest, circling her fingertips over his serpent ink. "I just wish it had done something with my PTSD, what you call battle madness."

"The battle madness may have saved you, lass. We think you were captured and tortured by the undead." He traced the lash welt on her shoulder, which no longer hurt at all. "They use thorned whips that leave such marks."

As the sun painted the surface of the loch with the last of its rays, the final veil of darkness lifted from Kinley's mind. She remembered the boy leading her into the cave, and transforming into a Roman.

"They were waiting for me to come back to the grove," she said, frowning. "One of them made himself look like a kid, and lured me into a trap. They dug out a tunnel in a hill."

"The legion can take on the appearance of mortals they drain, but it lasts only for one night," Lachlan told her. "They wouldnae stand watch in such a place without reason. Did they tell you why?"

She met his gaze. "Yes. They wanted to know where Dun Aran is. That's why they tortured me. My fear, combined with the whipping, must have been what made me lose it. I burned them all to ash." It made her shudder to remember how savagely she had killed the undead.

He took hold of her hands. "You defended yourself against creatures who would have beaten you to death."

"I know, I just…" she stopped and shook her head. "I've spent my entire adult life saving people. I'm sick, Lachlan, but I'm not a killer. Crossing over did more to me than heal my injuries. It gave me this god-awful fire power."

"Which you have used only against the undead," he reminded her. "To save my life, and your own." He cradled her face between his palms. "'Tis a gift from the gods. What does that tell you?"

"That the undead shouldn't mess with me?" she tried to joke, and then sighed. "I don't understand it. I don't think I want to. What I want is to stay here, and be with you, if you'll have me."

"I've had you," he said and kissed the space between her brows. "I'll want you for as long as I walk the earth." He touched his lips to her right cheekbone. "I never wish to wake again without you in my arms." He kissed her mouth, slowly and thoroughly. "I love you, Kinley Chandler."

She wanted to jump on him right then, but there was more to be said.

"What about the druids wanting to lock me up? No matter how much I like it, they're right about me not belonging here. I have knowledge of the future. Aside from the fire power, I think that makes me more than a little dangerous."

"I am Laird of the McDonnels, and that is no small thing," he said. "Thousands of clansman answer to me. I protect mortals here and on the mainland. Druid kind are our allies, but they are no' clan. They have no power or sway over me and mine. They will honor your pledge to me, and my claim on you." He touched his brow to hers. "Or they will discuss it with the snake."

Kinley grinned and touched his ink. "It's good to be the snake."

"Aye," he said and hoisted her out of the water. He waded up to the embankment with her, where he knelt and placed her on a soft bed of cool moss. "We could return to the stronghold, but the men will get between us and our bed."

Our bed.

Kinley felt her eyes sting as he lay down beside her. "Can't have that."

Tiny red and amber lights winked around

them as fireflies came out to spangle the grasses. The heat from the cove rolled over the bank to cover them in a warm mist. Kinley felt it as she stroked Lachlan's shoulder and arm, and watched his dark eyes as he tugged her closer. Everything about the man was a holiday. Looking at him was Christmas morning. Feeling his hands on her was the Fourth of July. The way he made her feel as he touched his mouth to hers was all of her happiest birthdays, bundled into one.

When he eased her onto her back to kiss her breasts she breathed in the scent of him, the loch-kissed coolness that made her heat up so fast she felt as if she'd burned with fever. Seeing his mouth envelope her nipple, and feeling the tug of his hungry sucking, sent a bolt of sensation straight to her clit. The dull throb of her temple dwindled away to nothing as her whole body lit up with need.

"Lachlan," she whispered. She worked her fingers into his thick mane, and wavered for a moment as he nuzzled her other breast. She felt his hand press between her thighs and his thumb part her. "Oh, that's really not fair."

"You'll have your fun later," he muttered against her breast. "Right now 'tis time for mine."

Her nipples were all for that, but the rest of her was about to riot. Then he slid down, parting her legs and putting his mouth to her, and Kinley clamped a hand over her mouth to keep the shriek of delight in her throat. His tongue traveled and probed and licked, wandering and laving and making her hips rock back against him. Her back bowed when he slid two fingers deep inside her, pumping them in and out as he suckled her pearl and worked his thumb against her bottom pucker, all at once.

Lachlan watched her face, and dragged the edge of his teeth over her clit.

Kinley thrashed, trying to resist the bliss, and then it took her and flung her into the stars, reshaping her into this mewling, frantic, heaving shower of heat and light and pleasure. So much pleasure. She loved it, she loved him, and still it wasn't enough.

"Oh, please please I need you to come into me I need–"

"I ken, my lovely." Smoothly he came up over her, his mouth catching her cries and his cock finding her and pushing in deep. "There now, you have me, and you're so bonny, look at you."

The strong muscles inside her gripped him

like a fist, and when she dragged his head down to hers she took his mouth and let her tongue dance with his. This was what she wanted, this joining that made them one.

"Lachlan," she breathed his name into his mouth. "You make me beautiful."

He covered her face with kisses as he worked in her, his thick shaft filling every inch of her inside before gliding back out. "'Twas too much to have you gone from me. You'll no' do that again, if it means I keep you like this, under me, on me, every day, every night. Oh gods you're whiskey in my blood and hot honey on my cock."

He fucked her to another climax, muffling her whimpers with his deep, delicious kisses, and then drew up her leg to penetrate her even deeper. Once he had buried himself to his root he braced himself over her and began to pound her with hard, heavy thrusts that made them both gasp and shake.

As the fireflies danced around them Kinley wrapped her arms around his neck, clutching him as his chest heaved against her aching breasts and his back muscles tightened. Then a deep guttural sound erupted from him, and he plowed into her with one final, soul-shattering stroke.

"I love you," she whispered against his ear as his shaft swelled inside her. "I love your hands and your mouth and your beautiful cock. I love your soul. I'll always be in your bed, waiting for you. Naked and aching and wanting you, Lachlan. Always."

He tucked her face against his neck, his big body shuddering as he jetted into her pussy, unleashing stream after stream of his come to fill her softness. The warm, wet flood set her off again, so they finished together in the dark that only they shared, filled with stars that went on for eternity.

When Kinley opened her eyes she chuckled, and threaded her fingers through Lachlan's hair to dislodge a dozen fireflies sparkling in the strands.

"Looks like lightning bugs really love you, too."

"It's the serpent. Me they but tolerate." He rolled to his side, holding her against him so their bodies remained merged, and brushed away some bits of moss clinging to her back. His hand moved to her shoulder, and rubbed the spot where the lash mark had been, before he touched her temple. "There now. The gods heard me and answered. You're healed."

"Hooray." Kinley kissed his fingers. "Now, about our bed. Is there a back way to get to it?"

"We'll go sleep in the hayloft," he said. "I had Seoc build a bed there for me."

Chapter Twenty-Three

W HILE HIS MASTER prepared for the meeting of the conclave, Cailean Lusk checked the dovecote for newly-arrived birds. He found no messages from Dun Aran, but one pigeon held a hastily-scrawled note from a village near the settlement. As soon as he saw the writer's mark he hurried to the meeting house.

Inside Bhaltair stood arranging boughs of evergreen in a protective pattern, and looked annoyed when Cailean showed him the note. "We've no time to cater to fearful mortals seeing demons in every shadow. Come and help me with this. I shouldnae have chosen pine. It's too stubborn. We'll do naught but bicker."

"Evander Talorc sent the message, Master.

His mistress is weaver there." Cailean read the grim plea, and added, "He warned us about the Chandler woman. He would no' ask this of us lightly." When the old druid scowled at him he added, "If the undead have attacked the village, we must summon the clan. 'Twould be best to be sure before we do."

"Oh, very well," Bhaltair said and walked out of the house and peered up at the dark sky. "'Twill be dawn in a few hours. Saddle two horses, and be quick, Cailean. The conclave arrives at noon, and if I am late, Brother Fergus will never let me hear the end of it."

From their settlement the two druids rode along a trail hidden from the eyes of mortals. Cailean repeatedly tasted the air, drawing and holding it in his mouth in an effort to detect any trace of mortal blood. All his tongue found was smoke and fear, which was explained when they reached the edge of the village.

"Wait," Bhaltair said when he would have dismounted. In the bright moonlight, he peered at the smoldering ruins of the cottages. "There are no bodies."

"Mayhap they took them, to serve as thralls," Cailean said as he peered through the smoke. "Or they ran into the hills." In a louder voice he called, "Hello? Is anyone here?"

A white-skinned, dark-haired woman rushed out of hiding, falling on her knees in front of the druids' mounts. "Masters, the undead attacked us. They took everyone away on carts before they set fire to our homes." She knuckled away the tears streaking her soot-stained face. "I hid in the trees and watched it all."

"You are Fiona Marphee?" Cailean asked.

When she nodded Bhaltair swung off his horse and tugged the terrified woman to her feet. "Where is Evander Talorc?"

"That is what I would like to know," a cold voice said as dozens of undead trotted out of hiding places and surrounded them. "Do tell us, old man. Where are the McDonnels?"

Fiona screamed and tried to run, but a Roman wearing the battle armor of a prefect caught her and flung her to the ground.

"No, brother," Bhaltair said quietly as Cailean summoned his magic. "We were brought here for another reason." To the prefect he said, "We are monks, and ken naught of this clan you seek. Let us take the wench and be on our way, to trouble you no more."

"I am Quintus Seneca, Prefect of the Ninth Legion. Claiming to be monks is clever, but I know the difference between mortal priests of the one god, and druids who spill blood for their many." He made a gesture, and one of his men clouted the still-shrieking Fiona, who fell over in a silent, limp heap. "I am a reasonable man, and there is no need for bloodshed. I believe that you will tell me everything I wish to know."

"Do you now. Well, then." Bhaltair smiled gently, as if well-pleased. "Go bugger yourself, you pestilent pile of dung."

Chapter Twenty-Four

FIONA OPENED HER eyes, squinting until she adjusted to the dark. She was in the cavern. The iron chains of her manacles rattled as she moved, and a moment later a chalk-faced centurion loomed over her.

"This one is awake, Prefect." The Roman grabbed her hair and used it to haul her to her feet.

Sobs poured from Fiona as she saw the two druids being led away by guards, and met the dreamy gaze of the younger of the pair. Cailean Lusk didn't seem fearful, but the druids were a strange lot. She gave him a tremulous, tearful smile that vanished as soon as they were gone. She straightened and held her shackles to the guard yanking on her curls as she looked at Quintus and

Gaius, where they were conferring on the tribune's dais.

"Take these off me," she told the guard.

The prefect murmured something to his commander before he walked down to join her.

"Well done, Mistress Marphee. I am a little disappointed that we could not also take your lover this night."

"I told you he wouldnae come." She shook out her wrinkled skirts and tucked her curls back behind her ears. "He never does after we've swived like that. It guilts him."

"Wait here." He returned to Gaius.

Fiona's skin crawled, as it did every time she was obliged to come to the tunnels. Being brought in as a captive revived the old, hateful memories of when the undead had taken her the first time.

She'd been but a girl then, looking after her widowed father and learning to work the loom. She'd said her prayers that night before going to bed, and had fallen asleep without a care. The men who had taken her had come in so silently they'd had her bound and gagged before they carried her out into the night. Fiona had seen the blood on the floor by her da's room, and knew him to be dead. That was the moment her heart died with him.

In the tunnels they stripped her naked, touching her white skin as if she were a prize hog about to be slaughtered, and put her in the women's pen. Her young body had almost glowed in contrast to the filthy bodies of the captives. Some of the older women had pushed her to the back when the Romans came to choose, but they remembered her. They cast lots to decide who would have her. One tall, heavy soldier with a scarred face won her. He told her his name was Marius as he carried her off to his cave, but she would address him as Master.

Fiona never thought about that night, all those hours, what that monster did to her. It made her scream and cry and puke when she did.

She lay in a stupor in the pen for most of the next day. When the choosing time came again, the prefect ordered her brought to his chamber. There he had pierced her wrist with his fangs, and drank from her veins, but then had another man bathe her and wrap her in a blanket.

"What is your name, child?" the prefect asked.

She peered at him. He was not hurting her like the other one. He had kindness in his voice.

"Fiona Marphee, Master."

He nodded, and asked, "Fiona, how would you like to go home now?"

The real tears that spilled down her face were the last she would shed. "I would, sir. Please."

Quintus Seneca had told her what she would have to do, and took her back to the cottage himself. He had helped her clean up the blood on the floor, and arrange her father's body in the bed. He'd told her how to make it look like plague. Then he'd told her how it would be.

"If you wish to remain free, you must help us," the prefect explained. "I will call on you when I need you. You must do whatever I ask, Fiona, and I will keep you safe. If you tell anyone, or betray me in any way, I will take you back to the tunnels. I will make you Marius's blood thrall. Do you understand what that means?"

Fiona had. She'd done everything he'd asked of her. She'd spied on mortals and seduced important men and stolen and lied and hoored herself. She would have killed for Quintus Seneca, although he never asked that of her.

She hated him. He disgusted her with his false kindness. He had used her for ten years, and would go on using her for the rest of her life. She would never be free of him. Yet even now, as the prefect came to her, she knew she would do whatever he wanted.

"The tribune wishes to speak to you directly," Quintus said. He glanced at the dais before he added in a lower voice, "His blood thrall took her own life, so he is in a foul mood. Prostrate yourself before him, and say nothing out of turn, or you will be the next to feed him."

Fiona didn't doubt him. The prefect had been using her as his spy since killing her father, but she had no illusions about her importance. Mortals who failed the legion were easily replaced, and the undead especially liked pretty wenches and lads that they could fack while draining them. The only way she had survived this long was by using her wits to make herself more valuable than food.

Quintus marched her through the tunnel to the dais, where she stopped short of the steps and dropped to the cave floor, flattening herself against the stone.

"You've brought your little pet whore for a visit, Quintus. How delightful," Gaius said. "I take it she still hasn't fucked the location of the McDonnel stronghold out of that cunt-snared seneschal?"

"No, my lord," Quintus answered for her. "But she was helpful during our assault on the village, and lured to us two druids who may be important to the highlanders."

"Those heathens are useless to everyone," the tribune said as he came down to stand over Fiona, and nudged her with his boot tip. "You may rise, slut."

Fiona remembered not to look directly at Gaius as she stood. "Thank you, Tribune. Forgive me for no' pleasing you."

"I gave you no leave to speak." The tribune backhanded her with his gauntlet.

The heavy clout made her face hurt so much her eye began to tear, and blood pooled in her mouth where her teeth had cut the inside of her cheek. Fiona swallowed and hunched her shoulders. Quintus had warned her.

"I cannot imagine why the McDonnel would wish to put his cock in such a fat little cunt." He walked around her. "Still, you have done your best, I suppose, and I can be merciful. I think it pleases Quintus when I am. Can you send word to the McDonnels? Not to your swain, but to the laird himself?"

"Yes, Tribune." Fiona felt bile rise in her

throat as he fingered one of her curls. "What should I say?"

"Tell him that he and his men are to come to the grove of stones, before tomorrow dawn, and surrender to Quintus. If he does not, I will have all of the children from the village turned." He released her hair. "Now go back to your hovel."

"I cannae." Fiona cried out as he gripped the back of her neck. "Please, Tribune. Evander has the village watched. He will come as soon as he learns it has burned."

"Then you will fuck him one more time, and while he grunts over you, you will stab him, here." He pressed on a spot between the bones of her neck. "Drive the blade deep between the bones at the base of his skull. Then bring proof to me that he is dead."

Fiona nodded tightly. When he released her she looked down at her trembling hands. She had heard the Romans talk about how hard it was to kill the highlanders, and that only fire or a blade to the back of the neck could end them. Even now she carried a small dagger tucked between her breasts that would do the work. Evander didn't suspect her of being anything but a common, ignorant village wench.

But the thought of jamming her blade into his neck while he was naked and atop her made her belly go sour.

"I will return her to the village, my lord," Quintus said as he gripped her elbow.

"No, I need you here to question the heathens, for perhaps they know something of value to us. Give her a mount and send her on her way." Gaius walked back up to his throne and clapped his hands. "I'm bored. Bring me a thrall. Something with some fight left, but not too many teeth."

Quintus bustled Fiona out of the cave and through another tunnel that led to their underground stable.

"Do as the tribune says, and all will be well," he said. He drew his own dagger, and pressed it in her hands. "After the McDonnel is dead, cut off his manhood with this, and bring it to me. I will give it as proof of his death to Gaius, and we will talk about where next to move you."

Fiona chose a quiet mare from the legion's mounts, and led her out of the tunnels, where the sentries watched with greedy eyes as she mounted the horse. She rode sedately until she was out of sight, and then jumped down, falling to her hands and knees as she puked up everything in her stomach.

She had seen terrible things in her short life, and it had hardened her. It did not even shock her that Gaius had ordered her to murder her lover, or that Quintus had asked her to castrate his corpse. She had known from the moment she was told to seduce the McDonnel seneschal that it would come to a bad end.

Her only mistake had been to fall in love with him.

Chapter Twenty-Five

E VANDER READ ONLY once the message Fiona had sent by dove before he gathered his weapons and headed for the loch. He would be missed, leaving in the middle of the day, but he didn't care. His mistress's village had been attacked and burned by the legion, and she the only mortal left living.

Now he could bring her back to Dun Aran, and install her as his mistress. Having done the same with Kinley, Lachlan could say naught to him about it.

Never had Evander felt so powerful while diving into the loch and transforming to flash through the currents. At last he could show his lovely lass all of his secrets, and bring her to the safety of the stronghold. The bubbling water frothed about him, dancing as if it could feel his fierce glee.

As soon as Evander rose from the stream he ran straight to Fiona's cottage, which he found only a charred shell. The rest of the village had also been burned, and the bodies of slaughtered livestock lay everywhere. He saw no corpses, which meant the villagers had been taken, as the undead would not have disposed of the bodies. Fiona might have thought her neighbors killed, but the legion had likely captured and taken them to serve as blood thralls.

The thought of the same being done to his sweet lass made Evander's blood boil. If even one of those monsters touched her, he would find it and nail it to the door of her cottage. He should have brought her to Dun Aran, where she would have been protected.

This was all Lachlan's fault.

"Fiona?" He entered her cottage, and breathed in. He could smell her skin, and blood, and began searching through the scorched rubble. "Fiona, I'm here. Call out to me if you can. I'm here for you, lass."

A blade tip pricked the back of his neck. "Dinnae move," a cool voice said from behind him. "Or I will end you where you stand, Evander Talorc."

He stared at the burnt remains of her standing loom, and felt his heart ice over. "What have you done, lass?"

"Kneel." When he did she took his sword, dagger and cudgel, and tossed them out of reach. "Hands behind your back. Clasp them together." Once he had, he heard the clank of irons as they closed around his wrists and latched. "You're as blind as that druid boy and his auld master. They came calling before you. Now they're learning what manner of magic the legion wields. I'll tell you, there's none blacker."

When she came around to face him Evander took in her disheveled appearance. She had a dark bruise spreading from her cheek to her eye, and her hair and frock looked as if she'd been dragged through swill. The cunning expression on her face he had never seen, nor the Roman blade she clutched in her hand.

"Am I no' fetching, my lord?" she demanded, and spread her skirts as if she wanted his admiration. "Your sweet Fiona, here and back from Hell. Och, what's the matter, sweetheart? Do you no' wish to fack me now?"

He spat at her feet. "I'd burn off my hands before I'd touch you again."

"You men do love your fires."

Fiona went to retrieve something from a singed dresser, swearing under her breath as she plunged it into her washing basin. She removed the small metal box and pried open the lid, peering in at the coins before she tucked it under her arm.

"Counting your silver, Judas?" Evander asked.

"Oh, I earned every penny, from my weaving." She glanced around the ruined cottage, and tucked her bottom lip between her teeth for a moment. "I never thought they'd torch my father's house. I've done so much for them, and asked so little." She looked up at the broken, burnt timbers of her collapsed roof. "'Twas the only place in the world I was ever happy, so when they told me about you, I said, I'll use my Da's cottage. There, I thought, I could be happy for a time. Until I was finished with you."

Now he understood why she had kept asking him to bring her to Dun Aran. "You've been spying for the legion."

"Longer than you think," she said, her voice hardening again. "Did you never wonder why you kept seeing me all pretty and primped at the market, and in the street? 'Tis how they use me, lover. I'm the bait they dangle at the prize catch. That would be *you*, stupit. You might have ken it, if you'd ever pulled your brain out of your cock."

Evander thought of how she had peeped up at him, all virtuous innocence, and the trembling of her voice as she had first refused him her bed. "You were no maiden."

"No' since that night I was taken. 'Tis an easy thing to feign. Some shaking and blushing, a nick on the inside of the thigh, and lo, I'm a virgin again, and so I have been, five times now." She brought the dagger to press against the back of his neck. "Stand and walk out the back door. There's a cart waiting."

"I'll no' let you deliver me to the legion," Evander told her. "If that is your intent, stick your blade in me."

She laughed. "Even now, you're naught but a great thickhead."

The tip of the dagger left his neck, but as he braced himself for the blow he heard Fiona screech, and turned to see her struggling against the arm Neac had clamped around her waist.

Behind the chieftain a dozen Uthars rushed into the cottage, swords drawn and faces grim.

"If you mean to go wenching, Seneschal, you should take us with you," Neac said and handed Fiona off to one of his men, who carried her out. Then he unlatched the irons and let Evander's hands loose. "We've better taste in lassies." When Evander would have gone after Fiona the chieftain planted a big hand on his chest to stop him. "We stood outside while she made her confession. We need her alive so we might find Cailean and his master."

"She's mine to question," Evander said and picked up and sheathed his sword. "No one puts hands on her but me."

Outside, Fiona looked up at him. "I should have facked you and cut off your cock."

"Aye," Neac said, grimacing. "I dinnae think anyone will wish to touch her."

EVANDER FELT a grim joy as he marched Fiona to the stream. Taking her back to Skye to be questioned and killed instead of installed as his mistress did not make him bitter. Away from any chance of the undead retrieving her, he could take his time with her. He also wanted her to see Dun Aran before he throttled the life out of her. She would weep when he told her that he had meant to bring her to live at the stronghold that day. How close she had been to learning exactly what her masters needed to wipe out him and his clan.

Fiona struggled at the edge of the water. "You'll no' drown me."

"Quiet," he ordered. He hated pulling her into his arms, and binding her to his thoughts, but it had to be done. As he jumped into the current, he felt her wild struggling as he transformed. But he held her fast as he went liquid and whisked the two of them from the mainland to Skye. When he walked up out of the loch with her flung over his shoulder, she choked out some water and twisted until he put her on her feet.

"What did you do to me?" she shrieked, stumbling away from him and staring in horror at the water. "You pulled me through the stream to here? How?"

"I'm no' mortal," he said with a steely grin.

Neac and his men surfaced and strode from the water.

New fear danced in her eyes. "You'll no' eat

me alive, Evander. Snap my neck and be done with it."

"That will wait a wee bit. Here's what you wanted to find for those blood-sucking leeches." Evander grabbed her and gave her a shove toward the steps leading to the underground vaults. "Do you ken where you are? Behold, the Black Cuillin mountains of Skye. They've kept our castle safe for more than a thousand years."

She wouldn't look at the stronghold until Evander pulled her head back.

"I dinnae care about where 'tis," she said. "I never did. Fack you and your castle."

"Then why were you forever nagging me to bring you home with me? So we could be together, you said. Because you missed me so much after I left you." He had to let go of her or rip the hair from her head. "How well you played your bed games. When you weren't spreading your legs for the Romans."

"Aye, I've facked the undead," Fiona said and smirked. "Are you feeling jealous, my lord and master? Did you think of me as yours alone, a little mortal doll for you to stroke and cuddle and make you feel adored? Has anyone but me ever really wanted you, Evander? I'm thinking no'."

He was going to kill her, right here and now, in the same place where the Romans had slit his throat. A more fitting place to spill her traitorous blood he could not imagine.

"Do it," she told him through her teeth. "End me and my miserable life."

Neac caught his hand up as he reached for his dagger. "No' yet, lad. You'll have to tell the laird about her, and what she's done."

Aye, and how Lachlan would gloat over his stupidity. "I will," he told the chieftain, "as soon as I learn what she's told the legion."

Neac's gaze shifted to Fiona's sullen face. "You'll learn naught if you beat her to death, Evander, which I think you will the moment you're alone with her. Allow me—"

"*No*," he said through clenched teeth. He felt like an old pot riddled with crazing and about to shatter. In a lower voice he said, "This was my doing, Neac. It must be me."

"As you say, then." The chieftain clapped a hand on his shoulder before he turned and called to his men, "Whiskey and ale for the lot of you. Where's Mistress Talley? I've a powerful hankering for her honey and nut cakes."

Evander lit a torch before he took Fiona down

the steps that split off in one direction toward the hot cistern, and in the other to the vaults. In the first years after the awakening the clan had used the big, empty storage rooms as a dungeon for raiders, and villagers who had committed crimes against their neighbors. Lachlan had outfitted the rooms with all manner of torture equipment, claiming the sight of it was enough to scare the truth out of their prisoners.

Fiona seemed blind to the cobwebs that draped the corners over the stretching racks and hanging rows of iron Brank's bridle masks. He touched the whipping post, and traced some old, dark stains streaking the wood—likely chicken blood painted on it to make it seem realistic. To Evander's knowledge not a single prisoner had ever been harmed since the building of the castle. His mistress would be the first when he beat her to death.

He took down one of the iron masks, and toyed with the spiked flap meant to be inserted in the mouth, so the tongue and palette would be pierced every time the condemned spoke.

"Mayhap you should wear this while we speak. It may remind you to be truthful."

"Takes a brave lad to torture a helpless wench

unable to defend herself," she countered. "You're more like the undead than you think."

"Do you want to die?" he demanded hotly.

"I dinnae want to live anymore, that's for certain." Her shoulders sagged as he approached her. "Just go on and break my neck. I've earned that much."

"Earned?" He threw the mask across the room, where it struck a Catherine wheel and clattered to the ground. "You hoored yourself for the undead, you treacherous vulture."

She nodded, and slowly looked around the chamber to inspect the devices, as if she were in a garden admiring flowers.

The only question Evander truly wanted answered could be asked with one word. "Why?"

"'Twas a better prospect than ending as one of their blood thralls. I'd have lasted no more than a week after they murdered my da and took me."

Evander peered at her. "Took you?"

"I was but a girl the night they came. Came straight inside while we slept, and killed my da, and carried me off." She fell silent for a moment, and then jerked her shoulders. "One of them took me back to the cottage. I kept da dead in my house for a week before I called for the grave diggers. By then he'd swelled and blackened enough to make them think he'd died of plague, instead of being drained by the undead." She smiled at him. "That's what Quintus told me to do when he freed me. He's clever, that one."

"The legion released you," he said and uttered a sour laugh. "Of course they did. Did they bring you posies, and walk you to church every Sabbath as well?"

Fiona leaned back against a wall to watch him. "You McDonnels have no understanding of what the undead do to the mortals they take. They bind us, and drag us down into their tunnels, and pen us like animals. We were not fed or given water. Some of the others scratch and bite at the new ones, hoping the smell of our blood will save them from being chosen."

Despite his anger, his stomach churned to imagine a girl being forced to endure such horrors. "Chosen for what?"

"Attention. The Romans come every night to choose a thrall to feed on, and fack, and do whatever else they wish." She met his gaze. "I was a maiden when they took me, so they drew lots over who would have me the first time. Quintus Seneca chose me the second. He didn't fack me while he drank. Of course I was still bleeding from what Marius did. Would you like to hear that? What a full grown man does to a virgin?"

Evander stared at her. "And you were taking me to them, as you did the druids? 'Tis what you wished for me?"

Her laughter echoed around them. "No, you blind bastart. Dinnae you see? I kept the cart packed and ready so I could flee to England when I had the chance of it. They'd never have followed me all that way. I'm no' so important to them. They'd just teach another thrall how to take my place." She hung her head. "I'm a hoor, aye, but I'm a good weaver. I would have earned the coin to keep us. We'd have been safe."

"We?" he said, surprised at how hard the word was to say.

She raised her head and looked him in the eye. "But I had to tell you what I'd done. I couldnae have it 'tween us." She grimaced. "And then your friends showed up."

"You meant to take me with you," he said, as something flickered deep in his chest.

Tears welled up into her eyes. "The tribune told me I was to kill you. Quintus said I must cut off your manhood, and bring it back to them as proof." She started to say something else, and then shook her head. "Please, Evander. I'm so tired now, and I've naught more to tell. If you ever felt anything for me, make it quick."

He remembered the moment she took the knife from his neck.

"Why couldn't you kill me?" he made himself ask, almost afraid to hear the answer.

"Because it would be like ending myself." She inhaled a sob. "Because I'm in love with you." She covered her face with her hands.

Like thin loch ice under a careless boot, something inside him cracked. He saw now how the legion and the clan had made them enemies. He could no more beat her to death than she could have ended and mutilated him. She was not the woman he'd known. But he was not the man she thought him.

He watched her cry into her hands, the great sobs wracking her. For months he had wanted to bring her to Dun Aran. Now he couldn't put the place far enough behind.

Maybe together they could find a way.

Slowly, he gathered her into his arms.

"I'm sorry for the things I said to you," she

sobbed and buried her face against his neck. "I didnae mean them. But you cannae keep me here, Evander. Your clan will learn what I am, and what I've done. Quintus will see to that."

"Lass," he murmured, tilting her face up so he could see her wet eyes. "We will go, and make a life where no one shall find us. 'Tis the only way we can be together now."

She gazed up at him, wonder in her face. "Do you mean it?"

He smiled down at her. "You have my oath."

But almost as quickly as her face brightened, a cloud passed over. "The druids and the people of my village," she said. "Their lives are on my head."

Neither of them could make a fresh start with the thought of those poor souls as blood thralls— to suffer what his Fiona had.

"We must set free the druids and the villagers," he said quietly. How he was going to do that without his clansmen would be the trick. As a thought occurred to him, he held her at arm's distance. "Is there ever a time when they're no' guarded?"

"Aye." She gripped his hands tightly. "When the undead sleep."

Chapter Twenty-Six

RAEN HAD TO rise several hours
before dawn to see to the laird's duties
as well as his own. He didn't mind the
extra work. Dun Aran was an efficient household,
and their well-trained mortal retainers labored
diligently. None of the clan woke until sunrise,
which was why it surprised him to see Seoc Talorc
staggering across the great hall.

"Seoc, are you waking, or off to sleep?" Raen
joked, and then saw the blood streaking the stable
master's face and grabbed him. The other man
had a nasty gash across his pate and a broken
nose, and when he eased him down onto a bench
he swayed as if ready to topple. "Seoc, who
beat you?"

"I would have given him the coin. He dinnae

have to steal it." He peered at Raen. "Why would my cousin run off with a mortal wench? He doesnae even like them. That and I thought Neac said she was a traitor…och, my head."

Raen called for a night sentry to see to the injured man, and then grabbed a hammer and headed for the dungeon. Last night the Uthar chieftain had told him only that Evander had brought a mortal to the stronghold for questioning. If he'd known it was a woman, Raen would never have left the seneschal alone with her. But before he reached the stronghold he saw a dark-haired woman at the loch. Evander stood waiting in the water for her. He heaved the hammer, sending it sailing through the air between them. As it plunged into the water, both Evander and the woman recoiled from it. In those few moments, Raen surged forward to come between her and the seneschal.

"Stop there, Mistress. Evander, come out and explain yourself."

"Fiona," Evander called. "Dinnae move."

"Stand aside, McDonnel," the plump woman said and drew a dagger of Roman design. "We're going away now. We'll no' trouble anyone again."

Raen disarmed her with one blow that sent

her sprawling. As he plucked her from the ground, he turned to look at Evander.

"Are you mad to be—"

The spear that rammed through his throat cut off his voice, and drove him to his knees.

Evander rushed up to seize the woman, but paused and grimaced down at Raen.

"Why did you move? I was aiming for your shoulder." He reached for the spear, but then let his hand fall away. Instead he picked up the woman and carried her into the loch.

Raen grasped the shaft protruding from his neck, and tried to tug it out. Warm wetness poured down his chest as he fell over onto his side, as Evander and Fiona disappeared under the water. He tried to take a breath, only to choke on his own blood. He tried again, inhaling only a little, and was able to get some air in his chest.

Raen panted around the spear as the darkness lightened, and the sun rose over the water. If he was to live, he had to save himself. Painfully he crawled toward the loch, until the end of the spear collided with a stone. With the last of his strength he gripped the shaft again, but when he pulled on it something inside his neck snapped.

It was then he knew he would never see

Evander or his woman again. Because as all feeling left his body from the chin down, he knew he would be dead.

❧

As THEY LEFT THE STABLES, Lachlan tugged Kinley to his side. "You like sleeping in the hay."

"I like that bed," she said as they walked down to the loch. "We should have Seoc make a new mattress for your tower chamber. He knows how to make straw feel like– *Raen*."

As soon as he saw the big man on the ground, Lachlan ran for him. But when he saw the spear that skewered his bodyguard's throat, he fell to his knees beside him. Raen was barely breathing, and from the look of his body he couldn't move. The end of the spear protruded from the back of his neck, as did a shattered bone from his spine. Since he still breathed his spine had not been entirely severed, but the laird had seen many such injuries during his long life. Removing the spear would likely finish him off.

As Kinley reached for it, Lachlan stayed her hand. "He's done for, lass."

Kinley glanced at the water. "Can't we just put him in the loch to heal?"

"The spear went through his spine," he told her, feeling sick. "It willnae heal unless we take it out, which will kill him before the waters can mend it. There's no coming back from this."

"But there has to be something we—"

"Kinley," Lachlan said past the contraction in his throat. "'Tis the killing blow."

Lachlan stared at the ghastly wound trying to think how he could make Raen more comfortable.

"Wait," Kinley said and touched her face. "*Lachlan.*" She grabbed his arm. "Can you carry him and me through the loch to the oak grove where I crossed over?"

"He's almost dead, lass. Let his final…" He stopped when he saw the light in her eyes. The grove? "Hold the spear," he said, as he hefted Raen into a sitting position. Carefully, he drew the man up and onto his shoulder. "You think it will heal him, as it did you?"

"I don't know," she said taking his free hand as they waded into the water. "But we have to try."

Lachlan carried his bodyguard into the loch,

and emerged from the stream nearest the sacred grove. Kinley helped steady Raen as they hurried to the center of the ancient trees, where Lachlan carefully lowered the big man next to the stone.

Only then did he notice the mark carved on the shaft, and his blood ran cold. Evander, who could hit anything with a spear, always carved his with the same mark.

Kinley placed her hand over a winged serpent etched into the surface of the stone. The lines of it took on a green glow.

"We take out the spear," Kinley told him. "We go through to my time, and then we come right back." Kinley gripped the spear too. "Okay, now."

It took almost too long to tug the weapon out of Raen's neck, and as soon as Lachlan flung it away he heard a death rattle escape his body-guard's lips. Kinley snatched up both their hands, leaned close to the glowing stone, and pressed her cheek to the winged serpent. The green glow became a whirlwind of light that encircled them, shaping itself into a tunnel of curving oak boughs.

Lachlan landed hard beside Kinley and Raen, but this time the grove held no stones. A strangely-marked, bright yellow ribbon had been tied to the tree trunks to form a barrier. He heard something roar and looked up to see a huge, headless bird made of silver metal soaring over them. He turned his head to ask Kinley what it was, but saw another woman had taken her place.

She looked as if she had been torn apart and sewn back together by a shaking hand. Terrible scars covered her face, twisting her features and obliterating her beauty. The only feature he still recognized was her lips, which had somehow escaped unscathed—and made the damage done seem so much worse. Most of her hair had been cut away from the curving scars on her head. One of her legs stretched out so crookedly it didn't match the other, and the bandages wound around it had partially torn, showing the damage done. Bulky white stone covered one of her arms to the shoulder. Half her body weight had melted away from her, leaving her limbs painfully thin and wasted.

He peered into her thunderstruck blue eyes, which now appeared dull and clouded. "Kinley?"

She nodded. "Now do you believe I was a soldier?"

Lachlan had not wept since he was a boy, but

he paid no mind to the tears that spilled down his face.

"My sweet lass."

"It's okay," she said, and gave him a lopsided smile. "This is why I didn't want to come back. I suspected I'd revert to what I was before I crossed over to your time." She shivered as she looked at the yellow ribbon bound around the trees. "God, they must think I was abducted or murdered, or both. I hope Dr. Stevens isn't the prime suspect." Her voice slurred the last words, and her eyelids fluttered.

"*Kinley*," Lachlan said thickly and put his arm around her.

"It's okay. I forgot how weak I was back then. Now. Whatever." Her hand shook as she touched Raen's bloodied neck with her twisted fingers. "The good news is that he still has a pulse."

"He won't for long," Lachlan told her, and frowned as green light shimmered around them. "Does the grove take us back now?"

"I think so. It felt like this when I came through the first time." She gripped Raen's shoulder. "Hold onto me, and don't let go. This way is a lot rougher."

Lachlan gently took her hand, and braced himself for the second passage.

Would they return to his time, and if they did, would Kinley and Raen survive it? He should have asked her that, but they were falling through the bower of oak trees again, and tumbling through time until they fell back beside the sacred grove stone.

He pushed himself upright, and looked over at the glowing forms of his woman and his best friend. Light funneled into Raen's neck, streaking through him to emerge from the back. His exposed spine sank back into his flesh, which covered over the terrible wound.

The light faded, and Raen opened his eyes and dragged in a breath as he pushed himself upright. He touched the smooth skin of his neck where the spear had pierced it. "My lord."

"Welcome back, lad," Lachlan said.

"I was crawling toward the loch," the big man murmured as he stared down at Kinley. "I never made it." He gripped the back of his neck. "How…?"

"She saved you," Lachlan said and moved to Kinley's side, where he watched the much slower process of her healing.

The light saturated her from head to toe, gleaming as it filled in the recesses in her cheeks and brow. New hair sprouted from the bald patches on her scalp and grew into thick, soft golden tresses. Her shattered leg straightened, and her curves grew riper as her limbs filled out. By the time the light evaporated she looked as she had the first time he had seen her from across the battlefield.

"My lord," Raen gasped as his dazed eyes shifted to Lachlan's face. "How can this be? I could feel naught, I couldnae breathe. I swear, I was dead."

"You were, nearly," Lachlan said and helped Kinley sit up, and brushed his mouth over her temple. "Crossing over healed you." He held her tightly against him. "Anything you ask is yours, *faodail*. My castle. My clan. Even my horse, if you want the demon."

She drew back. "I don't want anyone to know I did this but you and Raen. Also, I never want to do it again."

Lachlan tried to smile. "I dinnae think I could survive another go."

"No, you don't understand. Someone taped off the grove on my side as a crime scene, and...

okay, that's trouble I'll explain later." She rubbed her brow. "The thing is, if someone had been there and saw us, they might have kept us from coming back. Then Raen would have died in the future, and when they found his body…"

"Even more trouble," Lachlan finished for her. "Raen, was it Evander?"

"Aye. He was running away with a wench who spied for the legion, and I tried to stop them." He touched the front of his throat before he looked at Kinley. "I saw your wounds, Kinley. You shouldnae have survived them."

"We have these things in the future called VA hospitals, and I guess someone up there likes me." She saw the way Raen prodded his chest. "Sure you're okay?"

"I'm fashed, is all." He extended his arms and touched the back of his neck, and then rubbed the side of his head. "My battle scars have vanished. As if they never were." He took off one boot and peered at his big foot. "There's the toe I lost chopping wood as a boy. 'Tis grown back." He looked at the stone. "What does it mean?"

"Mayhap the gods send us a missive," Lachlan said and lifted up his tunic to see his abdomen was as smooth as a lad's. So were his arms and neck.

He wouldn't miss his scars, especially the reminder of his own beheading, but Neac would likely make much of them vanishing. "To remind us that we shouldnae make the same mistakes again."

She nodded slowly. "That's the other reason I don't want to do this again. I could feel myself dying in the future, and death was much closer than it was the first time I crossed over here. If I make a third trip, I don't think I'd live long enough to come back."

Chapter Twenty-Seven

I N THE LAIR of the undead the light of day was never welcomed. But the sun's warmth soaked into the earth above, and crept into the caves and tunnels to warm the frigid air. Mist drifted and swirled near the roofs of the caves as the sun rose. As day dawned outside, the legion retreated to their stone chambers. There they slept without dreams, while the sentries and guards braced themselves at their posts and closed their black eyes.

Cailean Lusk bent down to look through the wooden grate covering the entrance to the holding pen. There were two Romans standing watch.

"The undead are no' moving now, Master," he said and squinted. "I dinnae think they are breathing." He grimaced as the horrible smell of the pen filled his nostrils. "I wish I didnae have to breathe either. Gods, this place reeks."

"When the sun rises, it may leech away the life they steal from mortal blood," Bhaltair said. "Then they would have to spend the daylight hours in stillness, like the dead that they are." He grunted as he knelt down beside him to peer out at the motionless guards. "If only we could reach one of those swords."

Behind them one of the tormented souls giggled. "If you touch them, they wake up, and they are very angry. They chop off your fingers, or your hand, or they drag you out and drain you until you are as a worm shriveled in the sun."

Cailean shuddered. "Perhaps no' quite as still as the dead then."

The old druid scuttled backward and stood, helping Cailean to his feet. "We should capture one of these fellows and study him. We could learn much."

"Or he could get loose and kill everyone in the conclave," Cailean said. "We need to discover where they took all the children before that cold-eyed one carries out his threat." He tried lifting the grate. "I am no' strong enough to dislodge it by myself." He turned to the other captives. "Is there anyone who will help me?"

"No." A pale, thin female covered in bruises cringed away from him. "They will hurt us. They will *eat* us."

The terror that the blood thralls felt frustrated Cailean. For him and Bhaltair, and all of druid kind, death was simply a journey to their next life. It was true that after rebirth they had to wait some years until they grew old enough to communicate, declare their identities, and practice their crafts, but that was the cost of reincarnation. Death, while sometimes unpleasant and painful, was never the end for them, so they did not fear it.

The mortals imprisoned with them might have attained the same enlightenment, had they been born to druid kind. Their ignorance and superstitions made them impossible to trust, much less teach. But they were terrified, and he should not judge them. He'd been a captive for less than a day and already he wanted to kill himself.

"I see some movement," his master said, and stood on his toes to look through one of the vent holes that allowed air into the pens. "'Tis that woman taken with us from the village, and the

McDonnel seneschal." He frowned. "An odd alliance."

"'Tis what our brothers and sisters have always said about us," Cailean said.

He didn't want to risk waking the slumbering guards by calling out to them. Instead Cailean got on hands and knees and shoved his hand through the grate, waving it as best he could.

"You'll wake them," the woman behind him whimpered. "Stop."

"Master, these poor folk are very frightened. 'Twould help if they were to pray for our safe release."

"'Twould be better," Bhaltair grumbled. He turned and began tapping the mortals one by one. "You will pray now. In silence. Without fear." The soporific tone to his voice made their eyes half-close as his touch-charm went to work on them. "Pray. You will pray now."

One by one the captives dropped on their knees and clasped their hands together.

Two big hands gripped the bottom of the wooden grate and began to lift it. Two smaller, feminine hands reached for Cailean's and helped him as he crawled through and stood.

"Master Talorc," Cailean whispered. "Mistress Marphee. You are a welcome sight." He turned and bent to help his master out. "How did you free yourself, Mistress?"

"I was never a captive. I have been a spy for the legion," Fiona told him bluntly. "I am no more now, and I am sorry I brought you to this."

"Quickly," Cailean whispered, gesturing to the mortals still in the pen.

Coaxing the prisoners out took precious minutes, but when the last came through Evander replaced the grate. As they made their way into the tunnel one of the women slipped and fell heavily, crying out as she looked down at the broken bones under her.

The nearest sentry sleeping at his post snapped to attention, saw the woman and bared his fangs.

"Escape!" he shouted. "To arms, to arms!"

"Run," Evander bellowed as he snatched up Fiona.

As the undead swarmed around them, Bhaltair murmured under his breath, releasing the mortals from his calming spell. Seeing the guards rushing into the tunnel sent all the mortals fleeing after Evander and Fiona. Cailean quickly worked a light spell, creating the illusion of a

wall of sunlight, from which the undead staggered back. It lasted only a few moments, but
gave them time to herd the mortals after
Evander and Fiona into an empty passage with
daylight at the end. As they staggered out, the
captives from the pens embraced each other, fell
to their knees or simply stood and wept in the
daylight.

Cailean asked Evander, "You didnae find the
villagers' bairns?"

The highlander shook his head. "We found
you first."

The ovate regarded Fiona. "Where would the
undead take them?"

"The tribune turns mortals in the Temple of
Mars, beyond the great cavern. 'Tis what he
means to do to the bairns."

Horrible snarls came from deep in the tunnels.
Grim-faced, Evander drew his sword and made to
enter, but Fiona clutched his arm.

"You cannae, my love. They have awakened
now. They will kill anyone who goes inside." She
turned to the druids and told them how to find
the Temple of Mars before she added, "We are
outlaws now, and can stay no longer. You must ask
the clan to help you rescue the bairns."

Cailean eyed the highlander. Evander looked frustrated, and strangely ashamed.

"We will send word to them," Cailean said. "Where do you go now, Mistress Marphee?"

Fiona looked up at Evander. "Far from here."

"Ovate Lusk," the highlander said. "If you hurry, you may find the laird in the grove of the old Pritani stones. We saw him go there before we came for you." Another, more intense flash of guilt shone from his eyes before he took hold of Fiona's hand and led her away, disappearing into the trees.

Cailean felt a tingle of premonition. What good Evander Talorc had done to balance the weight of Fiona's evil, he suspected, was not enough. The pair might have their freedom, but the gods were not finished with them. He did not envy them their lot. When the gods decided to punish those who transgressed, they could be very cruel.

Bhaltair spoke with two of the mortal men who seemed sanest, and instructed them to take the other thralls to the nearest town to seek shelter. He and Cailean backtracked to where they'd tethered their horses and rode to the sacred grove. Lachlan, his bodyguard and a golden-haired woman were just leaving it. All three of them seemed to glow in the sunlight.

"My lord, are you hurt?" Cailean said and he dismounted and hurried over to them. But he stopped when he realized what radiated from them was not light but time magic. "You have crossed over."

Bhaltair stared at the woman. "She has, and taken them with her."

"Aye, and brought us back again," the laird said and inspected them with a frown. "Why are you in such a state, Master Lusk?"

"We were lured to a burned village, and there captured by the undead." He quickly related their rescue by Evander and Fiona, and the ultimatum issued by the tribune. "My lord, we cannae permit the legion to turn so many innocents. You ken what bairns who are made undead are like."

"Aye, as rabid dogs," Lachlan said.

"I saw the little ones before we were penned," Bhaltair said. "They took more than fifty, and near half of them babes that cannae walk. They will have to be carried out."

"But how can we save them before they are turned?" Cailean demanded, and then said to the laird. "To go back in those tunnels now is suicide, and as soon as the sun sets, the rest of the legion will wake. When you dinnae surrender, they will turn the little ones."

"We don't go in after the legion," the woman told him before Lachlan could reply. "We make them come out to us."

Chapter Twenty-Eight

KINLEY STOOD BY Tormod at the window of the map room, and glanced back at Lachlan, who was conferring with Cailean and Bhaltair. She wasn't sure how to feel about the druids, who looked like regular guys and yet had the power to raise an army of Pritani tribesmen from the dead and make them immortal. The younger man looked like a tallish high school freshman, and kept staring at her when he thought she wasn't looking.

What was seriously strange was how much the older one reminded Kinley of her grandmother. Voice, hair, eyes—all were exactly like Bridget's, as if he were a long-lost twin brother. But her grandmother wouldn't be born for another seven hundred odd years. Since that side of Kinley's family had come to America from Skye, it wasn't too much of a stretch to imagine Bhaltair Flen as a very, very distant relative. But why did he keep looking at her as if he wanted to punch her in the head?

She needed to quit worrying about the wand-wavers. Instead she turned to the Norseman.

"Just how much trouble are you in for helping me run away?"

"The laird hammered me good, and Neac will no' permit me to heal in the loch." The Norseman gingerly touched the dark purple bruise ringing his right eye, and then tapped his split lip. "I've woken with worse after a long night of drink." He glared at her. "My pottage every morning now is fish bones and water. Washing water, as it happens."

"I'll have a word with Meg," Kinley said and nodded at Bhaltair. "That old one keeps giving me the stink eye. What's his problem?"

"Master Flen still thinks you dangerous," Raen said as he joined them. "The laird has no' told him why we crossed over and back, but he suspects. The groves are sacred to the druids, and only they are permitted to use them."

"I'm good with that," she said and turned to

Tormod. "I need some ideas that will work in this time, and you were a raider. To save these kids our best bet is to get the undead out of the tunnels before we go in. We need a lure, something they can't resist."

"Blood would work, but only if they were starving." He thought for a moment. "When my clan once raided a monastery, we first sent our scouts in disguised as monks. They hid themselves until the brothers went to sleep, and then came to open the gates for us." As she started to reply he shook his head. "Dinnae go there, Kinley. The undead can smell us. No disguise would deceive them."

Kinley glanced over at the druids and their voluminous robes, and then studied Raen's tartan. "But can they smell the difference between different types of people? Like druids and McDonnels?"

Raen shook his head. "We are all alive. They would smell our blood, but no' who we are. For that they must see us."

Kinley nodded. "Then maybe we don't have to go inside at all."

She went over to Lachlan, who was still listening to Bhaltair's long-winded lecture, and smiled politely. "I'm sorry to interrupt, but we're running out of daylight, and I have an idea on how to get to the children. We'll need more people, which is where you druids come in."

Bhaltair's mouth puckered with disapproval. "This is a clan matter, Mistress Chandler. You would do well to leave this to the men folk."

"I'm a trained combat search and rescue officer. The men folk? Aren't." She turned to Lachlan. "We need more druids. A lot more. As many as you can get together before sunset. Here's why."

As she explained her plan, Bhaltair looked horrified, but Lachlan listened intently, as did Cailean. She used a piece of parchment and a charred sliver of wood to sketch a quick map of the area, showing the undead lair in relation to the sacred grove. Finally she used lines and arrows to mark the movements of the clan and the druids as they carried out the rescue.

"There is an older road at the back of the grove, here," Cailean said, and pointed to the spot on the map. "It leads around to the mouth of the stream. That would be the best direction of retreat."

"Aye," Lachlan said, and borrowed Kinley's

makeshift pencil to encircle another area. "We can set up a blind here to disguise it."

"To pull this off, we'll have to work very fast," she warned him. "But as long as our friends here don't freak out, it should work." She glanced at the two druids. "What do you think, friends?"

Bhaltair drew himself up to his full height. "I think you should remember to whom you speak. I am no' your friend. I am a member of the conclave. We rule all of our kind, no matter their family. A word from me, and I can have any druid placed in restraints, imprisoned, punished, or even disincarnated."

"Really? Awesome," Kinley said and turned to Cailean. "Why is he telling me this?"

"Only druid kind can use the magic of the groves. We ken the laird and his man couldnae have crossed over into your time without one of us to activate the time spell." The younger man gave her a pained smile. "That would be you, Sister Chandler."

"So I'm druid kind. Okay. Goes with the Scottish heritage, I guess." She leaned closer to murmur, "Does that mean I have to wear the hideous robe?"

Cailean winked at her. "I think no'."

Bhaltair cleared his throat. "If you two striplings have finished your bantering, we have brothers and sisters to summon." To Lachlan he said, "When they arrive, we should assemble in the great hall. There we may make the exchange quickly, and address everyone at once."

Kinley felt a little taken aback by his enthusiasm. "You're okay with my plan?"

"Why should I no' be?" he countered, and sniffed. "'Tis brilliant. And when 'tis done, we will teach you proper manners. I've no doubt you can be trained. Most savages can." He swept out of the map room.

"So, now, Kinley," Tormod drawled. "No more a McDonnel. You're to be a floor-duster. A savage one."

"I heard that," Bhaltair said, his voice floating in from the corridor.

Lachlan pressed his lips together and looked at the ceiling rafters, while Cailean had a coughing attack. Raen unbelted his tartan and tossed it at the younger druid, who staggered under its weight. Their antics made Kinley grin.

Tormod tugged the tartan off the druid's head and folded it neatly. "If you're wanting me in this fight, my lord, I should heal first." He gave Lachlan a wary look. "Just so I'm at my best."

"Aye, off to the loch with you," the laird said, and tugged Kinley into his arms. "Seems you may have to wear the hideous robe after all."

"Not this time," she said and tugged at a fold of his tartan. "Tonight I'm leading the clan into battle."

ONCE THE DRUIDS arrived and joined the clan in the great hall, Kinley watched from the edges. Lachlan addressed them briefly and turned over the explanation of the mission to Bhaltair and Cailean. As they began, he took Kinley with him to his tower chamber to change.

"No one is talking about Evander," she said as she sat on the edge of the bed to tug off her boots. "Or how he almost killed Raen before he took off with his legion spy honey for parts unknown."

"Aye, but the seneschal freed the druids and the blood thralls," he reminded her. "And Raen said that he turned into the path of the spear after 'twas thrown."

"Sure he did, right before Evander left him to bleed out." She saw the look he gave her and held up her hands. "I'm just saying."

"If Raen wishes to pursue Talorc and his woman, and bring them back to be judged, by clan law, I will go with him, and hunt them. Their sentence will be death, and while I have never executed a McDonnel, I will see it done." Lachlan came to sit beside her. "That is why no one speaks of it."

"It's not always good to be the laird, I guess." She looked around them. "Damn. I need a come-back."

He smiled. "What does that mean?"

"When soldiers in my time are about to go on a mission, they leave behind something that still needs to be done. Dirty clothes that have to be washed, or a half-written letter, or a borrowed tool that has to be returned to a neighbor. It's like saying they know they'll come back to do it, which is why we call it a come-back." She laced her fingers through his. "It's just a silly superstition."

Lachlan brought her hand to his lips. "Lass, we are no' so different as you think. My tribe let their fires go out the night before a battle. 'Twas thought to be good luck, so that we might return to light them again." He drew her to her feet. "We've no' much time left. There's something I want to ask you."

"All questions must wait," Kinley said and pulled her tunic over her head. Then she unlaced her trousers and dropped them. She knelt down at his feet. "Until after I get you naked."

Lachlan stripped to his waist, and sat back down on the bed while she worked his trousers down his long legs. She wanted so much to take her time, and kiss every inch of his now-flawless skin, but there wouldn't be time until after the op. Kinley caught his thick, erect shaft between her palms, savoring the warmth and steely hardness of him before she pressed her lips to the glistening eye of his cockhead.

His serpent tattoo began to move, swiveling its head to look down at her.

Tasting Lachlan while his ink watched her made her hungry for more. She took him in her mouth, curling her tongue around his satiny bulb as she sucked.

"You'll make me spill, lass," Lachlan said as his hand tangled in her hair. He worked his fingertips against her scalp in a soothing motion, before he withdrew from her mouth. "And I want to fill you while you come with me."

"I don't know," she said and reached up to touch his ink. The serpent's tongue flickered against her fingers. "I think the snake wants to come out and play."

"Tonight the snake must watch."

He lifted her up as he lay back on the bed, and slowly lowered her onto his slick cock. She reached down to guide him in, catching her breath as he parted and penetrated her. He impaled her as she engulfed him, and for a moment she thought she would climax as she felt her folds stretch around his root.

Bracing her hands on his shoulders, Kinley slowly lifted herself, clenching around him so he felt her pussy caressing him as she did. As his dark eyes lit up, she thrust back down on him, driving him deep and taking his full length. The groan he uttered resonated in her chest as she did it again, harder and faster, her fingernails scoring his shoulders and her breasts bobbing wickedly. She bent down to rub her hard nipples against his mouth, teasing him but not allowing him to catch them and suck. Relentlessly she worked herself on him until the sweet friction had him swelling inside her.

"Kinley," he groaned.

With a savage growl he rolled with her, pressing her knees up and plunging into her with a single, brutally delicious thrust. He held her gaze as he plowed in and out, his big body tight and shaking over hers. He dragged his hand to her breast, catching her hard nipple and pinching it as he stroked in and out.

Kinley knew she couldn't win this battle, and she didn't want to. She wanted them both to fall together, with each other and into each other, where they would never be apart or alone again. She reached up to touch his mouth, feeling his heaving breaths warm her fingers.

"I love you."

Lachlan gathered her up, plunging one last time before he held his cock deep and kissed her mouth. She melded herself to him, gripping his hair and taking his tongue and squeezing his shaft. They both cried out as the dark, sweet heat they shared turned into an inferno of bliss.

It seemed as if she came forever, trembling and moaning and shuddering on him. He jerked and grunted and shook in return, and when they fell together they didn't let go. Kinley didn't think that she could, not now, not ever.

He kissed the tears from her cheeks, and the sighs from her lips. He didn't have to tell her it was time to set this aside and that the world outside was waiting. They both released each other and climbed off the bed.

She didn't want to stop touching him, even when they were dressed and ready for battle, but once he belted her tartan she took a step back. "All right. I'm ready for battle now. What did you want to ask me?"

"'Tis too soon, mayhap, but I cannae sleep at night for thinking on it." Lachlan took hold of her hands, and went down on one knee. "Kinley lass, to me you are like the stars shining on the loch, and warm rain on my face, and the smell of meadow just bloomed. I'm no' always a patient man, or an easy one, but I'm yours now, for as long as you'll have me. Will you be mine, and marry me?"

She'd needed something to give her luck, and he'd given her the best come-back ever. "I'll tell you my answer," she said, grinning like a fool, "after the battle."

Chapter Twenty-Nine

THE DAPPLED PEARL of the full moon rose in the cloudless, star-speckled sky over the sacred grove. Night seemed to imitate day as thin, colorless light illuminated the ancient stones, and their guardian oaks. Every living creature that inhabited the grove had already fled.

If time had possessed breath, it would have held it.

Kinley reined in Tama, and held up her torch to wave it from side to side to signal the all-clear. She then dismounted, taking care to adjust the edge of Lachlan's tartan to cover her hair. Behind her the hundreds of tartan-clad fighters marching in three ranks merged into single-file to follow her in.

She stopped beside the time-spelled stone. It was strange to be leading an attack. She'd never fought anyone except to defend herself or others. If this went the wrong way a lot of blood would be spilled, and it would be her fault. How had Lachlan done this for centuries?

An archer trotted up to her and nearly tripped over his own feet. Once he righted himself, he said in a loud, overly-gruff voice, "We are assembled, my lord, and prepared for your commands."

"Ready for orders," she corrected him in a low murmur. "No offense, Cailean, but if I'm going to make them believe I'm the laird, I need someone with a deeper voice."

"Will I serve?" Bhaltair said. He wore Neac's tartan and chain mail. "Stand up straight, brother. You're supposed to be a McDonnel."

"Aye, Master…I mean, Chieftain." Cailean frowned and waved his hand before he rejoined the ranks of the druids behind them.

"Do you truly believe the undead will think us the clan?" Bhaltair asked as he watched the shadows moving through the oaks.

"As long as they don't come too close, and everyone keeps covered up, we should be able to fool them long enough for Lachlan to get the kids from the tunnels."

At least that's what she hoped.

Having the druids swap their clothing with the McDonnels had been the key to the success of their plan. While they pretended to be the highlanders surrendering to the legion in the grove, Lachlan and his men would enter the lair and grab the children.

"The legion's sentries must have spotted us coming into the grove," the old druid said. "Do you think the commander will order all of his men out of the tunnels?"

"Probably not, but he'll want most of them to see this. Lachlan and the guys can deal with the guards they left behind." Kinley peered as she saw the glint of metal shields, and the first line of undead soldiers emerge from cover. "Okay, it's show time."

Romans marched into the grove, spreading out in neat ranks around two men on horseback.

"I need you to do your best imitation of the laird now," Kinley told Bhaltair. "Don't let them see your lips moving."

The druid nodded and pulled up a fold of his neck scarf to cover his mouth.

"Tribune of the Ninth Legion," Kinley whispered, and waited for Bhaltair to shout her words at the Romans. "I am Lachlan McDonnel, Laird of the McDonnels. My clan and I have come to surrender to you, once you have freed the mortal bairns, as you promised."

The two mounted men trotted their horses toward the center of the grove. Both wore heavy armor, plumed helmets and red cloaks. One had festooned himself with glittering objects. They both removed their helmets and handed them off to soldiers on the ground. Kinley could see the younger Roman sneering, but his older companion had a shrewd, detached look that immediately troubled her.

"Tribune Gaius Lucinius," Bhaltair muttered to her, nodding at the younger of the pair. "The other is his prefect, Quintus Seneca."

"I promised you nothing, Highlander," Gaius shouted, sounding almost excited. "You will surrender to me, or I will have my men butcher you where you stand."

"Put down your weapons," Quintus said in a cold, calm voice that carried clearly. "Once you have disarmed, and kneel before the tribune, we will consider releasing the children."

Kinley hoped Lachlan and Raen had already found the kids, because she suspected this was going to be over in about a minute. She extended her arm, and rolled her fist. Behind her the front line of the druids pretending to be the McDonnels did the same, signaling all of their troops to prepare to run.

"Well?" Gaius rode closer, stopping only a hundred yards from Kinley before he dismounted and drew his sword. "Will you kneel before me, or must I lop off your legs, Highlander?"

Kinley swatted the air, signaling for the druids to run.

"We dinnae kneel before walking corpses," Bhaltair shouted, and turned only to stop and backpedal. "Oh, gods, no."

He and the other druids hurried toward Kinley as dozens of undead came out of the trees behind them, cutting off their escape route.

LACHLAN CARRIED the last two infants out of the tunnel. He handed them off to the clansmen who were waiting with the carts they had filled with the other children.

"Drive them to town," he ordered over their pitiful shrieks. "Guard them and their parents until dawn."

Raen pulled off his druid robe and used it to cover the sobbing babies before the cart pulled away from them.

"I set fire to the bodies," he declared. "And the altar, the pens, the dais, and anything else I passed that would burn." He spat on the ground. "Facking Romans."

It would be a long time before Lachlan could forget what they'd seen below in the legion's lair. The bones of their victims lay everywhere, as if the bodies had been left to rot where they dropped. The pens where they had kept captives as blood thralls had been carpeted with filth and rags. The worst sight had been the Temple of Mars, where they had found the bairns in cages, and a charnel pit filled with the decomposing bodies of sacrificial victims. The stench of rotting flesh had been so thick it made the air taste like poison.

He'd let the woman he loved more than his own life lure the undead from the lair, for she had convinced him that her plan would save the villager's bairns. Now that it had, he felt ice creeping through his veins.

"Kinley and the druids should be here," he told Raen, scanning the empty woods around them. "Something has gone wrong. We must get to the grove, *now*."

Lachlan rode as if chased by demons, pushing Selon as hard as he could to cover the distance quickly. As he reached the edge of the grove he saw the druids who had disguised themselves as the clan, surrounded on all sides by the legion. The undead jabbed at them, driving them as cattle to the slaughter, but the magic folk were gathering in small clusters, kneeling before the Romans, and joining hands as they looked up at the stars.

Kinley was in the very center, held between two Romans.

KINLEY TRIED to shove the tribune away, but his grip on her arm only tightened as realization dawned on his colorless face.

"You are not the McDonnels," Gaius said, his voice growing shrill as he looked at the faces of the druids around them. "You but dressed in their clothes. Quintus, how can this be?"

"It was a trick, Tribune," the prefect said, and backed away from Kinley. "We must go back to the lair. That is where the highlanders will be waiting."

"No, we shall not walk into our own graves," the legion's commander screeched. He grabbed Kinley by the hair, and jerked her around to see the druids kneeling in the grass. "Now you will watch them die, as the highlander did his men."

"You were the one who did that to him?" She smiled a little. "How did you like getting kicked in the balls? Did they fall off before the druids cursed you and your boys?"

The tribune's eyes went squinty-crazy as he looked at the men and women kneeling before his legion. "You know about the curse."

"It's your own damn fault. If you hadn't slaughtered the clan, they would never have been able to cast their deaths on you." She saw him smile, and felt suddenly uneasy. "You think it's funny?"

"I think if my men kill all these druids as tribute to Mars, the Great God, we shall be released from the curse." He turned her and dragged her back against him, pressing the edge of his sword against her throat. "You will watch them die."

"Gaius, leave her. The McDonnels are coming," Quintus said before he fled for the trees.

"Coward. Mars will not release him this night." He turned her around to see Lachlan and the McDonnels running toward the grove. "Ah, the Pritani scum are arrived. They can watch the heathens die, too."

Kinley struggled to free herself, but went still as the blade cut into her neck. In the next moment Gaius would shout the order to execute the druids, who were doing nothing to save themselves. All of them would die. Their blood would stain the sacred grove and her hands forever, unless she stopped the tribune from giving the order, and bought them a little more time.

"Let's give them something else to see," she muttered and lifted her flaming hands.

As fury and fear twined inside her, the flames raced up her arms. In moments they engulfed her and the tribune.

Gaius screamed, flung her to the ground, and thrust his sword down at her chest. She tried to avoid it, but the blade rammed through her shoulder. Though agony exploded through her, she kicked viciously at the tribune's ankles. As he collapsed on top of her, the weight of him and the blade held her pinned.

The flames spread to her tartan, and for the first time Kinley felt the heat of fire. When the tribune lifted his head as if to call out, she wrapped her arm around his neck and pulled him back into the blaze. Her hair was burning now, charring and falling away, but still she held on. The fire swelled around them so that they became the center of a giant geyser of flame. Through it she saw the other undead back away from the druids, turn and flee.

The smell of burning flesh choked her, and Kinley knew she was dying along with the repulsive tribune. But somehow it didn't hurt. Nor was she afraid.

These things we do, that others may live.

It was her time.

I love you, Lachlan.

Tribune Gaius Lucinius gurgled something as he rolled away from her into the blackened grass. His body glowed red and white as it was reduced to charcoal and finally ash.

Kinley felt her own body growing lighter and

lighter as she burned, until all that was left was a final prayer. She reached up to touch the winged serpent on the Pritani stone.

Thank you for Lachlan. Thank you for his love. Watch over him.

ॐ

LACHLAN FOUGHT the undead as he always had, with unrelenting speed and power. Raen and the clan joined him, spreading out to meet the legion's line on both sides and preventing it from flanking them. He worked both blades as he cut down every Roman who came at him, and strode over the fallen to move closer to the center of the grove. He kept his eyes on his woman, convinced he would reach her in time.

But seeing the huge burst of flames that consumed Kinley and the Roman made the laird go mad.

The battle became a nightmare of heads and limbs and screaming mouths as Lachlan hacked his way through the men between him and Kinley. He tried to plow through the line, only to be dragged back again, and nearly gutted Raen as he turned.

"Head down, arse up," Lachlan ordered.

His bodyguard lowered his interlaced fingers, and Lachlan planted his boot on them. With a colossal heave Raen tossed him over the heads of the legion attackers. When his heels touched earth he ran for Kinley, and roared her name.

"*Kinley.* I've come, I'm here, I'm—"

Lachlan stumbled to a halt as he saw the two burned bodies by the sacred stone. He heard the men fighting behind him, and the blast of the Romans sounding their retreat horn, but all he could do was stare.

"*No.*"

One corpse had fallen into heaps of ash. The other was Kinley. She had rested a slender hand against the ancient etched lines, that even now glowed red from the intensity of the flames. She didn't move or breathe. The flames had burned off her hair and clothes and skin, leaving a blackened husk.

Lachlan's swords fell from his hands to thump on the ground. His knees rammed into the earth as he dropped beside her.

"Oh, no, lass, no."

He thought of his mother and sister, holding each other as they coughed away their last breaths to the white plague; his men on the shores of the loch, silently going to their deaths; the mortals they had not been able to save from the legion, their bones carpeting the undead's lair.

And now his sweet lass. His love. His Kinley —*gone*.

He wanted to drive his fists into the stone until it shattered, but instead he reached for her burned hand, and gently held it between his.

"You couldnae wait for me, my darling? I would have gone with you. Gladly." A sob tore from his throat. "You cannae leave me behind, lass. I've naught without you."

Lachlan pressed her hand to his face, weeping against her poor charred palm until he felt magic pressing in all around him. He lifted his head to see every druid in the grove standing in a perfect circle around the stone, their hands joined and their eyes glowing with the white light of the moon.

"My lord."

When Lachlan looked up, Cailean Lusk had tears in his eyes. They were dreamy, and yet as ancient as the grove stones, and full of sorrow for this woman warrior who had saved them all.

"Give her my life," Lachlan begged him. "Let me go instead of her. I beg you."

Bhaltair came to stand beside the ovate. "Come, Cailean. 'Tis time."

Like the loch where Lachlan had awakened, moonlight bathed the grove in its cool white glow. The druids stood as they had then, hands joined. Light traced the carvings on the ancient stones, and suddenly rayed out to form an enormous circle over Lachlan's head. It floated down to the druids and poured over them like water, drenching them in power as they murmured in low, hushed voices.

Kinley's hand slipped from his as her burned body floated up from the earth. Slowly it turned until it was upright, and became infused with the druid's power. Her form glowed for a moment with a white-hot intensity that made Lachlan's eyes hurt. But he could not look away. Instead he watched, slack-jawed, as her form drifted back down to stand by the stone.

The druids dropped their hands and stepped backward from their circle, all eyes on Kinley.

Lachlan staggered to his feet. "Kinley?"

She opened her eyes as the last of the light faded from her body. She wore the pale robe of a druid initiate, and her golden hair hung down to her waist. He looked into her eyes, and saw love so pure and powerful that it nearly drove him to his knees again.

"Don't faint," Kinley whispered as she reached for him. "It'll make you look bad in front of the guys."

Lachlan simply grabbed her, and held her against his heart as he touched her face and wept into her hair and kissed her smiling lips.

Bhaltair Flen cleared his throat, and when Lachlan and Kinley finally looked at him, said, "Mistress Kinley Chandler, you went willingly to your death, that we might live. Now you are reborn, our daughter of the dragon, and you shall never die."

"Really? You made me…?" Eyes wide, she touched her cheek. "Thank you."

All of the druids bowed to Lachlan and Kinley and silently retreated from the grove.

"The legion has fled, my lord," Raen said as he joined them, and smiled at Kinley. "My lady, you look…much improved."

"I feel like a new woman. Again," she said, and glanced down at her robe. "But this thing has to go. I don't do robes. Someone bring me boots, trews and a decent tunic, please."

"We'd be glad to, my lady," Neac called, and waved in the direction the druids had gone. "Only they took all of our clothes with them, the magical scoundrels."

"Well, I'm no' wearing this back to the castle," Tormod announced as he divested himself of his robe. He swung his tattooed arms out to stretch before he strode, naked, back to the stream.

Raen went after him. "You cannae come naked out of the loch, you shameless Viking. You'll scare all the maids witless."

Kinley shook her head. "And I get to live forever with them. Okay." She looked up at Lachlan. "You do an excellent come-back, you know."

"I had some help," he said smiling. For which Lachlan would offer thanks every day of his eternal life. "Have you an answer for me, then?"

"Aye. Yes. Of course." Kinley erupted with laughter as he picked her up and swung her around. "I will marry you, Lachlan McDonnel, Laird of the McDonnels. My lord. My love."

Chapter Thirty

✧❈✧

SOME WEEKS LATER Cailean Lusk brought a tankard of ale to his master, who sat on the edge of the glen watching the wedding feast. Every mortal on Skye had come to share in the food and drink and merriment, and every tree fluttered with colorful ribbons and the McDonnel triskele banner.

"'Tis a happy day for Lachlan and Kinley, and the clan," he said to his master. "We should dance."

"At our age?" His master made a rude sound. "We'd look the proper fools. Well, I would. Did you speak with the laird?"

"Aye," Cailean said and sat down beside him. He watched Kinley who was being whirled about by Neac Uthar. The chieftain wore a flowered crown on his bald pate, and had a face reddened by laughter. "They've found no trace of the legion since we sealed off their lair. He doesnae believe they sacrificed themselves to the sun. There have been small raids on the mainland since the night we saved the bairns. No mortals are being taken, but they are still killing for blood."

"That is what the evil bastarts do," Bhaltair said and took a swallow of ale. "Now that Quintus Seneca will command them, 'twill be different, and the undead much more dangerous."

Cailean's dreamy eyes took on an older caste and he nodded at the highlanders. "Will we tell them what we learned while we worked our spell in the grove?"

"What would you have me say? That it has made itself a gateway for others like Kinley? That more women with druid blood may be brought back, and since they have never incarnated they will have powers unknown to them? And that we have no idea why?" The old druid set down his ale. "How do I explain to the laird that the gods are no' finished meddling with him and his men?"

"Mayhap 'tis no' meddling," Cailean said. "I think the gods wished to save the clan as well as

Kinley. To make all of them whole again. That could be why this has happened."

His master patted his arm. "'Tis a happy thought, but we cannae ken the minds of the gods, lad. There may never again be another woman to cross over from the future."

Cailean looked at Lachlan, who had seized Kinley and taken her from Neac, and was kissing her breathless now.

"We shall see."

THE END

• • • • •

Another Immortal Highlander awaits you in Tharaen (Immortal Highlander Book 2).

For a sneak peek, turn the page.

Sneak Peek

Tharaen (Immortal Highlander Book 2)

Excerpt

Raen had hoped the laird and his lady would have returned by now, so they could decide what to tell the lieutenant. Instead he would have to guard her another night.

Tormod met him at the base of the tower stairs. "She's gone from her room." He grimaced. "She wanted to see where the river empties into ocean, but I told her 'twas too late for a walk. 'Twas why she sent me to fetch her bathing water, so she could steal away. A *jötunn* would be easier to keep penned."

"She is bored," Raen said suspecting that Diana had finally grown impatient with her confinement. "I'll bring her back and watch her for the night. Go and get some sleep."

"You'll want chains for her," the Norseman predicted. "And mayhap a large cudgel for yourself."

Raen sent a guard to inform Neac he was leaving the stronghold, and took the path through the ridge peaks that led down to the river. Tormod's solution to every problem with females involved fetters and raiding tactics, but if he could not convince Diana to cooperate, Raen might very well have to put her in shackles.

As he reached the edge of the estuary, he saw a torch that had been wedged upright between two large rocks beside Diana's shoes. He stared at the odd footwear, for they made no sense to him. Why would she remove them here, unless…

"Diana." He rushed to the edge of the water, yanking off his boots and vest as he peered out at the dark, cold waters. "Where are you? Call to me."

He heard a splash as he stripped out of his trews, and looked over to see a pale figure sinking beneath the surface. He waded in and dove deep, dissolving into his water-bonded form that made him as fast as light. He streaked through the murky depths until he felt the warmth of her, and surfaced.

Several yards away Diana did the same, gasping as she wiped a hand over her face. "Boy, I'm glad I grew up by the Pacific. This water makes frigid sound cozy."

Raen changed back and swam over to her, only to see her submerge and dart beneath him. He spun, blinking the sting of salt from his eyes until he saw her again. "You can *swim*?"

"You thought I couldn't?" she said as her lips curved. "Aw, you jumped in to save me? That's adorable. I should mention that I was a real jock in college. I lettered in distance swimming, softball and track."

"I thought you were drowning." That he shouted the words made him feel even more the fool. Clamping down on his temper, he said, "The sea is too cold. You cannae swim here."

"I can't swim, I can't leave the castle, and I can't walk around without a guard." She made a rude sound. "What *can* I do?"

"No' scare me like this. 'Twould be very good to do that." He reached out and pulled her into his arms, and then stiffened the moment her skin brushed his. "Diana, why are you naked?"

"You haven't invented the swimsuit yet. Or the wetsuit, for that matter." She lifted her arms and linked her hands behind his neck. "You're naked, too."

"I was saving you, no' seducing you." He tried to put some space between them, but she curled her long legs around his. "We will sink."

She leaned close to press her cheek against his and whispered, "I don't care."

Raen felt the lightning spirit awakening, and quickly turned his head to break the contact with her skin. "I ken what Cailean told you, but you are no' my wife. You dinnae belong here. 'Tis a mistake."

"Doesn't feel like one at the moment," she said but drew back a little. "We're naked and alone, Big Man. We've both wanted this since you tied me to that bed." She slid her palm up to cover his marked cheek. "Feel it? It's like you're already inside me."

Raen clamped her against him and swam one-armed until he could touch bottom. Then he trudged out of the water. When he set her on her feet her breasts grazed his chest, and the soft curls of her sex clung to the throbbing base of his erection. He would do the decent thing and set her away from him, as soon as he had warmed her, as soon as she stopped touching him, as soon as the spirit subsided–

He dragged her up against him, glorying in the feel of her resilient, slender form as he kissed her. Her lips parted for him, and he ravished her mouth, the way he had wanted to since the night she had come to the castle. His hands found their way down to her buttocks, and he clasped the firm curves, pressing her against his throbbing cock and rubbing her against his shaft. She made a small, sweet sound and hitched herself up on him, her breasts dragging against his chest as she grabbed a handful of his hair.

He wanted to fack her so badly he shook with it, and he wrenched his mouth from hers. "Diana, we mustnae…"

"Please find a place where we can stretch out," she said, sounding breathless and eager. "Grass, rock, glen, I don't care. I need you." She moved against him, letting him feel the slickness of her little quim. "See? You know you want it, and God, so do I."

"We cannae," he said, as he set her down and

backed away from her. "I am no' for you. I cannae have you."

"You can have me right now," she assured him. "I'm right here, I'm naked, I'm willing. Is there something else I need to do or say?"

Bright, hot power beginning to spark inside him. "Please," he said through clenched teeth. "Go back to the castle. Now. Hurry."

It was too late to stop it. He knew it as soon as he felt his face burn. The chilly air crackled around them as his ink came alive and spilled down over his heart, spattering her with its silver-white sparks of power.

"Oh, my god," Diana gasped and covered the flow with her hands as if to stop it. "What is happening to you?"

"It's awake now," Raen said tightly as he wrapped his arms around her, pressing her long, lovely body against his. "Be still, or the spirit will take what it wants from us."

• • • • •

Buy *Tharaen (Immortal Highlander Book 2)* Now

MORE BOOKS BY HH

For a complete, up-to-date book list, visit
HazelHunter.com/books.

Get notifications of new releases and special
promotions by joining my newsletter!

Glossary

Here are some brief definitions to help you navigate the medieval world of the Immortal Highlanders.

Abyssinia - ancient Ethiopia
acolyte - novice druid in training
addled - confused
advenae - Roman citizen born of freed slave parents
afterlife - what happens after death
animus attentus - Latin for "listen closely"
apotheoses - highest points in the development of something
Aquilifer - standard bearer in a Roman legion
arse - ass

auld - old

Ave - Latin for "Hail"

aye - yes

bairn - child

banger - explosion

banshee in a bannock - making a mountain out of a molehill

barrow - wheelbarrow

bastart - bastard

bat - wooden paddle used to beat fabrics while laundering

battering ram - siege device used to force open barricaded entries and other fortifications

battle madness - Post Traumatic Stress Disorder

bawbag - scrotum

Belgia - Belgium

birlinn - medieval wooden boat propelled by sails and oars

blaeberry - European fruit that resembles the American blueberry

blind - cover device

blood kin - genetic relatives

bonny - beautiful

boon - gift or favor

brambles - blackberry bushes

bran'y - brandy

Brank's bridle mask - iron muzzle in an iron
framework that enclosed the head

Britannia - Latin for "Britain"

brownie - Scottish mythical benevolent spirit that
aids in household tasks but does not wish to
be seen

buckler - shield

Caledonia - ancient Scotland

caligae - type of hobnailed boots worn by the
Roman legion

cannae - can't

cannel - cinnamon

canny - shrewd, sharp

catch-fire - secret and highly combustible Pritani
compound that can only be extinguished by sand

Centurio - Latin for "Centurions"

century - Roman legion unit of 100 men

chatelaine - woman in charge of a large house

Chieftain - second highest-ranking position within
the clan; the head of a specific Pritani tribe

choil - unsharpened section of a knife just in front
of the guard

Choosing Day - Pritani manhood ritual during
which adolescent boys are tattooed and offer
themselves to empowering spirits

chow - food

cistern - underground reservoir for storing rain water

claymore - two-edged broadsword

clout - strike

cohort - Roman legion tactical military unit of approximately 500 men

cold pantry - underground cache or room for the storage of foods to be kept cool

comely - attractive

conclave - druid ruling body

conclavist - member of the druid ruling body

contubernium - squad of eight men; the smallest Roman legion formation

COP - Command Observation Post

cosh - to bash or strike

couldnae - couldn't

counter - in the game of draughts, a checker

courses - menstrual cycle

cow - derogatory term for woman

Coz - cousin

croft - small rented farm

cudgel - wooden club

da - dad

daft - crazy

dappled - animal with darker spots on its coat

defendi altus - Latin for "defend high"

detail - military group assignment

dinnae - don't

disincarnate - commit suicide

diviner - someone who uses magic or extra sensory perception to locate things

doesnae - doesn't

dories - small boats used for ship to shore transport

draughts - board game known as checkers in America

drawers - underpants

drivel - nonsense

drover - a person who moves herd animals over long distances

dung - feces

EDC - Every Day Carry, a type of knife

excavators - tunnel-diggers

fack - fuck

facking - fucking

faodail - lucky find

fash - feel upset or worried

fathom - understand

fere spectare - Latin for "about face"

ferret out - learn

festers - becomes infected

fetters - restraints

fibula - Roman brooch or pin for fastening clothes

filching - stealing

fisher - boat

fishmonger - person who sells fish for food

floor-duster - Pritani slang for druid

foam-mouth - rabies

Francia - France

Francian - French

free traders - smugglers

frenzy - mindless, savagely aggressive, mass-attack behavior caused by starving undead smelling fresh blood

fripperies - showy or unnecessary ornament

Germania - Germany

god-ridden - possessed

Great Design - secret druid master plan

greyling - species of freshwater fish in the salmon family

gut rot - cancer of the bowel

hasnae - hasn't

heid doon arse up - battle command: head down, ass up

Hetlandensis - oldest version of the modern name Shetland

Hispania - Roman name for the Iberian peninsula (modern day Portugal and Spain)

hold - below decks, the interior of a ship

holk - type of medieval ship used on rivers and close to coastlines as a barge

hoor - whore

huddy - stupid, idiotic

impetus - Latin for "attack"

incarnation - one of the many lifetimes of a druid

isnae - isn't

jeeked - extremely tired

Joe - GI Joe shortened, slang for American soldier

jotunn - Norse mythic giantess

justness - justice

kelpie - water spirit of Scottish folklore, typically taking the form of a horse, reputed to delight in the drowning of travelers

ken - know

kirtle - one piece garment worn over a smock

kuks - testicles

lad - boy

laird - lord

lapstrake - method of boat building where the hull planks overlap

larder - pantry

lass - girl

league - distance measure of approximately three miles

Legio nota Hispania - Latin name for The Ninth Legion

loggia - open-side room or house extension that is partially exposed to the outdoors

magic folk - druids

mam - mom

mannish - having characteristics of a man

mantle - loose, cape-like cloak worn over garments

mayhap - maybe

milady - my lady

milord - my lord

missive - message

mormaer - regional or provincial ruler, second only to the Scottish king

motte - steep-sided man-made mound of soil on which a castle was built

mustnae - must not

naught - nothing

no' - not

Norrvegr - ancient Norway

Noto - Latin for "Attention"

Optia - rank created for female Roman Legion recruit Fenella Ivar

Optio - second in command of a Roman legion century

orachs - slang term for chanterelle mushrooms

orcharders - slang for orchard farmers

ovate - Celtic priest or natural philosopher

palfrey - docile horse

paludamentum - cloak or cape worn fastened at one shoulder by Romans military commanders

parati - Latin for "ready"

parched - thirsty, dry

parlay - bargain

penchants - strong habits or preferences

perry - fermented pear juice

Pict - member of an ancient people inhabiting northern Scotland in Roman times

pillion - seated behind a rider

pipes - bagpipes

pisspot - chamber pot, toilet

plumbed - explored the depth of

poppet - doll

poppy juice - opium

pottage - a thick, stew-like soup of meat and vegetables

pox-ridden - infected with syphilis

praefectus - Latin for "prefect"

Prefect - senior magistrate or governor in the ancient Roman world

Pritani - Britons (one of the people of southern Britain before or during Roman times)

privy - toilet

quim - woman's genitals

quoits - medieval game like modern ring toss

repulsus - Latin for "drive back"

rescue bird - search and rescue helicopter

roan - animal with mixed white and pigmented hairs

roo - to pluck loose wool from a sheep

rumble - fight

Sassenachs - Scottish term for English people

scunner - source of irritation or strong dislike

sea stack - column of eroded cliff or shore rock standing in the sea

Seid - Norse magic ritual

selkie - mythical creature that resembles a seal in the water but assumes human form on land

semat - undershirt

seneschal - steward or major-domo of a medieval great house

shouldnae - shouldn't

shroud - cloth used to wrap a corpse before burial

skelp - strike, slap, or smack

skin work - tattoos

smalls - men's underwear

SoCal - slang for southern California

solar - rooms in a medieval castle that served as the family's private living and sleeping quarters

spellfire - magically-created flame

spellmark - visible trace left behind by the use of magic

spew - vomit

spindle - wooden rod used in spinning

squared - made right

stad - Scots Gaelic for "halt"

staunch weed - yarrow

stupit - stupid

Svitiod - ancient Sweden

swain - young lover or suitor

swived - have sexual intercourse with

taobh - Scots Gaelic for "Flank"

tempest - storm

tester - canopy over a bed

the pox - smallpox

thickhead - dense person

thimblerig - shell game

thrawn - stubborn

'tis - it is

'tisnt - it isn't

toadies - lackeys

tonsure - shaved crown of the head

TP - toilet paper

traills - slaves

trencher - wooden platter for food

trews - trousers

trials - troubles

Tribune - Roman legionary officer

tuffet - low seat or footstool

'twas - it was

'twere - it was

'twill - it will

'twould - it would

Vesta - Roman goddess of the hearth

wand-waver - Pritani slang for druid

warband - group of warriors sent together on a specific mission

wasnae - wasn't

wee - small

wench - girl or young woman

wenching - womanizing or chasing women for the purposes of seduction

white plague - tuberculosis

whoreson - insult; the son of a prostitute

widdershins - in a direction contrary to the sun's course, considered as unlucky; counterclockwise.

willnae - will not

woad - plant with leaves that produce blue dye

wouldnae - would not

ye - you

yer - your

Pronunciation Guide

A selection of the more challenging words in the Immortal Highlander series.

Bhaltair Flen - BAHL-ter Flen
Black Cuillin - COO-lin
Cailean Lusk - KAH-len Luhsk
Dun Aran - doon AIR-uhn
Evander Talorc - ee-VAN-der TAY-lork
faodail - FOOT-ill
Fiona Marphee - fee-O-nah MAR-fee
Lachlan McDonnel - LOCK-lin mik-DAH-nuhl
Loch Sìorraidh - Lock SEEO-rih
Neacal Uthar - NIK-ul OO-thar
Seoc Talorc - SHOK TAY-lork
Tharaen Aber - theh-RAIN AY-burr
Tormod Liefson - TORE-mod LEEF-sun

Dedication

For Mr. H.

Copyright

Making Magic

Welcome to Making Magic, a little section at the end of the book where I can give readers a glimpse at what I do. It's not edited and my launch team doesn't read it because it's kind of a last minute thing. Therefore typos will surely follow.

This is the first full-length novel that I've published and it's because of readers like you. I regularly poll my newsletter members and ask them their opinions on all sorts of things. But one of the areas that surfaced over and over again was the desire for longer work.

Readers spoke and I listened!

I mean what would be the point of asking you what you wanted if I was going to ignore it? This has been fun for me, not only because of the different word count, but also because I can respond to reader's wishes. I feel like there's some dialogue between us, delayed maybe, stilted even, but still some sort of exchange. And that to me is fun.

Why medieval Scotland? If you know my books, then you've seen that I've been inching my way toward historical romance for quite a while. There was the whole time travel arc in Silver Wood Coven (Books 11 - 16) and even the ancient lives in Hollow City Coven. The past fascinates me, not too surprising since I was an archaeologist in a former career incarnation. The Immortal Highlander books give me the chance to indulge my penchant for history, but crossed with paranormal romance. The proverbial win-win for me —and I hope for you!

So that's it for now. I really hope you've enjoyed Lachlan and now it's on to the next in the trilogy.

Thank you for reading, thank you for reviewing, and I'll see you between the covers soon.

XOXO,

Hazel

Los Angeles, August 2017

Read Me
Like Me
Grab My Next Book?

CPSIA information can be obtained
at www.ICGtesting.com
Printed in the USA
LVHW052357280519
619390LV00019B/380/P

9 780578 458687